A LETTER, A KNIFE, AND A CORPSE

District Attorney Harry Dirkson, like many elected officials, had two faces, the genial, harmonious one he showed his constituents, and the other one. Dirkson's other one was something else.

"Now," Dirkson said, ominously. "Let's see if I've got this straight. yesterday the girl came to you with a blackmail note. You sent her away. You made no investigation whatsoever, and today she winds up with a corpse in her livingroom."

Farron sighed. "That's right."

"She asked for help. You didn't give it. Result—a corpse."

"Sounds like hell when you put it that way, doesn't it?"

"Well, how do you want me to put it? It's as if the girl, having failed to interest you in her blackmail letter, decides to see if she can attract your attention with a corpse."

"Come off it, Harry, " Farron said somewhat irritably, in spite of himself. "You're not arguing in front of a jury."

"No, but I will be, won't I?" Dirkson shot back. "How's it gonna sound then? You tell me. How's it gonna sound?"

Farron shrugged and shook his head. "It's gonna sound like hell."

"It's gonna sound like *shit*," Dirkson corrected.

THE BAXTER TRUST

J.P. HAILEY

LYNX BOOKS
New York

THE BAXTER TRUST

ISBN: 1-55802-404-2

First printing/1988
Lynx edition/May 1989

Published by special arrangement with Donald I. Fine, Inc.

This book is published by Lynx Books, a division of Lynx Communications, Inc., 41 Madison Avenue, New York, New York, 10010. The name "Lynx" and the logo consisting of a stylized head of a lynx are trademarks of Lynx Communications, Inc.

Printed in the United States of America

0 9 8 7 6 5 4 3 2 1

For Lynn,
Justin and Toby

1

SHEILA BENTON pushed the long, blond hair out of her eyes and peered at the clock.

7:20.

Damn.

She rubbed her eyes, sat up in bed and turned to the man sleeping next to her. She grabbed his arm and shook him.

"Johnny!" she said. "Johnny!"

John Dutton, twenty-eight, lean, muscular, pretty boy, stirred slightly and said something noncommittal like, "Mumph."

She shook him harder.

"Johnny! Wake up! You'll miss your plane."

"Good. Good. Miss my plane," he muttered.

She pulled the pillow out from under his head.

John grimaced, twisted his head around, opened a bleary eye and found himself staring at a magnificent pair of bare breasts.

The thing is, he hadn't seen them quite this way before. At times when he had been awake, they'd seemed impressive. In the early morning, they impressed him not at all.

"Johnny!" said the breasts. "Wake up! It's seven-twenty!"

"Fuck it," Johnny mumbled. He rolled his face into the sheet, away from the breasts.

Sheila hit him with a pillow. "Get up!"

John rolled over onto his back, opened his eyes, squinted at her and gave her the smile she found totally endearing.

"I haven't got the energy," he said.

She smiled back. A warm, friendly smile. A smile between lovers. But more than that. Between conspirators. Between people enjoying an in-joke.

Sheila turned and reached over to her night table. On it was a round shaving mirror. On the mirror was a pile of white powder, a razor blade, and a straw. Sheila took the blade and fashioned some of the powder into four white lines. She picked up the mirror and held it out to John. He took the straw and snorted two of the lines. She took the straw from him and snorted the other two. She put the mirror back on the night table, then turned back to Johnny.

"Feel better?"

"Uh huh."

"Got the energy to get up now?"

Johnny smiled at her impishly. "Now I don't want to get up." He rolled over on top of her and began kissing her.

"Johnny!"

She couldn't believe he was doing this. Jesus, how the hell were they ever going to make the plane, and—

Johnny suddenly rolled off her and jumped out of bed.

"Last one in the shower is a silly girl," he said, and bolted for the bathroom.

Sheila stared after him in total exasperation. Then she shook her head, laughed, rolled out of bed and followed him.

They soaped each other happily, with a great deal of giggling and fun. Sheila clung to him, kissed him.

"I wish you didn't have to go," she said.

He grinned. "You want me to get a divorce, don't you?"

"Silly question."

"Then I gotta go. What a pain in the ass to go all the way to Reno just to get rid of some lousy bitch."

Sheila smiled. "When you put it that way, it sounds kind of attractive."

"Hey. When I divorce you, it's gonna be right here in New York."

"Johnny."

"And then when I marry my third wife—"

Sheila stepped back and turned off the hot water. Johnny screamed and jumped back. Sheila turned the hot back on, but kept her hand on the knob.

"Are you going to be a good boy now?"

"Yes. Yes. I promise."

Sheila relaxed and let go of the knob.

Johnny held up the bar of soap, and mimicked a gas-station attendant.

"Soap your tits, lady?"

Ten minutes later they were both out the door of Sheila's brownstone on West Eighty-ninth Street, Johnny lugging his suitcase. The MG was right where they'd left it, halfway down the block. To Sheila, that seemed a small miracle. Even with the NO RADIO sign and the code alarm on the car, Sheila couldn't believe it had never been stolen off the streets of New York. Each time she found it still there, she attributed it to the fact that it was Johnny's car, and somehow Johnny seemed able to do anything.

They crammed the suitcase in the trunk, hopped in and took off, with Sheila driving.

She headed uptown to One twenty-fifth Street, went over the Triboro Bridge and took the Grand Central and the Van Wyck out to JFK Airport. Traffic was good, and Sheila pulled up in front of the terminal ten minutes before the plane was due to depart. Another miracle of the Johnny kind.

There was just time for a quick hug and kiss and then he was gone, and she was back on the Van Wyck heading home and thinking about what she was going to do with herself now.

Jesus. Two days. Two whole days without Johnny. It wasn't fair. And all because of that woman. *That woman.* The infamous Mrs. Dutton, whom Sheila hated as much as it was possible to hate someone one has never met. Why should she be causing them this trouble? Sheila could understand her wanting to hang onto

Johnny, though. He really was perfect. So handsome, and nice, and funny, and witty, and intelligent, and sexy and brilliant. Only twenty-eight years old, and already an influential stockbroker on Wall Street. A real Prince Charming. A perfect man.

Except for the cocaine. Sheila wished Johnny wasn't so fond of cocaine, hadn't introduced her to it. Of course, it *was* good, and Johnny wouldn't do it if it wasn't really all right, would he? Still, there was all that talk about it being psychologically addictive. Johnny said that was horseshit, and he ought to know. And *she* did cocaine, and she wasn't addicted. The hit she had taken was wearing off, and she did feel like another, but she didn't *have* to have it. It wasn't like the world would stop if it wasn't there.

Sheila began wondering how much cocaine was left in her apartment. They'd had a whole gram. How much had they done last night? Couldn't have been that much. She probably had at least half a gram to last her for the two days. That ought to be enough.

It had to be enough, she suddenly realized. Johnny hadn't left her any money. How much did she have? Thirty, forty dollars? Barely enough to eat on, let alone score any drugs.

Sheila drove back over the Triboro Bridge. She pulled the money out of her purse. Yeah. Forty-three dollars. Not nearly enough to score any drugs.

Shit. Sheila was angry with herself. Why was she thinking about scoring drugs? She didn't need them. Two days without Johnny was not the end of the world. Besides, she had a half gram left.

Sheila pulled onto her street. A block away, a car pulled out of a spot right in front of her building. The light on the corner was changing. Sheila gunned the motor, and shot across Columbus Avenue, causing a taxi to slam on its brakes and a pedestrian to dive for safety. Sheila felt no guilt at this. In New York City, you kill for a parking space.

Sheila parked the car and got out, after remembering to set the code alarm. She walked up the steps and into the foyer of her building.

The mail had come. Sheila could see the white of a letter through the slots in the box. She dug out her keys and unlocked the mailbox.

The letter was addressed to her. It was typewritten. There was no return address.

Sheila tore the envelope open and pulled out the letter.

And knew at once that something was wrong.

The letter was made up of words cut from newspaper headlines and pasted onto a sheet of paper.

It said: "I KNOW ALL ABOUT YOU."

Sheila stared at the letter with the disbelief a normal person feels when something like that happens to him.

She folded the letter, and went up the stairs.

Sheila unlocked the door and let herself into her apartment. The letter was still in her hand. She flopped down on the bed and read it again. "I KNOW ALL ABOUT YOU." What the hell did that mean? Was it a joke? One of Johnny's jokes, perhaps. She doubted it. Johnny had a terrific sense of humor, and he was always kidding around, but this wasn't like him. This wasn't funny. This was scary.

She folded up the letter and put it on the night table as if to dismiss it from her mind. *Screw the letter. It's nothing.*

She stood up and looked around. The apartment, of course, was a holy mess. It was a small studio apartment, and with the couch folded out into a bed, there was barely room to move around.

Sheila began to straighten up. She made the bed, folded it up and put the cushions back on the couch. She picked up the dirty clothes from where she had left them lying on the floor and stuffed them into the laundry bag in the bathroom.

The remains of the Chinese food she and Johnny had ordered the night before were still sitting on the table in the small kitchen alcove. Sheila dumped them in the garbage and wiped the table.

She realized she was doing all this to keep from thinking about the letter. Which, of course, made her think about the letter. The nagging thought that taunted her, of course, was what if it *wasn't* a joke? What if it was real? "I KNOW ALL ABOUT YOU." Knew all *what* about her? What was there about her that someone could know that could hurt her?

The answer, of course, was the cocaine. Someone could tell the cops about the cocaine. Or tell her uncle, which would be worse. Or actually, which would be the same, since if she got busted, her uncle would find out.

So what should she do? If this was a blackmail letter, she should go to the police. But what could she tell them? She couldn't say, "Hey, I do cocaine and someone's threatening to tell you about it."

Shit. She wished Johnny were here. Johnny would know what to do. She would too, if it weren't for the cocaine. That was the tricky part.

Thinking about the cocaine made Sheila realize she really needed another hit. She opened the drawer of her night table, and took out the plastic bag.

Shit. Almost nothing left. Had they really gone through that much? They'd had a whole gram last night. There was only enough left for a couple of good lines.

Sheila ripped the bag open, and dumped the coke out on the mirror. She chopped it with the razor blade, fashioned two lines, picked up the straw, and snorted the coke up her nose. She licked the powder off the inside of the plastic bag. There. That should make her feel better.

It didn't, however. And she'd known it wouldn't. Snorting the last line of cocaine never made her feel good. There was always the sense of loss.

Well, that was that. Two whole days without Johnny or coke. Well, it would be good for her. A chance to show herself that she didn't really need it.

The phone rang. Sheila walked over and picked it up.

"Hello," she said.

A gruff male voice said, "I know all about you."

Sheila felt as if the floor had suddenly disappeared from under her feet. She had a flash of absolute, total panic. What triggered it was the sudden realization, the sudden awareness. In that split second she knew, absolutely *knew*, that this was no joke, that this was real, and this was now, and this was happening. Happening to her.

"What?" she gasped. "Who are you? What do you want?"

The phone clicked dead. A dial tone buzzed in her ear.

Sheila knew that the man had hung up, but she couldn't help jiggling the button on the phone and saying, "Hello? . . . Hello?" Finally she gave up, and hung up the receiver.

She sat there for a moment, pulling herself together.

Okay. The letter was one thing, but this was something else. And Sheila realized she just couldn't take it. There was only one thing to do.

She picked up the phone and dialed 911.

2

LIEUTENANT FARRON turned the letter in his hands, glanced over at the stolid, impassive face of Sergeant Stams and thought, "Why is he bringing this to me?"

Lieutenant Farron, tall, thin, wiry, twenty-six years on the force, was a smart cop. A crisp, efficient, no-nonsense cop. Bright enough to handle anything. Brighter still in being able to quickly sort out and decide what to choose to handle.

Sergeant Stams, on the other hand, was a short, stout, bull-necked man. Less intelligent. A plodder. Still, he was a good cop, and he knew his job. And part of his job was keeping this type of stuff off Lieutenant Farron's desk. So why had he brought him this?

Lieutenant Farron glanced over at Sergeant Stams, hoping for an answer and expecting none. Sergeant Stams merely returned his gaze with the stolid, impassive look that seemed to be his only expression. But he did return it, with no wavering, no doubt. Which answered the unasked question: yes, Sergeant Stams had meant for the Lieutenant to concern himself with this, and still did, despite the inquiring look.

Lieutenant Farron turned his gaze to the girl. Blond, pretty, twenty-two, twenty-three, he guessed. What could there possibly be in the life of a girl like this that would warrant blackmail, if this was, indeed, a blackmail letter? Or, more important, what could there possibly be that could merit his attention?

Lieutenant Farron looked at the letter again. "I KNOW ALL ABOUT YOU." Damn skimpy for a blackmail letter. Most blackmailers weren't so reticent. So what the hell was it?

Farron looked back up at the girl.

"This came in the morning mail?"

"That's right. I drove my friend to the airport to catch a nine twenty-five plane. The letter was there when I got back."

"I see. And what do you make of it?"

"What do you mean?"

"What does it mean to you?"

"Nothing."

"You think it might be a prank?"

"It might."

"So why bring it to us?"

"I know it seems stupid. I wasn't going to. But then I got the phone call."

"The phone call?"

"Yes."

Farron frowned. This was like pulling teeth. He looked at Stams. The Sergeant's expression had not changed, but still, somehow he looked smug.

Farron turned back to the girl. "Tell me about the phone call."

"It was a man's voice. That's all I know. I'd never heard it before. I'm sure of that."

"Old? Young?"

"Not old. Not young. Just a voice. A deep, male voice. That's all I can tell you."

With just a trace of irony in his voice, Farron said, "Could you tell me what it *said?*"

Sheila caught the irony. "Oh," she said. She smiled in an "aw-shucks" way that men usually found endearing, but which was utterly wasted on Lieutenant Farron. "I'm sorry. The same thing. He said the same thing."

"What do you mean, the same thing?"

"The same as the letter. 'I know all about you.'"

"That's all?"

"Yeah."

"No 'hello,' no 'who is this?'"

Sheila shook her head. "Nothing. I said, 'Hello.' The man said, 'I know all about you' and hung up."

Farron frowned. "I see. When did you get the phone call?"

"Just now. Just before I came here."

Farron rubbed his forehead. "All right, let me reconstruct this. You went to the airport, you came back and got this letter."

"That's right."

"You opened it at once, right? As soon as you got home?"

"That's right. In fact, I opened it in the foyer. I picked up the mail on my way in."

"Okay. And then you went right into your apartment?"

"That's right."

"And how soon after that was the phone call?"

"Not long."

"How not long?"

"Right away. Maybe five minutes."

Farron stole another glance at Stams, as if to say, "Is that what you think is significant?" Of course, he got no response.

"You have any enemies?" he asked the girl.

She shook her head. "No. And I don't know anyone who'd want to blackmail me, either."

Farron looked at her. "You think this is a blackmail note?"

She smiled. "Well, what do you think it is? An invitation to dinner?"

Farron frowned. The girl was cute and spunky. Farron was beyond appreciating cute and spunky. He found girls like her a pain in the ass.

"Are you a likely candidate for blackmail?" he asked.

"Do you mean do I have any money, or do you mean do I have anything to hide?"

"Either."

"As to money, I have none. I'm an actress. All I've been able to get lately is some extra work. I have a trust fund that doles me out just enough money to get by."

A light went on. "A trust fund?"

"Yes. And you can stop thinking what you're thinking, because my dear departed grandfather fixed it so that I can't touch the money until I'm thirty-five. I'm twenty-four now."

"That's very interesting. Tell me about the trust fund."

"Why? I told you, I can't touch the money—"

"Nonetheless, tell me about it."

"I don't see what difference it makes."

"You also don't see why anyone would want to send you that letter."

"Oh . . ."

Lieutenant Farron smiled, which didn't come easy for him. "Humor me."

Sheila brushed the hair out of her eyes and frowned. She was no more used to men like Lieutenant Farron than he was to her. Like many pretty girls her age, she wasn't used to doing what men wanted. She was used to smiling sweetly, and having men do what *she* wanted. Still, she was scared, and she wanted help.

"Okay," she said. "I'm an orphan. My father died before I was born. My mother was killed in a car accident when I was four. My Uncle Max brought me up. My grandfather, that's my mother's and Uncle Max's father, died shortly after my mother was killed. In his will, he set up a trust fund for me. But I tell you, there's no way I can touch it until I'm thirty-five."

Farron pursed his lips. "Is it a large trust?"

"Yes."

"Could you be more explicit?"

"What?"

"How large?"

"What does it matter? I tell you—"

"Miss . . ." Farron had a moment of panic, as he realized he had no idea who he was talking to, not the best of procedures for a veteran police officer. He glanced at the address on the envelope the letter had come in. "Miss Benton. I'm a police officer. It's my job to determine what is and what isn't important. I take all the facts and sift through them. If I let someone else decide for me what's important and what's not, then I'm a lousy police officer and I'm not doing my job. Now, I just want to know the relative size of your trust fund. In my mind it's important. So tell me. Is it bigger than a breadbox?"

Sheila smiled. "All right. My grandfather was very wealthy. The trust is quite large. I have no idea how much is actually in it. The only one who would know is Uncle Max. But I know it's several millions."

Lieutenant Farron raised his eyebrows. "Several *millions?*"

"Yes," Sheila said, somewhat impatiently. "But I can't touch it. You know what I get? Two hundred a week. That's eight hundred a month, ten thousand, four hundred a year. Try and live on that in New York. The only reason I get by is I have a dingy, one-room apartment on the Upper West Side that's rent-controlled and costs me three hundred a month. Which I know I shouldn't complain about, because there are people who would kill for it. But that's it. I have nothing. I own nothing. I have no money."

"Except for the trust."

"Which I can't touch."

"Who is your trustee?"

"Uncle Max."

"And who is Uncle Max?"

"Uncle Max. Maxwell Baxter."

And suddenly Lieutenant Farron understood. Maxwell Baxter. One of the richest men in New York, in the United States for that matter. A wealthy man. A powerful man. A man with political connections. A man, perhaps, with connections to the commissioner.

Farron looked at Stams. Without changing expression, Stams seemed to be saying, "I told you so."

So he had. Stams' judgement was vindicated. This was why he'd brought him the girl. This was why he'd brought him this unlikely and unimportant case. The girl was Maxwell Baxter's niece, and therefore merited attention. There was no way to fault Stams on it. He'd done right.

But he'd done more than that. And both he and Farron knew it. Yes, he'd informed Farron, so Farron wouldn't be caught flat-footed if this developed into something. But more important, he'd covered his ass. He protected himself, by not turning the girl down. By not taking the responsibility. By leaving it up to Lieutenant Farron to turn the girl down.

He'd passed the buck.

"So," Farron said. "Maxwell Baxter is your trustee?"

"Yes."

Is he your sole trustee?"

"That's right."

"And he gives you two hundred dollars a week?"

"Actually I get a check once a month. Sometimes it's eight hundred, sometimes it's a thousand, depending on how the weeks fall. It all adds up to ten thousand, four hundred a year."

"What about inflation?"

Sheila made a face. "What *about* it? That's *with* inflation. I started at fifty a week. It's *up* to two hundred."

"Is the amount a provision of the trust?"

"Yes. Carefully worked out by Grandpa to keep me poor for as long as possible."

"And your uncle can't increase that amount."

She hesitated. "No."

"You hesitated."

"Did I? The answer is no, he can't."

"But he can give you money at his discretion?"

"In an emergency, yes."

"And blackmail would be considered an emergency."

Sheila was getting annoyed. This was not going the way she had hoped. "Look, let's get something straight. If someone were blackmailing me, the threat would be that if I didn't pay them, they would tell my uncle. Can you really see me going to my uncle to get money to pay to a blackmailer to keep him from telling my uncle something?"

Farron smiled. "No. Which brings me to the second part of my question. What would this man tell your uncle? What is it you have to hide?"

Sheila looked at him with wide-eyed innocence. "Nothing."

"Nothing?"

"Nothing that I'd pay a dime for, even if I had it."

"Publish and be damned, eh?" Farron nodded. "Quite proper attitude."

Farron had had enough. He got up to indicate the interview was over.

"Well, Miss Benton, we'll do what we can."

"What do you mean by that?"

"If you get any more calls or letters, get in touch with us immediately."

Sheila stood up. "You sound as if you're washing your hands of the whole thing."

Lieutenant Farron came around the desk. He smiled at her, but he also took her arm and guided her to the door.

"Well, Miss Benton," he said. "You must admit it sounds rather unpromising. You have no money to pay blackmail. You've done nothing to be blackmailed about. And so far, no one's made any demands on you."

"Some people want other things besides money," Sheila protested.

"That they do, Miss Benton. That they do."

Farron opened the door. She gave him a look, then stalked out of the office.

Farron closed the door, went back, and sat at his desk.

"Well," Stams said. "What do you think?"

Lieutenant Farron thought Sergeant Stams had successfully passed the buck. But he wasn't going to acknowledge that to him.

Farron shrugged. "Could be nothing. Practical joke. Could be something else. What I don't like is the fact the phone call came as soon as she got home. It could mean our man's watching the house."

Stams nodded. "So what do we do?"

Lieutenant Farron knew that sarcasm would be lost on Sergeant Stams, but he couldn't help himself.

"What do we do?" he said. "We put three bodyguards on her at all times, assign five squad cars to the area, and tap her phone."

He looked up to see Sergeant Stams looking at him, impassive as always.

"What do you think we do?" Farron said. He snorted and handed him the letter. "File it."

3

SHEILA BENTON spent a restless night.

Johnny called around seven o'clock to tell her he'd arrived safely and everything was going fine. Sheila would have loved to have told him all about what was happening, but she didn't have

the heart. He had his wife's attorneys to deal with, and he didn't
need the added distraction. Besides, he'd kidded her on the way to
the airport that she wouldn't be able to get along for two days
without him, that she'd be calling him up for advice. Well, she'd
handled this herself, hadn't she? She'd reported it to the police.
She'd done everything she could do. And what the hell could *he*
do, a million miles away?

And the other thing was, Johnny was never serious. He treated
everything as a joke. He wouldn't take this seriously. He'd just kid
her about it.

That started Sheila off on a bad train of thought. Johnny was
never serious. How could she be sure he was serious about her?
Nonsense. She knew he loved her. Didn't he? Wasn't he in Reno
divorcing his wife so he'd be free to be with her? So what if he was
never serious. She *liked* the way he kidded around. That was part
of what had attracted her to him in the first place. So what was
she worrying about?

It was a bad night. A night without Johnny. A night without
coke. Jesus, she hadn't thought it was going to be this hard. By
eleven o'clock she was climbing the walls. She had ransacked the
refrigerator and the kitchen shelves, and found damn little. Some
orange juice. Some Wheaties. Some stale crackers. What she
found, she ate, but it wasn't nearly enough. She wanted something
exciting, like pizza. But she couldn't eat a whole pizza, and no one
would deliver a slice. And she wasn't that keen about walking out
to Broadway, not alone, not at night, and not now. But she really
wanted something.

What she wanted, of course, was coke. She didn't really want to
admit that, but it was true. And when she finally did admit it,
when she finally said to herself, "Jesus, I need a hit of coke," she
rationalized. It would have been all right, she told herself, if it
hadn't been for the letter. That was what was throwing her. If it
hadn't been for that, she wouldn't have needed the coke. She
wouldn't have felt this anxious and desperate. She could give up
the coke easy enough, that wasn't the problem. But not *now*. Not
with Johnny gone and this thing happening to her. This scary

thing that she didn't understand. There was plenty of time to stop taking coke when everything was all right. That was the time to do it. Not in the middle of a crisis. Not with so much else on her mind.

By one in the morning she had convinced herself that there was nothing wrong with buying coke at this particular juncture in her life, and, considering how things stood, she should simply go ahead and do so.

With this conviction, she was finally able to fall asleep.

She awoke the next morning at nine o'clock. She got up, showered and dressed, folded up the bed and set out to accomplish her purpose.

On her way out, she checked the mailbox. The mail hadn't come yet, and she was glad. She wasn't up to another letter, if one happened to be in it.

Sheila walked out to Broadway and hailed a cab. Aside from cocaine, taxies were her one extravagance. Sheila couldn't stand public transportation. It was so filthy in the subway. And so inconvenient, particularly getting from one side of town to the other. You had to take the subway to Times Square, shuttle, and then take a third train where you wanted to go, which was usually blocks from a subway stop anyway. So Sheila splurged a lot on cabs.

The cab took her through Central Park at Eighty-sixth Street, down Fifth Avenue and across to the address she had given on Park Avenue.

Sheila dug in her purse and discovered she had twenty-one dollars. She gave the driver a twenty and a smile. He grumbled over the twenty, which Sheila felt was uncalled for. After all, the meter had been five-seventy. She'd been about to tell him to keep seven bucks, but when he bitched, she made it six-fifty.

A doorman opened the door of the cab and said, "Good morning, Miss Benton," as Sheila got out. Sheila favored him with a smile. It was nice to be greeted by name in such a posh setting.

Sheila went into the lobby and waited for the elevator. When it arrived, the elevator man also greeted her by name. She smiled at him also. The fact that she knew neither his name nor that of the doorman bothered her not at all, nor did it seem to bother them.

The elevator stopped at the eighth floor and let her off, not in a hallway, but in the spacious foyer of the floor-through apartment. The double doors to the living room were open, and Sheila could see someone sitting on the couch. She frowned and had an uncharitable thought for the doorman and the elevator man. They should have told her Uncle Max had company. That didn't suit her purpose at all.

Sheila walked in and the person on the couch heard her and turned. He was a young man, about twenty-five, dressed in a tweed jacket and slacks, which coupled with his glasses immediately identified him as a student.

Sheila, who had been prepared to dislike the intruder, whoever he might be, nonetheless, broke into a smile.

"Phillip!"

"Hi, Sheila."

"What are you doing here?"

He smiled. "What do you think? I want to go to summer school." He jerked his thumb toward the door to the study. "Dad's in there making the touch now."

"You study too much."

"I don't study enough. You know how long it takes to get through law school?"

Sheila looked at him. "You really want to be a lawyer, Phillip?"

Phillip shrugged. "Uncle Max will support me through school. He wouldn't give me a dime if I quit."

"You have your trust fund."

Phillip grinned. "Yeah. Just like yours. And what brings you here, cousin?"

Sheila grinned back. "What do you think?"

They both laughed, as they shared their own, special in-joke.

"Can't wait to be thirty-five, can you?" Phillip said. "Well, I've got it all figured out. By the time I'm thirty-five, I'll either be a wealthy lawyer or I'll still be in school."

The door to the study opened and Max and Teddy Baxter came out.

Sheila looked up at them, and thought the same thing she always thought when she saw them together. It was hard to believe that they were brothers, and only a year apart, too. Moreover, it was hard to believe that Teddy was the eldest. Maxwell Baxter, hearty, robust, assured and confident, looked like what he was—a wealthy powerlord. Teddy Baxter, slim, emaciated, tentative, and apologetic, looked like what he was—a poor relation.

Secretly, Sheila liked Teddy, Phillip's father, better. Uncle Max was a cold, cultured, condescending, affluent snob. Uncle Teddy was a real person. But Sheila, who like Teddy and Phillip depended on Maxwell Baxter for everything, was careful never to let this show.

Uncle Teddy spotted Sheila first.

"Sheila!" he said. "What a pleasant surprise."

"Hello, Uncle Teddy. How are you."

"Fifteen hundred dollars richer, that's how he is," Max said dryly.

Sheila gave him a playful scolding. "Uncle Max, that's not nice."

"It's a crime, but there you are," Max said.

Teddy, feeling called upon to justify himself, said somewhat stiffly, "Education is very important—"

"Yes it is," Max cut him off brusquely, without taking his eyes off Sheila. "You know, Sheila, if you'd just go back to school, I'd be happy to pay your way."

Sheila smiled. "Somehow I remember. You tell me every time I see you."

"How's the acting world?" Teddy asked.

"Great," Sheila said. "I'm going to be on TV next Thursday. An ABC Movie of the Week."

"No kidding."

Sheila smiled. "Yeah. In the banquet scene, I'm the girl with her back to the camera at the third table from the left."

Teddy and Phillip laughed.

"We'll watch for you," Teddy said.

Phillip looked at his watch. "Come on, Dad. We'll miss my bus."

"Right," Teddy said. "We've got to get going."

They walked out into the foyer and rang for the elevator, which arrived promptly.

"Well, so long," Teddy said. "And thanks again."

"Don't mention it," Max said dryly.

As the elevator doors closed, Maxwell Baxter wheeled around to regard Sheila. There was accusation in his eyes.

Sheila didn't like dealing with Uncle Max, but she could do it. She handled him the way she handled all men, by being cute and witty and adorable, by kidding him along with light irony and gentle sarcasm.

Still, she always hated to take the initiative, especially under that steely gaze.

But she had to, so she did.

"Uncle Max—" she began.

He cut her off with a voice as cold as ice. "How much?"

Sheila smiled, one of her most adorable smiles. "Uncle Max, don't be like that."

"How much?"

"A hundred."

"For what?"

"Rent."

"It's the middle of the month."

"I'm late."

Maxwell Baxter turned and walked back into the living room. Sheila followed behind. He sat down on the couch, arranged himself comfortably, and assumed what Sheila well knew was his lecturing pose.

"You know," he said, "a girl your age needs something more than just acting. Do you know how many unemployed actresses there are in New York City?"

Sheila sat on the couch next to him and smiled, playfully.

"Uncle Max," she said. "That's your five-hundred-dollar lecture. I only want a hundred."

4

SHEILA SNORTED the stuff up her nose. She straightened up and sniffed twice.

Michael Croft leaned back in his desk chair and watched her. Croft, thirty-five, lean, tanned, neatly dressed in a stylish tailored suit, was an advertising executive and junior partner in the firm of Hoffman, Whittiker, and Croft, but fancied himself a Hollywood agent. For him the coke was just part of the image.

Croft cocked his head at Sheila. "Well?"

Sheila took her finger and wiped the residue of the line she had snorted from the top of his desk. She stuck her finger in her mouth, licked it off.

She smiled. "Pure milk sugar. It'd be great in coffee."

"I didn't cut it at all."

"This could be competition for NutraSweet."

"Come on. Before I ground this up it was solid rocks."

"Yeah. Sure. And you got it from a little old lady who only snorted it on Sundays."

Croft laughed. "How did you know?"

"Lucky guess."

"Are you saying this is the worst coke you ever had?"

"That would be flattering it."

"I see. How much do you want?"

"A gram."

Sheila emerged from the office building on Madison Avenue and hailed a cab.

It was one-thirty by the time the taxi dropped her off in front of her building, and Sheila would have been hungry had it not been for the line she'd snorted in Croft's office. As she went up the front steps, she realized it was just beginning to wear off, and she was in a hurry to get upstairs and snort another one. So she was halfway up the stairs before she remembered.

The mail. The thought filled her with a sudden dread. She hadn't picked up the mail. What if there was another letter? A more specific letter. A letter that told her what this was all about. Sheila wanted to know, and yet she dreaded to know. Not with Johnny gone. Please. Just keep this on hold till he gets back.

Sheila went back down the stairs and looked in the mailbox. Shit! There was a letter in it. She dug her keys out of her purse and unlocked the box.

It was a bill. Sheila had never been so happy to hear from ConEd.

Sheila stuck the letter in her purse, locked the mailbox, and went back up the stairs.

She unlocked the door to her apartment, walked in, and stopped suddenly.

The body of a man was lying sprawled on the floor. He was lying on his stomach, with his head twisted to one side, so that Sheila could see his face. He was a thin, gaunt man, somewhere in his fifties. Sheila didn't recognize him—she had never seen him before.

But she did recognize the large carving knife which should have resided in the rack on the wall in her kitchen alcove, but which now resided in the unknown gentleman's back.

5

SHE DIDN'T scream. Sheila could count that to her credit. And, considering her state of mind, that was quite an accomplishment.

If she had screamed, she realized, she would have been fucked. That snoopy Mrs. Rosenthal from next door surely would have heard—she heard every time Johnny slept over, so how could she miss a scream? And that would have been that. The fat would have been in the fire. Mrs. Rosenthal would have knocked on her door, and she would have had to call the police.

Sheila knew she had to call the police, but not yet. Not now. Not until she got a grip on things.

Who *was* this guy? She had just received a blackmail letter, so presumably he was the blackmailer. Which would make her the number-one suspect. But what the hell was he doing here?

The question had no answer. No one writes you a blackmail note, comes to your apartment, and sticks a knife in his own back. It just didn't make any sense. The way Sheila saw it, the only way it made sense was if the guy came there to blackmail her, and she killed him. And, she realized, if that was the only thing that made sense to her, it was sure as hell gonna be the only thing that made sense to the cops.

But she had to call them. What the hell else could she do? The guy was in her apartment. Dead. That made him kind of hard to ignore. Unless she ditched the body, which she realized was beyond her—she had to call the cops.

She took a deep breath, got control of herself. All right, what did she have to do first?

She went in the kitchen alcove and checked the knife rack on the wall. Sure enough, the slot for the large carving knife was empty. He'd been killed with her knife.

Sheila had a sudden mad impulse to pull the knife out of the man's back, wash it, and put it back in the rack. She quickly stifled it. That would be suicide. She was in enough trouble already. If she got caught trying to cover up, she'd be screwed.

She went back into the main room and looked down at the man. Christ, she must know him from somewhere. But she didn't. He was a total stranger. A dead total stranger, murdered in her apartment. Great.

She pulled herself together again. Okay, the cops are coming. They'll search the place. More trouble.

Sheila ran back to the kitchen alcove and got a paper shopping bag from the ones she had wedged in beside the refrigerator to save to use for garbage.

She ran back, detoured around the body on the floor and went to her night table beside the couch. She took the mirror and the straw and put them in the paper bag. Then she went to her bureau, jerked open the drawer, and began fumbling through it. She pulled out a small plastic grinder, a gram scale, some gram bottles, some straws, and other assorted drug paraphernalia, and put them in the bag. She pulled the clothes out of the drawer and threw them on the floor, just to make sure she hadn't overlooked anything. When she'd made sure she'd emptied the drawer of anything incriminating, she crammed the clothes back in and closed the drawer.

Okay. Was that everything? Yes. Shit! No. The gram in her purse. She grabbed the purse, fumbled in it, pulled out the small envelope with the small plastic bag.

She started to throw it in the paper bag, but stopped. Damn.

She couldn't throw it away. It wasn't fair. She'd gone through too much to get it. Sucking up to Uncle Max. And she'd need it to get through this crisis, what with Johnny being gone, and all.

But she couldn't. She didn't dare leave it in the apartment, and she didn't dare carry it on her. Not the way things stood. Because, much as she hated to admit it, she realized there was a damn good chance she was going to be arrested.

Sheila had a moment of near hysteria. She was trapped. Everything was coming down on her.

Then she had a flash of inspiration. She ran to her desk, jerked open the drawer, and pulled out an envelope. She took a pen and addressed the envelope to herself. She put the gram of coke inside, sealed the envelope, found a stamp and put it on.

Sheila grabbed up the envelope and the bag. She grabbed her purse and went out the door, locking it behind her.

Her mind was racing as she hurried down the street: *"I called from the corner because I didn't want to use the phone in the apartment. I knew you weren't supposed to touch anything, and—"*

She reached the corner. There was a phone booth, a mail box and a garbage can.

Sheila dropped the letter in the mail box. She was about to throw the paper bag in the garbage, when she realized she was going to tell the cops where she called from. Suppose they searched the garbage?

She realized she was being paranoid, but she also realized she had good reason to be paranoid.

Sheila hurried up the block to the next corner. There was a trash can there. She dropped the paper bag in it.

She hurried back to the corner on her street.

She picked up the phone. It worked. She dropped in a quarter and dialed.

6

LIEUTENANT FARRON pulled his car to a stop behind the other police cars double-parked in front of the apartment. He got out, slammed the door and checked the address, since everyone else seemed to be already inside.

Farron was in a foul mood, and had been ever since he got the call. He hoped the information was wrong, that somehow, someway, someone had gotten it wrong. Though in his heart of hearts he knew that wasn't true. Sheila Benton. That was the name. That was the girl. That was Maxwell Baxter's niece.

As Farron walked up to the building he noticed that one of the police cars parked on the block was, indeed, occupied. Through the rear window, the backs of two heads could be seen. One wore the cap of a uniform cop. The other had blond hair.

Farron angled his body to avert his face from the car as he went into the building.

Flashbulbs were going off as he entered the apartment. Farron stood back, to let the detective finish photographing the body. He snapped off a few more shots and stood up.

"Okay, doc, he's all yours," he said.

The medical examiner, who'd been standing with the other cops, moved in and bent over the body.

Sergeant Stams spotted Farron, and moved over to him.

"Okay, what have we got here?" Farron asked.

"A dead man."

"I can see that. Who is he?"

"Can't tell. He had no identification on him."

"Nothing?"

"Nothing in his pockets except this."

Stams held up a key. Farron started to take it, then stopped.

"Oh, you can take it," Stams told him. "There's no prints on it."

Farron took it and looked it over. It appeared to be a simple door key, and fairly new.

"Okay," he said. "Trace the key and find out who he is."

"I traced the key," Stams said, somewhat smugly.

Farron stared at him. "How the hell did you do that?"

Stams pointed to the front door to the apartment. "It fits that door there."

Farron whistled. "What does the girl say?"

"Says she's never seen him before. According to her, she just came home and found him lying there."

"That's helpful."

"Isn't it."

Farron frowned, rubbed his forehead. "Tell me . . ."

"Yes?"

"Is she . . . I mean, it's her, isn't it?"

"Her?"

"Sheila Benton."

"Oh, yeah. It's her."

"Shit."

"Yeah."

The medical examiner stood up.

"What have you got, Doc?" Farron asked.

"Offhand, I'd say he was killed within the last two hours. I can pin it down better when I get him to the morgue."

"Pin it down, Doc. It's gonna be important."

Stams looked at Farron. "Your three bodyguards didn't do too well, did they?"

Farron sighed. "What a mess. Wrap things up here, will you?"

"Where you going?"

"I'm going to take the girl downtown, hunt up the D.A. and see if I can get us out of the shithouse."

7

DISTRICT ATTORNEY Harry Dirkson, like many elected officials, had two faces, the genial, harmonious one he showed his constituents, and the other one. Dirkson's other one was something else. Police officers walked softly around him, and for good reason. This plump, bespectacled, balding man was a tiger when aroused. His sarcasm could put Lieutenant Farron to shame, and Farron was no slouch in that department himself. But under Dirkson's gaze, the usually unflappable Farron actually found himself beginning to squirm.

"Now," Dirkson said, ominously. "Let's see if I've got this straight. Yesterday the girl came to you with a blackmail note. You sent her away. You made no investigation whatsoever. And today she winds up with a corpse in her livingroom."

Farron sighed. "That's right."

"She asked for help. You didn't give it. Result—a corpse."

"Sounds like hell when you put it that way, doesn't it?"

"Well, how do you want me to put it? It's as if the girl, having failed to interest you in her blackmail letter, decides to see if she can attract your attention with a corpse."

"Come off it, Harry," Farron said somewhat irritably, in spite of himself. "You're not arguing in front of a jury."

"No, but I will be, won't I?" Dirkson shot back. "How's it gonna sound then? You tell me. How's it gonna sound?"

Farron shrugged and shook his head. "It's gonna sound like hell."

"It's gonna sound like *shit*," Dirkson corrected. He took a deep breath, blew it out again, and shook his head. He collected himself, and went on in a quiet tone of voice that somehow managed to seem more intense than if he'd shouted. "I don't know if that means anything to you, Lieutenant. You are a *hired* official. If you go on the witness stand and make an ass out of yourself, people may laugh at you, but you'll still have your job. I'm an elected official. I'm responsible to the *people*. I've got ten million fucking morons out there watching me who have the power to kick me out of office if they don't like what they see."

Farron nodded. All this was true, and more direct than he would have expected Dirkson to put it. It was no secret that Dirkson had political aspirations, though no one was sure just how high those aspirations were. But Dirkson had made a point of seeing that the district attorney's office piled up an impressive percentage of convictions, particularly in cases he handled personally. And if there was anything in the world he didn't want, it was to be made to look foolish.

"I know how you feel," Farron said.

Dirkson raised his eyebrows. "Do you, Lieutenant? All right, then, let me ask you one thing. If you had followed this up yesterday, do you think the murder might have been prevented?"

Farron shrugged. "It's possible."

"There you are."

Farron reached into his briefcase, pulled out a thick manila file, and threw it on Dirkson's desk.

Dirkson eyed it suspiciously. "What's that?"

"Glad you asked. That's our file for the last thirty days. Blackmail letters, threats of bodily harm, crank phone calls. I don't run 'em all down. If I had a hundred more men I would. I don't, so I don't."

Dirkson shook his head, condescendingly. "Lieutenant. It's not a question of what's fair." He pointed to the file. "These letters are trash. You could take 'em out and burn 'em. I wouldn't say a word." He picked up the blackmail letter. "This letter is important. And you should have done something about it."

Farron sighed. "In hindsight, even I know that."

Dirkson frowned. "I'm not talking hindsight. You knew who the girl was, didn't you?"

"Yes."

"You knew she was Maxwell Baxter's niece?"

"Everyone's related to someone."

"Everyone is *not* related to Maxwell Baxter."

"I know."

Dirkson sighed and settled back in his chair. "Well," he said. "There's nothing to be gained by going into all that now."

Farron's smile was somewhat strained. What the hell did Dirkson think they'd *been* doing?

"No sir."

Dirkson pressed the intercom. "Send her in."

An officer ushered Sheila into the office. A stenographer entered with them and began setting up a small table.

Dirkson immediately reverted to his constituent face. "Sit down, Miss Benton," he said, smiling graciously, as if it were a social occasion. "Now, I just need to ask you a few questions."

Sheila smiled back, but her attention was diverted by the stenographer, who had opened his notebook.

Dirkson, noticing this, said, "Just routine. In a murder case we never trust to memory. We take down the statements of all the witnesses."

Sheila fidgeted, nervously. "I really don't know what I'm a witness to."

Dirkson smiled, reassuringly. He picked up the letter. "Well, let's start at the beginning. Yesterday, you received this letter."

"Yes. Also a phone call with exactly the same message."

"Did you recognize the voice?"

"No. I'd never heard it before. It was a man's voice, but that's all I could tell."

"Could it have been the voice of the dead man?"

"It's possible. I have no way of knowing."

"You never saw him before?"

"No. I came back to my apartment, and there he was."

"Where had you been?"

"What?"

"Before you discovered the body. Where had you been? What had you been doing?"

Sheila's eyes flicked for just a second. "Window-shopping."

Dirkson noticed. A veteran interrogator, he knew he'd hit something. He didn't know what, but something about her answer had made her uneasy. It could have been a lie, an evasion, or simply an incomplete answer, but it was something.

"Window-shopping?" he said. "Where?"

Sheila smiled at him. "In windows."

Dirkson smiled too, but it was a forced smile, and in that moment he felt more sympathetic toward Lieutenant Farron. Jesus. Another of these nitwits who are so young and cute and pretty that they think that's all they ever have to be.

"What windows?" he asked.

"On Fifth Avenue."

"What stores?"

"I can't recall offhand. Stores in the fifties."

"How long were you window-shopping?"

"I've no idea. I'm very poor about time."

Dirkson would have been willing to bet she considered it an adorable habit, too. "More than an hour?"

"It's possible."

"Why were you window-shopping? Were you looking for anything in particular?"

"No. You see, I'd been to my uncle's on Park Avenue. I thought since I was in the neighborhood, I'd browse."

"Your uncle?"

"Yes. Uncle Max. Uh, Maxwell Baxter."

Dirkson shot a glance at Farron. "Ah, yes. Maxwell Baxter. You called on him this morning?"

"Yes."

"Why?"

Sheila smiled. "He's my uncle. And my trustee and guardian. I call on him all the time."

"You had no particular reason for calling on him this morning?"

"No."

"It was purely a social call?"

"Yes."

"And what time did you get to his apartment?"

"I have no idea. Uncle Max could probably tell you."

"Was anyone else there at the time?"

"Yes. Uncle Teddy and Phillip. That's Teddy and Phillip Baxter. Teddy is Max's brother. Phillip is my cousin. Teddy's son."

"I see. And were they there when you left?"

"No. They had to run. Phillip was on his way to Boston. He's going to summer school at Harvard. Teddy was taking him to the bus."

"So they left first?"

"Yes."

"And what time did you leave the apartment?"

"There again, you would have to ask Uncle Max."

"Well, how long were you there?"

She shook her head. "I tell you, I'm terrible with time."

"At any rate, you left his apartment, you went window-shopping, and then you went home?"

"Yes."

"How did you get home?"

"By taxi."

"And what time did—" Dirkson broke off. Smiled. "Never mind. What happened after you got there?"

"I walked in and found the body."

"So what did you do?"

"I was scared. I didn't know what to do. I ran out and called the police."

"You didn't call from the apartment?"

"No. It was awful. He was lying there, with the blood and everything, and— No. I ran out and called from the corner."

"You didn't touch anything in the apartment?"

"Are you kidding? I got out of there fast."

"You didn't touch the body?"

Sheila looked at him in surprise. "God, no. Why would I do that?"

Dirkson shrugged. "I don't know. Feel for a pulse? See if he was dead?"

"Oh. I see." Sheila considered this. "That's funny. I never thought of it. I just assumed he was dead. I mean, he looked dead, you know." A thought struck her. "Was he alive? I mean then?"

"He was dead when the police got there," Dirkson said. "That's the best we can do."

"You mean he might have been alive when I found him, and then died? Oh."

"And you have no idea who he was?"

"No. Who was he?"

Dirkson shook his head. "We don't know."

"You don't know?"

"No. He had no identification on him."

"Oh. Isn't that a little strange?"

"Yes it is. But he had nothing in his pockets."

"Nothing?"

"Nothing at all."

"Oh."

Farron stole a glance at Dirkson. Nothing but the key, he thought. He saw the way Dirkson's mind was running.

"You have any idea how this man got into your apartment?" Dirkson asked.

"No, I don't."

"You keep your apartment locked?"

She gave him a look. "In New York City? Of course I do."

"Then how could he have gotten in?"

"I have no idea."

"Anyone else have a key to your apartment?" Dirkson asked casually.

Sheila's eyes flickered. Johnny had a key. But that was none of their business.

"No," she said.

Dirkson caught it again. But he didn't press the point. He just made a mental note to find out to whom she'd given a key.

"All right," he said. "Let's get back to the letter. Can you think of any reason why this man would have sent you the letter?"

"I can't think of any reason why *anyone* would have sent me that letter."

The phone rang. Dirkson picked it up, listened and said, "Okay. Thanks. Send in Tucker."

He hung up the phone and turned back to Sheila. "All right, Miss Benton. That's all for now. I may need to talk to you again later. The police are finished with your apartment."

Sergeant Tucker entered. Dirkson came around his desk, helped Sheila to her feet and gestured to Sergeant Tucker.

"Now," Dirkson said, "if you'll just let Sergeant Tucker take your fingerprints, you're free to go."

Sheila paled. "My fingerprints . . ."

"Well, now," Dirkson said, suavely. "We've taken a lot of fingerprints from your apartment. We need yours so we can tell which of them are *not* yours."

"I see," Sheila said. She didn't look happy.

Sergeant Tucker escorted her out.

Dirkson's frozen smile lasted only until the door was closed. *"Damn,"* he said.

Farron looked at him with a wry smile. "Helpful, isn't she?"

"She certainly is."

Farron cocked his head. "I would hate to comment on the veracity of the D.A.'s office, but I notice you mentioned there was *nothing* in the dead man's pockets. I don't believe you mentioned a key."

"You're damn right I didn't, and you're not going to, either. I want you to clamp a lid on this key bit, and I mean now. If it leaks out, I will hold you personally responsible. You got that? If I end up having to prosecute the girl, I don't want her to know about it until I hit her with it in court."

"You think we'll end up charging her?"

"I don't know. You got any other suspects?"

"Not at the moment."

"Okay. Get on it. And get the dope on the girl. Find out if she really saw her uncle. Find out when she left. Trace the cab that took her back to her apartment. Get the driver to identify her. Pin him down on the time. Then dig into her personal life and give me everything you can. I want to know where she buys her food, who fixes her teeth, what kind of toilet paper she uses."

"It's already being done. Just routine."

"Yeah," Dirkson said. "Just like checking out that letter."

Farron looked at him. "All right. Tell me something. If that girl walked into *your* office with that letter, and told you what she told me, what would you do about it?"

Dirkson considered. "Off the record?"

"Of course."

Dirkson smiled and shook his head. "I'd say, 'Fuck her,' and forget about it."

8

SHEILA BENTON rode uptown in the taxi and assessed her performance, which wasn't easy to do, seeing as how she was a nervous wreck.

Well, she'd gotten through it. That was the best she could say about it. That damn district attorney, with his oily, ingratiating manner. He hadn't believed a word she said, she was sure of it. Particularly the window-shopping part. That was so feeble. But she'd had to say something. She couldn't have said, "No, I was out buying cocaine, so I couldn't possibly have committed the murder."

Shit. The cocaine. They hadn't arrested her. They hadn't searched her. She could have had it on her all the time. She hadn't had to mail it to herself, after all. And she really could have used it now. Christ, how long did the mails take, anyway? Forever, probably. But, hell, it wasn't like she'd sent it to Alaska. The mailbox was half a block from her house. The post office was two blocks from that. So how long could it possibly take?

The answer was, no time at all. But that didn't matter. Because there were no more mail deliveries *today*. And tomorrow seemed an eternity away.

The cab pulled up in front of her building. Sheila paid it off and noted with regret that after paying a hundred for the elusive gram, she now had only twelve dollars left. Well, that was the least of her worries.

Sheila looked at her mailbox on the way in. She couldn't help doing it, though she knew nothing could be there. She went up the stairs, unlocked the door and went in.

Christ. What a nightmare. But it was real. The body was, of course, gone, but there was a chalk outline on the floor around where it had lain, just like in the movies.

Sheila stood, looking down at it, and shuddered.

Then it all came apart for her. She'd held herself together for too long, and now it all let go. She went over and threw herself on the couch, weeping uncontrollably.

She cried for several minutes. Finally she managed to stop. She went in the bathroom and splashed water on her face. She looked at herself in the mirror. God! She looked awful. Well, why not? Who wouldn't, after all that?

She went back and sat down on the couch.

She reached an immediate decision. It was too much to take alone. She needed help. She needed reassurance. She needed Johnny.

He'd told her he was staying at the Wilshire. She called information, got the phone number and dialed.

There was no John Dutton registered there.

Sheila hung up the phone in a cold sweat. Jesus Christ, hadn't he said the Wilshire? She was sure he had. So why the hell wasn't he there? And where the hell was he?

She called information again, and told them to give her the phone numbers of all the hotels in Reno. The woman at information couldn't believe it. Was she crazy? There were three whole pages of 'em. Sheila told her to forget it and hung up the phone.

Sheila thought fleetingly of calling Johnny's wife. Her name was Inez. Inez Dutton. She'd probably be listed. But Inez wasn't supposed to know about her, of course. Well, Sheila could pretend she was a secretary or something, pretend it was a business call, couldn't she?

No, she realized, she couldn't. She could never pull it off. Not in the shape she was in. She'd break down. She'd blow it. Inez would know she wasn't a secretary. In fact, Inez might even know Johnny's secretary.

Shit. Of course. She was being stupid. Johnny's secretary. Sheila didn't know her name, but that didn't matter.

She picked up the phone, called the investment firm and spoke to a secretary who informed her that John Dutton was out of town and would be back tomorrow. She said it was urgent, and asked if there was any place he could be reached. The secretary said, sure, in Reno at the Hotel Wilshire.

Sheila hung up the phone as if in a fog. What was happening? Was it a conspiracy? Was everyone against her?

She shook her head to clear it, and got control of herself. Okay, she had to think. Her biggest problem right now was, sooner or later she was going to be arrested for murder. She was sure of it. The D.A. hadn't bought her story, there were no other candidates and they were going to get her. She couldn't reach Johnny, and she needed help.

A certain kind of help was immediately available, Sheila knew. All she had to do was call Uncle Max, and he'd take care of everything. He'd swing into action, hire teams of lawyers, call the commissioner, maybe even buy the cops off, if such a thing were possible in a murder case.

But that was just the trouble. *He'd* take care of everything. He'd be in complete control, doing everything, telling everyone what to do. She'd have no say in anything. In fact, he probably wouldn't even let her know what he was doing. He'd keep her in the dark, treat her like a child. And his stranglehold over her life would tighten and tighten.

Even so, this *was* murder, and she was so scared she probably would have called him if it hadn't been for one thing. The coke. If Max hired lawyers for her, she'd have to tell them about the coke. Or even if she didn't tell them, they'd find out. They'd question her, and she'd have to pretend to be cooperating with them, so she'd have to answer, and eventually they'd catch her in a lie and break her, and they'd find out.

And then Uncle Max would know. Sheila shuddered at the thought. Uncle Max. Her trustee. Uncle Max would know.

And that would cost her her inheritance.

No, damn it. Bad as the situation was, scared as Sheila was, Uncle Max was out. If anything was going to be done, *she* would have to do it.

Sheila got up, went in the kitchen alcove, and got out the Yellow Pages. Hell, which was it? Lawyers or attorneys? A damn stupid way to go about it, but at the moment she couldn't think of anything else to do.

9

STEVE WINSLOW was dreaming.

He was in a play, but the thing was, he hadn't rehearsed it. He hadn't rehearsed it, and he didn't know the lines. He wasn't even sure what the play was. It seemed to be a Chekhov, but he didn't know which one. *Uncle Vanya? The Cherry Orchard? The Sea Gull?* No. Damn.

He wasn't on stage. He was in the wings, waiting to go on. Waiting and watching the action. There was a girl on stage, and he was listening to her dialogue, trying to get a clue. Christ, if she'd just say she wanted to go to Moscow, she'd be Irina, and the play would be *Three Sisters*. But she wasn't saying that.

But what she was saying was right there in the script he was holding, the script he had now, but could not take on stage. And there, just a page later, was his entrance. For a long, long scene. Lines and lines and lines, more than he could ever learn in time.

The odd thing was, the script in his hand didn't tell him the name of the play, didn't even give him a clue. But he didn't even think of that. That didn't even bother him. That wasn't part of the dream. In the dream it never occurred to him that the play's title should be on the script, that all he had to do was look at the cover. In the dream the script only told him the lines, the lines that he didn't know. That and how soon it would be that he would have to say them.

And suddenly it came, and he was on stage, and the girl was talking to him, and in the void beyond the footlights were a thousand eyes all staring at him, waiting for him to reply, waiting like the girl for an answer that would not come, for a performance that would not happen. And here was this girl talking to him, and he didn't even know her name. Christ, he didn't even know *his* name. And the girl was talking, and the people were watching, and a phone was ringing, and—

A phone? A phone in a Chekhov play? Wait. What was going on? Something was not right. Couldn't be a phone. A bell, maybe. Yeah. A bell. Saved by the bell. He didn't have to go on. He didn't have to answer. The play was called off, down but not out, saved by the bell at the count of nine and—

Steve's eyes popped open. He blinked, stared. Where was he? What was that?

His eyes blurred. Then focussed.

A battered bookcase. The top two shelves taken up with worn, dog-eared, Perry Mason murder mysteries—paperbacks, some with their spines cracked, and the pages separated so that the titles were no longer legible; others, in slightly better repair, dating themselves with twenty-five- and thirty-five-cent prices. The middle shelves filled with books of plays, including several Samuel French scripts. The lower shelves filled with newer-looking law books.

Posters tacked to dirty, cracked, off-white walls. Faded posters from summer stock theatre productions: "Mayfair Theatre presents *A Streetcar Named Desire*"; "Roundtree Summer Theatre presents *The Homecoming.*"

A window with the blind drawn, light spilling through the cracks, offering the only illumination in the room.

The room where Steve lay stretched out on the couch.

Listening to the phone ring.

His room. His couch. His phone.

Phone.

Shit.

Steve rolled onto one side, reached over the end of the couch and grabbed the receiver from the end table.

"Hello," he muttered.

An adenoidal voice said, "Mr. Winslow?"

"Yes."

"This is your answering service. A Miss—"

"Wait a minute. Wait a minute," Steve said. "Lemme get a pencil."

He hung the phone over the end of the couch, sat up, and threw the blanket off him. He rubbed his eyes and looked at the clock. 4:30. Damn.

He got to his feet and pulled up the blind to let the light in. He turned and looked around, helplessly.

Steve's apartment was a one-room affair not unlike Sheila's except for the fact that his couch did not fold out into a bed, he slept on it as is, and, while Sheila kept her apartment fairly neat, his was a holy mess.

He plodded to the desk, pawed through the litter on top, and pulled open the drawers.

No pencil. Letters, books, magazines, newspapers, everything else but a pencil.

He was about to give up and just try to memorize the message, when he spotted a pencil on the floor. He scooped it up. The point was broken. He began picking at it with his thumbnail. He grabbed a letter off his desk and hurried back to the phone.

"Okay," he said. "Shoot."

"A Miss Sheila Benton called and wants you to call her right back. She said it was urgent."

"Wait a minute. What did you tell her?"

"Just what it says on your card—'Mr. Winslow is in conference with a client right now. Could I have him call you back?'"

"Fine. What was the name?"

"Sheila Benton."

"And the number?"

She told him and he wrote it down as best he could with the unsharpened pencil. It was poor, but it was legible.

He hung up the phone and dialed the number.

The first ring had barely begun when the phone was snatched up and a voice said, "Hello?"

"Sheila Benton?"

"Yes."

"Steve Winslow, returning your call."

"Oh, Mr. Winslow. Thank god you're there. I need an attorney."

"What's the trouble?"

"A man was murdered in my apartment this afternoon."

There was a moment's pause while Winslow digested the information. Murdered! Really? Was this a crank phone call? Was this one of his friends playing a joke on him?

"Murdered?"

"Yes. A man I'd never seen before. And yesterday I received a blackmail letter."

Jesus. If this was a prank, it was too good not to bite.

"Miss Benton, I'd better see you right away. Where are you now?"

"In my apartment. Do you want me to come to your office?"

Steve instinctively glanced at the cluttered room. He smiled slightly. "No. Don't come to my office. I want to see the scene of the crime anyway. I'll come there."

"All right. It's 193 West 89th Street. 2B."

He almost said, "Or not to be," but controlled himself. Instead he said, "Be right there."

He hung up the phone and shook his head. Holy shit. Was it possible? A client.

He stumbled into the bathroom, turned on the light and splashed water on his face. He gazed at his reflection in the mirror.

Though he was thirty-five, he looked younger. Part of the reason was his shoulder-length dark hair, which made him look like a hippie from the sixties. The hair framed a lean, expressive, sensitive face. Damn. An artist's face, not a lawyer's.

Steve pulled off the t-shirt and undershorts he had been sleeping in, and jumped into the shower. He washed quickly, got out and toweled himself dry.

Now what to do? His hair. Jesus, his hair. He had kept it long since his acting days out of force of habit—you could always cut it for a part, but you couldn't grow it overnight. Well, no time for a haircut now. He left it wet, combed it back, plastered it to the back of his neck. There. He could tuck it into his shirt collar.

If he had a clean shirt. Shit. He groped through the closet. Yes. A white shirt. Could use an ironing, but not bad. He grabbed it off the hanger, put it on, tucking the hair under the collar. He buttoned it to the neck, to hold the hair in place.

He went and looked in the mirror. Not bad.

Of course, pants would help.

He went back, jerked open a drawer of the bureau, found a pair of jockey shorts, pulled them on.

Great. Now the suit.

Steve rummaged through the whole closet before he remembered. Shit. He'd lent the suit to Arthur for that wedding last year, and he'd never gotten it back. And Arthur'd moved to California.

Jesus, what to do? Improvise. Pants, jacket, tie—throw it

together, get it done. If you're going to do it at all. If not, call her
back and tell her to forget it. What are you, nuts? The first client
in a year. Come on Winslow, you big schmuck, this can't be
that hard.

He continued to rummage through the closet and dresser
drawers.

10

SHEILA BENTON opened the front door and stared.

Standing in the doorway was a young man with his hair slicked
back from his head, wearing blue jeans, a tan corduroy jacket and
a green tie.

Sheila blinked. "Yes?"

"Sheila Benton?"

"Yes."

"Steve Winslow."

Sheila blinked again.

Steve wasn't going to take the chance of having the door
slammed in his face, not by a potential client, and not in a
murder case. He pushed right by her and into the apartment.

Sheila, as if in a daze, closed the door and locked it. She turned
to find the young man standing looking down at the chalk outline
on the floor.

"This is where you found him, eh?" Steve said.

"Yes."

"How was he killed?"

"With a knife."

"In the front or the back?"

"The back."

He frowned. "Hmm. That probably rules out self-defense. So he was lying on his stomach?"

"Yes."

"Where'd the knife come from?"

"It was mine. From that set on the wall."

Sheila pointed to the kitchen alcove.

"Uh huh." He crossed to the alcove. He pantomimed taking a knife out of the rack, turning and stabbing the man. He followed the man's fall down to the chalk line.

As he bent down, some of the hair tucked under his collar came loose and swung down.

Steve stood up. The hair hung down the left side of his face, giving him a lopsided look.

"Well, that's a break," he said.

"What?" Sheila said. She had only half heard him. She was staring, hypnotized, at the dangling hair.

"The position of the knife rack to the body," he said. "The circumstantial evidence would indicate that the murderer grabbed the knife from the rack, turned and stabbed the victim."

"So?"

"If worse comes to worst, that would probably rule out premeditation." He glanced around the room, then back at her. "Okay," he said. "Let's get the facts. Tell me exactly what happened."

Sheila blinked again, seemed unable to speak.

"Well," he said. "What's the matter?"

Sheila shook her head. "I'm sorry. It's just that . . . I don't know. You're just not my idea of a lawyer."

He looked at her, smiled. "Well," he said. "You're not my idea of a murder suspect, either."

It was a weak comeback, and it wasn't working. The girl just kept staring at him.

He noticed the dangling hair. He pushed it back. He gave up, sighed. All right, so much for bluffing it through.

"All right, look," he said. "I'm not what you expected. You think of a lawyer as someone in a three-piece suit with a haircut and a manicure and probably about sixty years old. Well, I'm not. But I didn't call you, you called me. That doesn't mean you have to hire me, and if you want to tell me to get lost, you certainly have that right. But the thing is, you can tell me to get lost at any time. So since you got me over here, why don't you tell me what this is all about, and we'll see if there is anything we can do about it. And *then* you can tell me to get lost, and you can go out and find some guy who dresses right and looks constipated, which I'm sure is your idea of what a lawyer ought to be."

She smiled, and he knew the battle was half over.

11

DISTRICT ATTORNEY Harry Dirkson was worried. He was worried because of what had happened and because of what hadn't happened. What had happened was Sheila Benton, niece of Maxwell Baxter, had gotten involved in a murder. What hadn't happened was Maxwell Baxter's attorneys hadn't called him and/or the commissioner, raising merry hell and demanding that the situation be cleared up as quickly and quietly as possible, keeping Sheila Benton's name out of it.

If that happened—and Dirkson was sure that it would—then he would be in a no-win situation. If he kept Sheila Benton out of it, which would be a pretty impossible job, and it got out, as it surely would, the press would crucify him. By the time the media got finished with him, his chances for reelection would be virtually nil.

On the other hand, if, god forbid, he should end up having to prosecute the girl, it was even worse. He would have Maxwell

Baxter, the commissioner, and maybe even the mayor on his back. No one would condone his actions. He would be the fall guy, pushed out front with no room to maneuver, and no expectations except to take grief from all sides until his head was finally, mercifully, chopped off.

Dirkson sat and stewed.

There were only two ways out, he figured. The first was the best. Clean it up. Exonerate the girl. Find conclusive proof that she wasn't involved. In short, find the murderer.

The second was terrible. Nail the girl. Prove she did it. Prosecute her and prove her guilty in a court of law.

It was a frightening proposition, but, Dirkson realized, it was something he just might have to do. It would be messy. He would take a lot of grief over it from all sides. But if she were guilty, really guilty, and he proved it, he just might survive. More than just surviving, he might emerge a hero, a fearless, crusading D.A., who forged ahead regardless of political pressure and personal interest, believing in equal justice for all.

Dirkson thought of that image a while, and he liked it. It scared the hell out of him, but he liked it. Prove the girl guilty. Done right, it could be quite a coup.

But too risky. Dirkson came back to reality. Jesus. Too damn risky. A last resort, and nothing more. You don't proceed against the girl unless it's an ironclad case. A sure thing.

You don't proceed against the girl unless you have no choice.

Having made that decision, Dirkson immediately felt better. Yeah, that was the ticket. The burden of proof was on the police department. They had to come up with it all. And it had to be airtight. Motive, means, opportunity. It all had to be there.

Well, the means was already there. The knife. It was presumably from the rack on the wall, which made it the girl's knife. Not good, but not bad. The knife was there at hand. Anyone could have used it.

Opportunity? That would depend on the autopsy report and the testimony of that damn cab driver, if the cops ever found him.

Shit, why the hell hadn't they found him yet? How the hell long could it take the damn cops to run a simple procedure like that? Dirkson realized it probably didn't matter. The preliminary report indicated that the victim had been killed not long before the police arrived on the scene. So, unless something spectacular and unforeseen showed up in the autopsy report, there was no reason why she couldn't have come home, stabbed him and run out and called the cops.

Dirkson was starting to feel slightly queazy. Shit. Means and opportunity were falling into place just fine.

Which left motive.

There, on his desk, sat the blackmail note. That's what it was, Dirkson conceded. Despite what some clever defense attorney might argue, despite its vagueness, despite the lack of any hint of violence or any demand for money, this was a blackmail note.

If it should tie up to the dead man.

The dead man. Another sore point. Who the hell was he? Why hadn't he been carrying any identification? Why hadn't the police been able to track him down yet?

If there should be anything to tie him to the girl . . .

Dirkson chuckled, in spite of himself. That *was* kind of funny. Tie him to the girl, indeed. He was found in her living room with the key to her apartment in his pocket, but, if there was anything *else* to tie him to the girl.

To Sheila Benton.

Maxwell Baxter's niece.

Shit.

Dirkson grabbed up the phone, pushed the intercom button and buzzed his law clerk.

"Sir?"

"Reese, who are Maxwell Baxter's attorneys?"

"I don't know, sir."

"Find out."

"Yes sir."

Dirkson hung up the phone, frowned, looked at the clock.

Damn. It was getting late. Something should have happened by now. Either the police or Baxter's lawyers or—

Shit! *Late.* This was the afternoon he was scheduled to play golf. Two of the guys in the foursome were heavy campaign contributors. And the main reason they were was because they liked the prestige of being able to hobnob with the bigwigs, to be able to say in passing, "Oh, not tomorrow, I'm playing golf in D.A. Dirkson's foursome." Jesus Christ, he was due to tee off in fifteen minutes. And this *was* an election year.

Dirkson lunged for the phone.

"Reese."

"Yes, sir, I'm working on it."

"Never mind that. Get me Dunwoody Golf Course."

"Sir?"

"*Now.*"

Dirkson slammed down the phone.

Hell. What should he do now? Wait for the phone call? Or hop in a cab and leave it to Reese to explain? How the hell long would it take to get up to Yonkers, anyway? A lot more than fifteen minutes. Can't let Reese explain, he's an idiot. Gotta wait for the call, explain the emergency, meet 'em for cocktails at the nineteenth hole and—

The phone rang.

Dirkson lunged for it. "Reese. You got the golf course?"

"No sir. The police lab. Kramer."

"Shit." Dirkson pushed the button. "Yeah, Kramer, what you got?"

"I've got good news and bad news."

Dirkson sighed. Shit. Everyone was a fucking comedian. "Yeah. Let's have it."

"I classified the victim's fingerprints and ran them through the computer. There's no record on him."

"Great. What's the good news?"

"The girl's prints are on the knife."

"Okay. Thanks."

Dirkson hung up. He put his elbows on the desk, put his head in his hands and rubbed his forehead. He seemed to be getting a terrible headache.

Yeah, sure, he told himself.

Good news.

12

"IT STINKS."

Sheila Benton frowned. "What?"

Steve Winslow shook his head. "Your story stinks."

That bothered her. Sheila had spent the whole time she was waiting for him working on her story, and she thought she'd done a pretty good job. She'd told him everything. That is, she'd told him more than she'd told the cops. She hadn't told him about the cocaine—she couldn't bring herself to do that. He was a lawyer and all, and he was supposed to be on her side, and everything she told him was a confidential communication, and all that, but still.

But she'd told him everything else. In particular, she told him the times everything had happened, times she actually knew, but had felt she shouldn't tell the cops. Somehow the times things happened had seemed incriminating to her.

And for good reason. Because it included the time she had taken out of her schedule to buy cocaine.

Sheila was seated on the couch. Steve was standing. He had been pacing back and forth in front of her as she told her story. He hadn't been looking at her though, aside from an occasional glance. For the most part he was thinking, just staring off into space. That bothered her. She was accustomed to being looked at.

For his part, Steve was distracted, but not so much that he hadn't heard her story. And not so much that he couldn't tell that it was a story with significant gaps. But still.

Maxwell Baxter, that was what was distracting him. Jesus Christ. This girl was Baxter's niece, for Christ's sake. It was like saying she was a Rockefeller. Which meant this was not just a murder case, this was a *sensational* murder case. For someone who'd been out of work just hours before, it was a lot to take in.

Glamour. Publicity. And a whopping retainer. Twenty-five thousand at least. It was wrong to be thinking that now, Winslow knew, but he was only human, and what human being could hear what he had just heard and help thinking that?

"What's wrong with my story?" Sheila asked.

That brought him back to earth. The job was only his if he earned it, and that was very much in doubt. Stop fantasizing and get down to brass tacks. Show her how her story won't stand up.

He looked at her then, and she immediately wished he hadn't. Because somehow the look in this strange man's eyes frightened her, more than the policeman's had, or even the district attorney.

It was as if he knew she was lying. As if he could see right through her.

And of course he jumped right on the time element.

"You left your uncle's at eleven forty-five. You didn't get home until almost one-thirty."

"I was window-shopping."

"For an hour and forty-five minutes? That's a long time to be window-shopping."

Sheila smiled at him. She raised her eyebrow ironically. "Mr. Winslow, take a look at this apartment. I am not a rich girl. I can't afford nice things. But I happen to like nice things. So I window-shop."

"They'll trace the cab you took back here. They'll find out when it picked you up, where it picked you up, and what time you got back here."

"So?"

"So if the time the cabbie says he dropped you off here is much earlier than the time you called the cops, nothing I can do is going to save you."

"But if the times check, I'm in the clear?"

"No. He could have been waiting for you when you returned. You could have killed him, then dashed out to call the police."

"But what if the doctor can prove he'd been dead longer than that?"

Steve thought a moment. "If he was killed before noon you're all right. You couldn't have gotten back from your uncle's before then. If he was killed after noon and before one-thirty, they'll claim you killed him, then rushed out to Fifth Avenue by bus or subway so that you could build up an alibi by taking a taxicab back."

Sheila frowned. "You talk as if I were going to be arrested."

"Of course you're going to be arrested. Your story stinks. You were being blackmailed. The man who is presumably the black-mailer is found in your apartment, stabbed with your knife. If you were a cop, who would you arrest?"

"When will they arrest me?"

"Probably as soon as they identify the body. They may wait till they find out what he had on you, but I doubt it."

"He had nothing on me."

Steve shrugged. "Yeah. Sure. He probably just wanted to sell you insurance, or something."

Sheila looked at him. "You don't believe me, do you?"

"I told you, your story stinks. It'll never stand up under cross-examination."

"Why not?"

Steve turned his back on her, paced away then turned back.

Sheila suddenly realized what was coming.

A cross-examination.

"All right," he said. "You say you were window-shopping?"

"Yes."

"On Fifth Avenue?"

"Yes."

"Which stores?"

"Well, Bloomingdales."

"That's Lexington, but I'll take it. That's one store. Did you spend an hour and a half at that one store?"

"Of course not."

"Well, what about Saks Fifth Avenue? How did you manage to miss that?"

"I didn't miss that."

"You window-shopped it?"

"Yes, I did."

"Fine. Now tell me one item you saw in the window at Saks Fifth Avenue."

Sheila tossed her head and gave him her most endearing smile. "Aw, come on."

He bored right in. "No. *You* come on. You tell me window-shopping is important to you, you love rich things, it's a big deal in your life, so this is not a casual thing and you're going to pay attention to what you see. So tell me one thing you saw in the window at Saks Fifth Avenue."

"Well . . ."

"Yes?"

"Damn it, I'm thinking."

"Good plan."

"What?"

"Nothing. Keep thinking."

"Damn it—"

"Thought of it yet?"

"Yes!" She practically screamed it at him.

"Good," he said calmly. "What was it?"

"A swimsuit."

"What kind?"

"A bikini."

"What color?"

"Blue."

Steve smiled, shook his head and locked his eyes onto hers.

"The reason I asked about Saks," he said gently, "is that I passed by there this morning. The window display is devoted to evening wear."

Her eyes faltered. "Well, maybe I'm wrong. Maybe it was Bloomingdales where I saw the swimsuit. Yes, I'm sure it was Bloomingdales."

He smiled again. "You see. Your story won't stand up. Not under cross-examination. And that's just a sample of what the D.A.'s gonna throw at you. He'll eat you up."

"No fair," Sheila said. "That's just dumb luck. If you hadn't happened to know what was in the window at Saks—"

Steve laughed. "Are you kidding me? You think I have the faintest idea what's in the windows at Saks Fifth Avenue? You think that's something I would really notice? That was a bluff, and not a very good one at that. The D.A.'s gonna fire a million questions at you, and sometimes he'll be bluffing and sometimes he won't, and you're not gonna know which is which."

Sheila bit her lip.

"Now," Steve said. "I certainly don't want to advise you, but if I were you and I were going to tell that story, the first thing I would do would be get my ass over to Fifth Avenue and find out what's in the goddamned windows."

Sheila hadn't realized it, but she'd made a decision. She realized it now. She realized it from the sense of loss she felt when she heard him say, "I certainly don't want to advise you." The decision, of course, was to have him act as her attorney. She wanted him. Strangely enough, she felt comfortable with this unconventional man who made her feel uncomfortable. There was something reassuring in the way he distrusted her. Something about him she liked. She took his statement to be a rejection of her case, and from her disappointment, she realized she wanted him.

"You don't want to advise me?" she said.

He smiled and shook his head. "I don't want to suborn perjury, compound a felony or conspire to conceal a crime." He looked at her and said, pointedly, "That's why I'm *not* advising you to look in those windows, and if you should look in those windows, it would certainly be without my knowledge. That advice I can't give you. I'm perfectly willing to advise you on legal matters."

"Then you'll be my attorney?"

"Just as soon as you give me a retainer."

Sheila bit her lip. "You'll have to get that from Uncle Max."

"All right. Get your purse."

Sheila looked at him. "We're going to see Uncle Max?"

"I'll call on him later. Right now I want you to take me to Fifth Avenue and show me where you were window-shopping."

Sheila looked at him, and a light dawned. "You mean you want me to—"

"I want to get the time element straight," he interrupted, pointedly. "The time element's going to be very important."

She stared at him, blinked. "Yes," she said, slowly. "I can see that it is."

13

DIRKSON GRABBED up the phone.

"Yes," he hissed.

"Maxwell Baxter's attorneys are Marston, Marston, and Cramden," Reese told him.

"Great. And could you tell me why it took so long to get that information?"

"Because I've been on the phone with the Dunwoody Golf Course."

"Oh, yes. And?"

"The gentlemen in question are not pleased. They seemed to take the attitude that *I* was preventing you from keeping your golf date."

"Yes, yes," Dirkson said impatiently. "How did you resolve it?"

"They'll meet you in the clubhouse after the round. They didn't mention future campaign contributions."

"Fuck you, Reese."

"Yes, sir. And Lieutenant Farron just came in."

"Send him in."

Farron didn't look happy, but then Dirkson wouldn't have expected him to. After all, Farron was pretty much in the doghouse over this one.

"What now?" Dirkson asked.

Farron shook his head. "We still haven't traced him."

"You came here to tell me that? Come tell me when you *have* traced him."

"You know the girl's prints are on the knife?"

"Yesterday's news. Anything else?"

Farron held out a paper. "Autopsy report."

"Why didn't you say so," Dirkson said irritably. He snatched it from him and looked it over.

"The only thing significant's the time element," Farron said.

Dirkson looked. "Twelve-thirty to one-thirty."

"That's right."

Dirkson looked at Farron. "Wasn't her call logged at one thirty-eight?"

"Sure was."

Dirkson frowned. "Well, that's sure cutting it a little thin. Can't we do any better than that?"

"Don't look at me. Talk to the medical examiner. Those are the times during which he says it could have happened."

"What time did she get home?"

Farron shook his head. "We haven't found the cab driver yet."

Dirkson looked at him. "Then what the hell are you doing here?"

Farron gave him a look, turned and walked out the door.

The phone rang. Dirkson scooped it up.

"Yeah, what is it?"

"Yes, sir," Reese said. "There's a Mr. Marston, of Marston, Marston, and Cramden on the phone."

"Oh, shit."

14

SHEILA AND Steve Winslow stood in front of Saks Fifth Avenue.

"This is one of the windows you looked in?" Steve asked her.

"Yes."

"How long were you looking in this window?"

"Four or five minutes."

"What were you looking at?"

Sheila looked in the window. "I was particularly interested in a blue dress with silver trim on the sleeves and hem."

"Your memory is excellent," Steve said, dryly. "Now then, it would have taken you about ten minutes to walk here from your uncle's apartment. The cab ride home would be about fifteen minutes. That leaves an hour and twenty minutes you must have been window-shopping."

"That's right."

"So, I want you to retrace your path to all the stores you visited this afternoon and try to remember how long you stayed at each of them."

"I understand," Sheila said.

"Good. First you can walk me to Uncle Max's. You should start from there, anyway."

"Okay."

They walked off down the street.

Realizing they were on the way to Uncle Max's made Sheila uneasy. She stole a glance at Winslow. She'd been relating to him as a person, because she was caught up in her own problems. So she'd forgotten what he looked like, what her first impression of him had been. God. This man was going to call on Uncle Max. This man was going to ask him for money.

"Do you want me to go in with you to talk to Uncle Max?" Sheila said. She tried to make the question sound casual.

"No, you don't have to," Steve said. "I can introduce myself. You just start from outside the building and retrace your path to all the stores."

"Okay," she said.

He grinned. "You sound relieved."

She flushed. Damn. She couldn't hide anything from him. "Well, I have to warn you," she said. "Uncle Max is going to be difficult."

"You mean about the money?"

"More than that. He'll probably insist on hiring his own lawyer to represent me."

"Well, why don't you let him?"

Sheila's eyes flicked for a moment as she thought of the real reason—the cocaine.

Steve noticed. He said nothing, but as with the window-shopping bit, he made a mental note that for some reason the girl was holding out on him.

She recovered quickly. "Because I don't want him running my life. I want my own lawyer who's working for me, not some stooge of Uncle Max's who's taking his orders and reporting back to him."

"Lawyers don't do that," Steve told her.

"You don't know Uncle Max. He's stinking rich, and he uses his money to control people. He controls my money, and tries to use it to control me. He thinks just because he's my trustee he can run my life."

"And you won't let him?"

She looked at him and laughed. "Why do you think I live in that stinking apartment? My trust fund pays me two hundred a week. Uncle Max would give me more if I did what he wanted. I don't, so he doesn't."

"Tell me about the trust," Steve said. "Who set it up, your father?"

"My father died before I was born. My mother was killed in a car accident when I was four." Sheila sighed. "It was in Vermont. One of those twisting mountain roads. The brakes failed, and the car went off a curve. Suddenly I was an orphan.

"After that, I lived with my grandfather at his house in Vermont. Actually, we'd been living with him before, my mother and I. Before she died, I mean. I'm not telling this well. What I mean is, I was already living there.

"Anyway, my grandfather died a year later. He left a third of his money to Uncle Max, a third to my cousin Phillip, and a third to me. He designated Uncle Max sole trustee for the two of us."

"Wait a minute. I thought you said your cousin's father was still alive. You saw him yesterday with Phillip at Uncle Max's."

"That's right. Uncle Teddy was completely disinherited."

"Why?"

"Uncle Teddy was pretty wild when he was young. Of course, I was too young at the time to understand what was going on. But I do know when grandfather died, Uncle Teddy was in jail."

"Uh huh. So Uncle Max owns the whole shooting works."

"That's right. And you're going to have to hustle to get your retainer."

Steve smiled. "You have no objection to taking money from Uncle Max, I see."

"None at all. I just don't want him telling me what to do. But as long as I can hire my own lawyer, I'm perfectly willing to let Uncle Max pay him."

Steve nodded. "I'm perfectly willing to let Uncle Max pay him too."

15

MAXWELL BAXTER, "casually" dressed in a thousand-dollar, tailor-made suit, regarded Steve Winslow as one might regard some rare species at the zoo. Corduroy. A green tie. Blue jeans. Really!

Maxwell Baxter was showing none of this. His manner to Winslow was infinite politeness and elaborate condescension, which, coupled with his icy reserve, was as irritating as he had hoped it would be.

"Mr. Winslow," Max said with a thin smile. "I don't wish to seem rude, but you are not my niece's attorney."

Steve was seated on the couch. He had declined Baxter's offer of a brandy, correctly realizing the offer was only an ironic attempt on Max's part to make him ill at ease. Uncle Max had made himself a drink, and was standing near the bar holding it.

Steve looked up at him, realizing Baxter was standing just so he would have to do that.

They'd exchanged opening remarks. Steve had introduced himself, and begun to explain the situation Sheila had found herself in. Baxter had interrupted to say he knew all about it. He'd followed that by the condescending offer of a drink, and then the flat denial that Winslow was Sheila's attorney.

"She has asked me to represent her," Steve said.

Max waved this aside. "Doubtless she has. However, you must

be aware of the fact that she has no money with which to pay you. I assume you have no desire to work for nothing."

"She has her trust fund."

Max smiled. "Of which I am the sole trustee. The disbursement of Sheila's money is entirely at my discretion. You will receive a fee only if I choose to pay you. And I do not choose to pay you."

Steve smiled back. "Did it ever occur to you that I might represent Sheila anyway, sue you for my fee and attempt to upset the trust?"

Max shook his head, pityingly. "Mr. Winslow, I am afraid my niece has not been entirely frank with you. She had lawyers look into the trust three years ago. They found it was impregnable."

Steve frowned. That seemed strange. Sheila had no money to hire lawyers, and Uncle Max certainly wouldn't have paid them. Maybe with a trust of that size at stake, lawyers would be willing to work on contingency. But then, if Sheila already had lawyers, why had she called him?

"That may well be," Steve said. "I haven't seen the trust yet."

"Implying you think you could do better? Excuse me a moment."

Max turned and walked into the study. He was back a minute later carrying a file folder. He presented it to Steve.

"Here's a copy of the trust. Don't read it now, it's quite lengthy. Take it with you and peruse it at your leisure."

"That's very considerate of you."

"Not at all. Merely expedient. Letting you read the trust is the best way to convince you that any action you take is bound to be fruitless."

Max smiled coldly and sat down in the easy chair. "The attorneys that Sheila had look into the trust are Poindexter and Brown. Perhaps you're wondering why Sheila called you rather than them in this matter. The answer is simple. She owes them money. They have never been paid for their services. I know because, having failed to collect from Sheila, they billed me as Sheila's trustee. Naturally, I declined to pay. They have not sued. And the reason they have not sued is because, having studied the trust, they know it to be judgmentproof and realize such suits would be futile."

Steve nodded. "I see. In that case, I might attack the will."

"The will?"

"That's right. Your father's will."

Max was genuinely surprised. "But the will has been proven genuine. There's no question about it."

"Oh no? Your brother was disinherited by that will. And I understand he's your older brother. Now, any will that disinherits the firstborn son is particularly open to attack. You just might find yourself out in the cold with Uncle Teddy in the driver's seat."

Max smiled, back in control again. "Mr. Winslow, once again you are speaking in ignorance of the facts. Before you get yourself out on a limb, let me try to explain this to you."

"For my own good, of course," Steve said sarcastically. Maxwell Baxter was one of those people he instinctively disliked.

Max took no notice. "My father was an eccentric man in many respects," he began. "But he was a good man, a kind man and a very honest man. He had very high scruples and a great sense of right and wrong."

"All right, all right, he was a saint. So what?"

"Alice, Sheila's mother, was his eldest child. The proverbial apple of his eye. In his original will, the bulk of his estate went to her. Alice was killed in a car accident when Sheila was four. Teddy, being the next eldest, should have become the principal heir. But Teddy was rather wild in those days. It happened that the day Alice was killed, Teddy was in New York promoting a fraudulent business deal. He was arrested the following day. Father was outraged, of course, and so, when he changed his will, Teddy was left out in the cold."

"And, wishing to provide for Sheila, he set up the trust fund, with you as trustee."

"Exactly. He set up a similar fund for Teddy's son, Phillip. And to make sure that Teddy couldn't get his hands on the money, he made me trustee and provided that Phillip couldn't touch the money until he turned thirty-five."

"And the same is true of Sheila."

"Exactly. So if you have the patience to wait eleven years for your retainer, feel free to take the case."

"Sheila gets the entire principal when she turns thirty-five?"

"Not necessarily. My father put a provision in the trust that if Sheila is involved in any serious scandal that would bring discredit on the family name, the money is to go to charity."

"Terrific. An open invitation for blackmail. That's all the police will need to give them an airtight case."

"That's why I've hired the best lawyers in town to represent her."

"Who?"

"Marston, Marston, and Cramden."

Steve shook his head. "Corporation lawyers. Have they ever handled a murder trial?"

"They'll handle it so there *is* no trial."

Steve stood up. "Don't kid yourself. Within twenty-four hours your niece will be in jail charged with first-degree murder. The only reason she isn't there right now is because the police haven't identified the body yet so they don't know just who the hell to charge her with killing."

"And when she is," Max said calmly, "Marston, Marston, and Cramden will represent her."

"We'll see about that," Steve said grimly. He headed for the door.

"Going so soon, Mr. Winslow?" Max said as he passed.

"I have work to do, Mr. Baxter."

As Steve rang for the elevator, Max followed as far as the foyer door for a parting shot.

"So glad you can afford to work for nothing, Mr. Winslow," he said. "So few people can."

16

STEVE WINSLOW came out the front door of Maxwell Baxter's building onto Park Avenue, and looked up and down the block. Christ. There were never any phones on the damn street.

Steve shook his head and chuckled. Hell, what could you do but laugh? After all, it was kind of funny. Here it was. Just what he'd always wanted. A real murder case. Why should he get a fee for it too?

He headed over to Lexington and spotted a phone on the corner. A woman with a huge load of fancy shopping bags was making for it. Steve Winslow cut in ahead of her. He knew from experience she would take forever, and he was in no mood to be a gentleman.

Steve punched in 411, and asked for the listing. The operator said, "Certainly," he heard the click and the recording began. Oh hell, the worst of these recording information services, where the hell was a pencil?

He dug in his pockets, pulled out a whole bunch of junk, and finally, an old ballpoint pen. He tried it on an old envelope. It worked.

By that time the recording had already given the phone number and instructed him to stay on the line if he needed further assistance.

An operator clicked on. "Yes?"

"The phone number for the Taylor Detective Agency."

"We just gave you that number."

"I missed it."

"All right."

There was a click, and the recording began again.

He got it that time. He broke the connection, got a dial tone and dialed the number.

A female voice answered. "Taylor Detective Agency."

"Mark Taylor, please."

"Who's calling, please?"

"Steve Winslow."

"One moment please."

There was a click, and Steve was on hold. He hated that. At least there was no recorded music. Another click, and Mark Taylor's slightly Brooklyn twang said, "Steve, hi. Good to hear from you. Where you been keeping yourself?"

"It's a long story. Listen, Mark. I got some work for you."

"Oh yeah? What kind of work?"

"A murder case."

"No shit. I thought Wilson and Doyle fixed it so you'd never work again."

"I got lucky. Now look. A man was found murdered in a Miss Sheila Benton's apartment this afternoon."

"Yeah. What about it?"

"You heard about it?"

"Can't say that I have."

"Well, you will. It happens to be the biggest thing going."

"Oh yeah? And why is that?"

"Because Sheila Benton happens to be Maxwell Baxter's niece."

Taylor whistled. "You mean to say you got a piece of that action?"

"That's right."

"Who's the client?"

"Sheila Benton."

Taylor whistled again. "How the hell'd you get involved?"

"That can keep. The thing is, I need information, and I need it fast. The police haven't identified the body yet. When they do, I want you to go to work on him."

"How strong?"

"As strong as you can. I want to know everything the police know, and some things they don't know. Get men started. Work round the clock, if you have to."

"That's gonna run into a lot of money."

"Don't worry. I got a huge retainer."

Steve hung up the phone. He walked over to a townhouse, sat on the front steps and opened the file folder. Inside, as Baxter had said, was a copy of the provisions of the trust. Steve sat on the steps and read it through.

It was simple and straightforward. Sheila's entire fortune was in trust until she reached the age of thirty-five. Maxwell Baxter was designated sole trustee. In the event of his death, the power of trustee reverted to the bank, which was to administer the trust under guidelines specifically laid out in the document, which included the amount of money Sheila could receive each month. The only provision under which she could receive more was in the event of a medical emergency, or if she wished to attend school.

The morals clause was there too, just as Baxter had said: ". . . be convicted of any crime, or engage in any illegal, immoral or unethical act which should, in the estimation of the trustee, bring disrepute upon the family name, the entire trust is forfeit, and . . ."

Steve skimmed through the rest of the document and found the passage he was looking for: "This trust is held inviolate. No lien of any kind upon the said Sheila Benton shall be payable from or shall in any way reduce the amount of this trust. No judgment in any court of law against the said Sheila Benton shall be payable from this trust or shall in any way reduce the amount of this trust. Any debts incurred by the said Sheila Benton are hers and hers alone, and have no bearing upon this trust, nor shall any creditor of Sheila Benton have any legal recourse. . . ."

It went on in that manner for another page and a half. Steve read it through three times, looking for a loophole. In the end he was forced to admit that Baxter was right. There was no way he was going to get a dime.

Wouldn't you know it? He was hurting for cash right now. He checked in his pockets. Thirty-six bucks. Nothing in the bank. And the rent coming due.

Shit! Not only that, but he was late for work.

Steve drove a cab. This was another carryover from his acting days, just like his long hair and his answering service. Out-of-work actors waited tables or drove cabs. Steve had never had the temperament to wait tables, so as an out-of-work actor he'd driven a cab. And then, as an out-of-work lawyer, he'd driven a cab.

And he was due to drive one now.

With a sigh, Steve shoved the document back in the folder, got up and went back to the phone. He fished in his pocket, dug out another quarter and dropped it in. It rang three times, then a voice answered.

"Hello."

"Hello, Marty. It's Steve. Listen, can you drive for me tonight?"

"Sorry, pal. I got a date."

"Listen, Marty, it's important."

Marty chuckled. "So's the date."

The phone clicked dead.

Steve sighed and hung up the receiver. He picked it up again, dug out another quarter and dialed.

"Hello?" growled the voice of the dispatcher.

"Hello, Charlie. It's Steve. Listen. I can't drive tonight."

"Why not?"

"I'm sick."

"So get a replacement."

"I tried. No one's free."

"Then you gotta drive."

"I'm sick."

"Yeah. I'm sick too. Look. Show up or get a replacement. You don't show up, you're fired."

The phone clicked dead.

Steve hung up the phone. Shit. What was it he had? Thirty-six bucks? The cabbie job was his lifeline, the thing standing between him and eventual eviction. If there were any chance, any faint hope of getting a retainer . . . but he'd read the trust, and he knew enough law to know what it meant.

He couldn't afford to lose his job.

Which is why Steve Winslow, attorney for Sheila Benton in a premeditated-murder case, spent the first night of his employment driving a cab.

17

MARK TAYLOR was seated at his desk talking on the phone when Steve Winslow walked in. It was three in the morning, and Taylor looked it—stubble on his cheeks, and circles under his eyes. Steve, who had slept late and shaved late, looked better, if you discounted his clothes.

The stubble on Taylor's cheeks was red, and matched the curly red hair that framed his chubby face. Taylor was a man who had spent his twenties resisting the onslaught of fat, and now in his thirties had given up. Half a sandwich from the all-night deli lay unwrapped on his desk. Next to it was the inevitable cup of coffee, which, after years of being black, was now laced with cream and sugar.

Mark Taylor had been Steve's roommate their freshman year at Yale. Steve had gone on to major in drama. Mark had majored in economics, but that had been out of the necessity of majoring in something. To Taylor, Yale had meant just one thing: football. At six foot, two hundred twenty pounds, all muscle, Taylor had been an exceptional linebacker with not unrealistic professional aspirations. A knee injury that wouldn't heal right his senior year shattered the dream. He emerged from Yale with a "gentleman's C" in a subject that held little interest for him, and with limited prospects.

His salvation had been his beef, which landed him a job with a Manhattan detective agency run by the father of one of his former teammates. Taylor liked it fine, picked it up fast and within five years was running his own agency.

When Steve, who'd kept in touch, had gone to work for Wilson and Doyle, he'd promised to try to throw some work Taylor's way. Only Steve hadn't lasted long enough to do it.

"Hi, Steve," Taylor said. "Just a second." He spoke into the phone. "Okay. Good work. Call me back as soon as you know." He hung up the phone. "Steve. How you doing?"

"Hi, Mark. Any luck?"

"Yeah. The police just identified the body."

"Oh yeah? How?"

"Traced the laundry mark."

"Good for them. Who is he?"

"Don't know yet. I've got a pipeline into headquarters, though, and he'll call me just as soon as he can get the information."

"Good work."

Taylor shook his head. "What a case. Sheila Benton, for Christ's sake." He took a sip of coffee. "How the hell'd she come to hire you, anyway?"

Steve grinned. "Picked my name out of the phone book."

"What?"

"That's right."

"You shitting me?"

Steve shook his head. He sat in one of the clients' chairs, stretched out and rubbed his eyes. "When Wilson and Doyle fired me," he said, "I was up against it. No other firm would touch me, not with their recommendation. I made the rounds for a while, but it was no use. So there I was with a law degree and nowhere to practice. I had no money. I couldn't rent my own office. I couldn't afford to advertise. So I did the only thing I could think of. I got an answering service, and listed the phone number in the yellow pages under 'Lawyers.'"

"You're kidding."

Steve shrugged. "It's a big city. I figured with the law of averages, eventually someone would call me. It took a year."

Taylor nodded, chuckled, shook his head. He was amused, but he also seemed to be preoccupied with something, and Steve had a pretty good idea what it was.

Taylor picked up the half a sandwich, took a bite, chewed it and cocked his head at Winslow.

"So the *girl* hired you?" Taylor said.

"Yeah."

"Not the uncle?"

"No. The girl called me."

Taylor nodded. Swallowed. Pursed his lips. "I've dug up some information on Sheila Benton. Not much, but some. And as I understand it, her money is all tied up in trust."

"That's right. Her uncle is the trustee."

"That's what I heard. So she couldn't very well hire you without her uncle's consent."

"She's over twenty-one. She can hire anyone she wants."

"True. But she can't pay them. Unless her uncle authorized it."

"What's your point, Mark?"

"Well, as I understand it, a lawyer from Marston, Marston, and Cramden showed up at the D.A.'s office inquiring into the case."

"Oh. Sure. That's Maxwell Baxter's attorney. Probably trying to keep a lid on publicity."

Taylor seemed uncomfortable. "Could be. The way I heard it, the lawyer claimed to be representing the girl."

Steve smiled. "Yes. He would. Maxwell Baxter is a little impulsive. Wants to do everything himself. Don't worry. I straightened him out."

Mark Taylor was surprised. "You spoke to him?"

"I went to see him. Last night, at his apartment. Just between you and me, the man is a royal pain in the ass. But that doesn't concern you. As far as you're concerned, I'm your client. You leave Maxwell Baxter to me."

"Well, that's a relief," Taylor said. He didn't seem terribly convinced, but he let it drop.

"So what have you got?" Winslow asked.

"Well, if you're representing the girl, nothing good. Of course, we got nothing on the dead man yet, 'cause they just made the I.D. Which leaves us with the physical evidence."

Taylor reached for a yellow legal pad on his desk. It was covered with what appeared to be indecipherable scrawl marks. Taylor proceeded to decipher them.

"Autopsy report. According to the medical examiner, the guy died between twelve-thirty and one-thirty. That is not good because . . ." Taylor ran his finger down the page, located another scrawl. ". . . the police located the cab driver who drove her back to her apartment. The guy picked her up on Madison Avenue and Fifty-eighth Street at a little after one o'clock and dropped her off in front of her apartment at around one-twenty. So even if she happens to have an alibi from twelve-thirty on—which no one can confirm she has, by the way—it's still no good, 'cause she could have got home at one-twenty, found the guy in her apartment, killed him and then called the police."

Steve frowned and digested the information.

"The saving grace," Taylor went on, "is that the cab driver's recollection is hazy, at best. He doesn't give receipts. He doesn't write down the exact times on his trip sheets. So you can probably make mincemeat of him on the witness stand."

"For all the good that would do," Steve said. "What about the identification?"

"There you're in trouble," Taylor conceded. "The identification will probably stick. The way I get it, the cabbie's a young guy, fancies himself something an ass-man. I understand this Sheila Benton is something of a dish. I don't think there's a chance in hell you're going to make a jury believe this guy didn't take a real good look at her."

"It doesn't matter anyway. The police are going to have no problem proving she was in the apartment."

"Her alibi's no good?"

"I didn't say that. What else you got?"

"Fingerprints. The girl's fingerprints are on the murder weapon."

"Figures. It was her knife. Naturally her prints would be on it."

"Try telling that to a jury."

"I will. What else?"

"Well, as you said, it was her knife. Came from a rack on her kitchen wall. There were three other knives in the rack. Different sizes. Same make. Not much question that it was her knife."

"I could raise the point."

"Sure," Taylor said flatly.

"What else?"

"Isn't that enough?"

"You mean that's all you got?"

Mark Taylor stared at him. "What the hell do you want? I just got on the job today. The police identified the body about a half hour ago. Must have rousted some poor cleaner out of his bed and shook him down for his records. As soon as I get the name, I'll start working on it, but, for your information it's three in the morning and there's not going to be that much I can do."

"What about the girl?"

"What *about* her?"

"What have you got on her"

Taylor stared at him. "Shit, Steve, you didn't say anything about the girl. You said find out everything I could about the dead man. And why the hell would you want to hire me to investigate your own client?"

Steve smiled and shook his head. "You'd know if you met her."

The phone rang. Taylor scooped it up.

"Taylor . . . Yeah . . . Great. Thanks."

He hung up. "Okay. We got it. The name is Robert Greely."

"Mean anything to you?"

"Not a thing. I'll go to work on it."

Taylor snatched up the phone again and started to dial.

"Another phone I can use?" Steve asked.

Taylor pointed to a desk in the corner. Steve went over, pulled out his address book, picked up the phone and dialed.

The phone rang six times before the groggy voice of Sheila Benton said, "Hello?"

"Hi, Sheila. Steve Winslow."

"What?"

"It's Steve Winslow. You know. Your lawyer."

"Jesus Christ."

"No. Steve Winslow. The cops identified the dead man. Just thought you'd like to know."

"What? What's that? They identified him?"

"That's right. The name is Robert Greely. That mean anything to you?"

"No. Who did you say?"

"Robert Greely. You sure you never heard of him?"

"Sure I'm sure. What the hell time is it, anyway?"

"Three o'clock."

"Jesus Christ. Couldn't you have waited till morning?"

"If you're lying to me about knowing Greely it won't make any difference."

"Why?"

"'Cause you'll be arrested within the next hour." Steve hung up the phone.

18

SHEILA BENTON came down the stairs and checked her mailbox. As expected, the mail had not come yet. Damn, she thought. She really could have used a hit of coke, what with how things were, what with how much sleep she'd gotten.

At least Johnny would be back. God, she needed him. He'd been so strong and understanding on the phone last night, when he'd called her. And so sorry about the mix-up about the hotel. Though that wasn't really like him, to make a mistake like that. He was usually so precise about everything, which was surprising, considering how much he liked to kid around. Well, it just showed he was human. Told the wrong hotel to her *and* to his secretary. Because he'd stayed there before, and he'd confused the names. Could have happened to anyone. And he was a real brick on the phone. Not to worry about anything. He'd be there and he'd take care of it.

Sheila couldn't wait to see him.

She came out the front door, started for the car and stopped.

Steve Winslow was coming up the street. He was wearing the same clothes he'd worn the day before. He'd shaved, but his hair was poorly combed, his eyes were bloodshot and his jacket looked as if he'd slept in it.

He raised a hand in greeting. "Good morning, Miss Benton."

"What are you doing here?"

"Oh, I was in the neighborhood, I just thought I'd drop by."

"You look like hell."

"I don't feel so hot either. It happens that I've been working while you've been getting your beauty sleep."

"Oh?"

"Yeah. This guy Greely. The guy you don't know. The dead guy. Well, it happens the police don't know him either. He has no criminal record. His prints are not on file. That's the good news."

"Why is that good news?"

"Wake up. The theory is the guy was blackmailing you so you killed him. If the guy had a police record as a blackmailer that would just about sew it up."

"Oh. But he doesn't?"

"No. And that's gotta be worrying the police some. And at this point, keeping the police worried is about the best we can hope for."

Sheila looked at him. "Why do you say that?"

Steve shrugged. "Well, that's the bad news. The cops have located Greely's address. It's a dive in the Park Slope section of Brooklyn. But here's the thing. The cops have sewed it up tight. There's no information coming out whatsoever. I've got detectives crawling all over the place and they can't find out a thing. And that's strange, 'cause we got a pipeline into police headquarters— that's how we know the cops I.D.'d Greely and found his address —and we still can't get anything. Once the cops got the lead to Greely's apartment, they clamped the lid on tight. And that can mean only one thing. They found something."

"What?"

"Best guess is something that proves Greely wrote the blackmail letter."

"Like what?"

"Newspapers with words cut out would do it. I don't know. That's just the best guess, but it's not really a good one."

"Why?"

"'Cause you're here. The cops haven't picked you up yet. And if they had solid evidence that Greely wrote that letter, you would think that they would."

Sheila frowned. "So you don't think that's it?"

He shrugged again. "Maybe, maybe not. There's another factor to consider. The D.A. had a visit from Mr. Marston, of Marston, Marston, and Cramden yesterday."

"Who?"

"The attorneys for your Uncle Max."

"Oh."

"Yeah. Luckily I got that bit of information before the pipeline shut down. Anyway, that's the other explanation. If Uncle Max is throwing his weight around and leaning on the D.A. to keep you out of this, well, then it's possible the cops have linked the letter to Greely, but they're not going to make a move on you till they have an airtight case."

Sheila bit her lip. "I see. But if Uncle Max has hired attorneys—"

"Don't worry about it. Uncle Max can hire anybody he wants. As far as I'm concerned, I'm working for you."

She looked at him. "Wait a minute. Uncle Max didn't give you a retainer?"

"That's neither here nor there."

"But he didn't?"

"No."

"But I can't pay you. I have no money."

"Don't worry about it. If you want me, I'm your lawyer. That's all you have to consider. Uncle Max is going to pay me. He just doesn't know it yet."

She frowned.

"Unless you'd like me to bow out of the case. Which you have a perfect right to do. In which case, Uncle Max would be delighted to retain Marston, Marston, and Cramden to represent you."

"No."

"Okay. I'm your lawyer till you fire me. So, as they say in the singles bar, let's talk about you."

"What?"

"Let's assume the cops linked the letter to Greely. That makes him a blackmailer. You have a trust fund that you lose if your name is connected with any scandal. So all the cops would need to give them an airtight case would be to find out what he could have been blackmailing you about."

Her eyes faltered. "I see."

"Well? What could it be?"

She looked at him defiantly. "Nothing. Nothing at all."

Steve sighed. "You sure know how to boost a guy's confidence. All right. So tell me. Where are you going?"

"To the airport."

He smiled. "Flight is an indication of guilt," he said lightly.

"I'm meeting someone."

"Oh? Who?"

"John Dutton."

"Who's John Dutton?"

"A friend."

"That narrows the field. Now I know you're not going to meet an enemy. Is this John Dutton anyone special?"

"He's my boyfriend, if you must know."

"That's nice. Does he live with you?"

"He has his own apartment."

"He ever sleep over?"

"That's none of your business."

"As a matter of fact, it *is* my business. Any hint of scandal, remember?"

Sheila pouted, said nothing.

"Where's he coming from?"

"Reno."

"When'd he go there?"

"Two days ago."

"The same day you got the letter?"

Sheila bristled. "And just what is that supposed to mean?"

He shrugged. "Nothing. Just trying to get the time straight."

"Yeah, it was the same day. I dropped him at the airport. When I got home the letter was in my mailbox."

"And then you got the phone call?"

"Yes."

"Was his plane in the air at the time?"

Sheila glared at him. "Are you trying to imply—"

"Yes I am. Did you think it was him?"

"Now look here—"

Steve cut her off sharply. "No. You look here. I'm going to give you a little bit of advice, first of all because you need it, and second of all because that's what a lawyer's supposed to do. And it's this—stop being so outraged all over the place. This is just a sample of the type of questions the D.A.'s going to be throwing at you, and let me tell you, if you're going to react like this you're a dead duck. And this is nothing. These are pretty innocuous questions. Wait'll you get cross-examined by someone who isn't on your side.

"Now, stop being so hotheaded and emotional, and think rationally for a minute. You're just a normal, ordinary person going about your business, living your life. One day, as a bolt out of the blue, you get that letter. If, as you say, there is no reason for anyone to blackmail you, then your first reaction would be what any normal person's reaction would be under those circumstances—you would think it was a joke."

Steve paused and let that sink in. "Now, wasn't that your first reaction? Didn't you think it was a joke?"

"Yes. Yes, I did."

"Of course you did. And your next reaction would be to think who could have played this joke. Right?"

"I guess so."

"Well, it's only logical, isn't it? Wouldn't that be your next reaction?"

"Yes. I guess it was."

"This what's-his-name, this John Dutton—is he a funny guy? He like to kid around?"

"Yes. He's very funny."

"So you immediately thought it might be him."

"Well—"

"Of course you did. It's a completely natural reaction. You don't think it was him any more, not now, not after everything that's happened, not now that you know it's not a joke.

"But you did at the time. You thought it might be him. And that's why when I suggest it might have been him, you're outraged, you get angry, you fly off the handle. If you'd really never thought it might be him, when I asked you that you'd laugh and say, "John Dutton? Don't be silly."

"Instead you get angry. Which happens to be a guilty reaction. I know it, and the district attorney knows it. It's what we look for on cross-examination. Any time we can get the witness angry, we know we've got something, we know we've hit a nerve. And then we bear down."

Steve stopped and looked at Sheila. Her eyes blinked. She looked slightly pale.

"Hey, nothing to worry about," Steve said. "Don't let it bother you. You'll get better."

"Better?"

"Yeah. At lying."

Sheila's head snapped up. She opened her mouth for a terrible rejoinder.

"Ah," said Steve. "An outraged reaction."

Sheila wilted.

"Well," he said casually. "How you getting to the airport?"

She pointed to the M.G.

Steve looked at her in surprise. "You own an M.G.?"

"Of course not. It's Johnny's."

He looked at the car and nodded thoughtfully. "All right. You wait here. I'll go pick up Johnny at the airport."

"Why?"

"Frankly, I'd like to talk to him before you do."

She frowned.

He looked at her and grinned. "Besides, I've always wanted to drive an M.G."

19

DISTRICT ATTORNEY Harry Dirkson rubbed his eyes as he walked down the hall to his office. He had not slept well. In fact, he had hardly slept at all. The Sheila Benton case wouldn't let him. Damn. That one, silly, snip of a girl should cause so much trouble.

He'd had trouble falling asleep to begin with, just worrying about the damn case. And then there'd been the phone call at three-thirty in the morning, telling him the dead man was Robert Greely. And then the call at four-thirty, telling him the police had located Greely's apartment.

So it had been quite a night.

Dirkson shoved open the door of his outer office and walked in.

"Morning, Reese."

'Morning sir."

"What's up?"

"Lieutenant Farron's been looking for you. He's been in three times already."

Dirkson detected a note of reproach behind Reese's nerd-like features. "I overslept," he said. He was surprised to find he said it somewhat defensively. Christ, this case had him balled up.

"Yes, sir. And about Farron?"

"Call him. Tell him I'm in."

Dirkson went into his inner office and shut the door. There was a pot of coffee waiting on the warmer. Dirkson needed coffee. He poured himself a cup, splashed in cream.

He had just sat down and taken a sip when the phone buzzed. He picked it up.

"Yes?"

"Lieutenant Farron to see you."

"Send him in."

Dirkson rubbed his head and took another sip of coffee. Jesus. Let it be good news. Something that wrapped up the case. Something that cleared the girl.

Something that got him off the hook.

Lieutenant Farron came in.

"Good morning, Farron. What you got?"

"Morning sir," Farron said. "Well, to begin with, the lid's on tight. Greely's apartment's sealed up, just like you said, and no information is leaking out."

"Good. And the press?"

"We've released the fact that the dead man's name is Robert Greely, and that's it."

"Fine," Dirkson said. "Is that all you came to tell me?" He hoped it was.

"No, sir. I got the dope on the Benton girl."

Dirkson tensed. God, he hoped it cleared her. Though in his heart he knew it wouldn't. "What have you got?"

"Well, she has this trust fund of close to twenty million dollars that she loses if she's involved in any scandal that would reflect on the family name."

Dirkson waved his hand irritably. "Yesterday's news, Farron. You don't have to recap for me. What have you got?"

"Well, it seems that she is having an affair with a young man. A Mr. John Dutton."

Dirkson nodded. "She's twenty-four. I'm not terribly shocked. Anything else?"

"Yes, sir. John Dutton is married."

"Oh?"

"Yes. He seems to be in the process of getting a divorce, but at the moment he is definitely married."

Dirkson frowned. "I see."

Lieutenant Farron stood expectantly. But Dirkson said nothing. After a few moments, Farron went on. He did so somewhat hesitantly, as he was not sure why Dirkson was being so reticent.

"Yes," Farron said. "And of course, the thing now is motive. I mean, opportunity is tied up—according to the coroner she could have killed him just fine. And means is there—her knife. So, with Greely presumably blackmailing her, and her having a trust fund to lose, then the only thing left is a reason for her to be blackmailed, and now we've got it. She was having an affair with a married man. That would have been sufficient grounds under the terms of her trust for her to lose everything. Twenty million dollars. If there was ever a more convincing motive for murder, I never heard it."

Dirkson took a sip of his coffee. He rubbed his head. Damn. It was all coming down on him, wasn't it? The last thing he wanted. And there was Lieutenant Farron, standing there like an expectant dog who's just brought his master back his ball, waiting for the praise, the "Good job," the "Well done," or at least the acknowledgment of the effort.

Or for instructions.

What could he tell him? That he didn't *want* to find evidence against the girl? That he wished the whole Sheila Benton case would dry up and blow away? He couldn't tell him that.

So what could he do in the face of this new, damning evidence?

There was only one thing he could do. And much as he hated to admit it, Dirkson knew what it was.

Dirkson sighed. "All right," he said. "Pick her up."

20

JOHN DUTTON stood in the arrivals building at JFK Airport and looked around. Where the hell was Sheila? This wasn't like her. She had his flight number. She knew his arrival time. So where the hell was she? Sheila was dependable. She'd be here come hell or high water.

Unless . . .

There was a newsstand at the far end of the terminal. Dutton walked over to it.

There was nothing on the front page of the Post or the Daily News. That seemed odd. Dutton didn't know it, but Sheila had Marston, Marston, and Cramden to thank for that.

Dutton bought the Daily News. He stood in the terminal and riffled through it.

It was on page eight.

The body of a man had been discovered yesterday afternoon in an apartment on the Upper West Side. The man was identified as Robert Greely, fifty-two, of Brooklyn. The apartment was rented by a young woman identified as Sheila Benton.

Sheila Benton was described simply as an aspiring actress. There was no mention of any trust fund, no mention of any connection to Maxwell Baxter.

The police were investigating.

Dutton read the article twice. His mind was reeling. Yes, Sheila would be here to pick him up, unless . . .

Could the police have established a connection? Could they have tied this in to Sheila?

Could Sheila be under arrest?

As if in a daze, Dutton plodded mechanically down to the baggage claim. He was so distracted his suitcase went by him twice on the carousel before he recognized it and picked it up.

"John Dutton to the information desk, please," came the voice over the loudspeaker. "John Dutton to the information desk, please."

A chill ran down his spine. His first thought was, "Christ, the cops." Then he realized that was just paranoia. Sheila was late, so she'd paged him.

But that wasn't like Sheila, either. For all her kookiness, she was quite practical. If she were late, she'd go right to baggage claim.

But she hadn't done that.

Dutton hefted his suitcase, trudged toward the information desk.

He saw at once that Sheila wasn't there. On the other hand, neither were the cops, not even anyone who looked like a plainclothes cop. He walked up to the desk.

"You paged John Dutton?" he asked.

A man stepped up to him. "John Dutton."

Dutton turned, and his first thought was plainclothes cop. The thought was immediately dispelled. No cop would dress like that. "Yes?"

"Steve Winslow," said the man. "I'm Sheila Benton's attorney."

Dutton stared at him. Sheila had told him on the phone she'd hired an attorney, but *really*. This slovenly dressed young man with bloodshot eyes looked more like a Bowery bum than a lawyer.

"Sheila couldn't make it," Steve said. "So I came to pick you up. I've got your car. It's in the short-term parking lot."

Steve clapped him on the shoulder and guided him toward the door. Dutton walked along beside him as if in a daze.

"So," Steve said. "You've been in Reno the past two days?"

"That's right."

"And you called Sheila last night?"

"Yes."

"And she told you about the murder?"

"Of course."

"What do you make of it?"

"I don't know what to make of it. It doesn't make any sense."

"Yes. Everyone seems to agree on that. What about the blackmail letter?"

"What *about* it?"

"Who could blackmail Sheila?"

"No one."

"No one?"

"No one at all. Sheila's not that type of girl."

"What type of girl is she?"

"What do you mean by that?"

"Whatever you take it to mean. What's she like?"

"Don't you know?"

"I know what *I* think. What do *you* think?"

"She's a very straightforward girl. No one could blackmail Sheila. She'd laugh in their face."

"Spoken like a gentleman."

"What does that mean?"

"It means it's what I expected you to say."

Dutton gave him a look. Dutton instinctively disliked Winslow, and would have even if Winslow'd been properly dressed. Winslow was the type of guy that irritated the hell out of him. Because Dutton saw himself as a winner. And even in that innocuous little conversation, Dutton was left with the feeling he'd lost the exchange.

For his part, Steve didn't like Dutton much either. Dutton was too much of a pretty boy. And the thing was, Dutton knew it. He had that certain something in his manner that many pretty boys have, that attitude of I'm-god's-gift-to-women-so-the-world-is-my-oyster. He was the type of guy men hated, and women loved. In Steve's estimation, Sheila couldn't have done much worse.

They reached the car. Steve unlocked the trunk, and Dutton put the suitcase in.

"I'll drive," Steve said, and climbed in.

Dutton didn't like that either, didn't like the way this guy was just taking charge. He stood there a few seconds, wondering if he should make an issue out of it. He decided to let it go, and climbed into the car.

Steve pulled out of the lot and got onto the Van Wyck.

Dutton was waiting for Winslow to ask him some more questions, but there weren't any.

The silence became uncomfortable.

"So," Dutton said.

"Yes?"

"About the murder."

"Yeah?"

"Tell me about it."

"Oh, you're interested in the murder?"

Dutton gave him a look. "Give me a break, willya?"

"Okay. What do you want to know about it?"

"Who did it?"

"That's the sixty-four dollar question, isn't it? The police are going to say Sheila did."

"That's absurd. Sheila couldn't kill anyone."

"Oh, good," Steve said dryly. "Why don't you tell the police that so they can save themselves the trouble of arresting her?" Before Dutton could think of a comeback, Steve added, "By the way, do you have your ticket stub?"

Dutton, startled by this change of gears, said, "What?"

"Your plane ticket. Have you got the stub?"

"Yeah. Why?"

"Is there anybody who can prove you were actually in Reno?"

"Why?"

"I want to cross you off the list. If the police get tough about it, can you prove you actually went to Reno?"

"Of course I can."

"Who saw you there?"

"My wife."

Steve's head twisted around. "Your *what?*"

"My wife," Dutton said. "I went out there to see my wife's attorney about the divorce papers, and—"

Dutton's head snapped back and the car rocketed forward as Steve stamped the gas pedal to the floor.

21

"WHY DIDN'T you tell me he was married?"

Sheila Benton looked at Steve Winslow though the wire mesh in the visiting room at the lockup.

Steve had to admire her. In spite of her predicament, she wasn't crying, and she wasn't rolling over and dying either. Unhappy as she must be, scared as she must be, she was a fighter, and she was still scrapping.

"It was none of your business," she said defiantly.

"It was all of my business," he said. "It's the last link the police need to convict you of murder. Greely was a blackmailer. You have a trust fund that you lose if your name is connected to any scandal. Being named a correspondent in a divorce case would just fill the bill."

"I know that."

"Then why didn't you tell me?"

"I didn't think of it."

"Bullshit."

"All right, damn it," Sheila said. "I'm not stupid. What you just said—about losing my trust fund—you think I didn't know that? About being named correspondent. I know. It's the motive. It's all the cops need." Sheila shrugged helplessly. "I thought if the case looked too black, you wouldn't take it."

"I'm a lawyer," Steve said. "It's not my job to judge you. It's my job to take the facts and present them to the jury in the best possible light. But I have to know what they are first."

"Then you won't quit on me?"

"Of course I won't quit on you."

"That's good, because, well, there's something else I have to tell you."

"What is it?"

"I was lying about the window-shopping."

"So, what else is new? What were you really doing?"

"Buying cocaine."

Steve looked at her. "What?"

"I was buying cocaine."

He just stared at her for a moment. Then he began laughing. He shook his head and laughed, mirthlessly.

Sheila, who had been working herself up to this particular confession, and who had thought she had girded her defenses against any sort of reaction, was totally unprepared for this. She stared at him in irritation.

"What's so damn funny?" she said.

Steve waved apologetically, but continued to laugh. "Sorry," he said. "It's just my luck, somehow. I mean, how bad can things get? Now I've got a cokehead for a client in a hopeless murder case. You've made my day."

"What do you mean, hopeless murder case?"

"Well, I said if the cops found any grounds for blackmail you'd be sunk. Wait'll they find out about the coke."

"They won't."

"Don't count on it."

"So, what if they do? They already have a motive for blackmail. What difference does it make if they have two."

"Wake up," Steve said. "I don't know if you're aware of it or not, but there's been a tremendous backlash against drugs lately, and particularly against cocaine, what with crack and all. Not only will this give the prosecution a motive for blackmail, it'll turn the whole jury against you."

"So?"

"So that changes our whole strategy. Before, we could stall around, buy some time, get a few postponements and continuances. Now I gotta rush this thing to trial before anyone figures out you're a junkie."

"I'm not a junkie!"

"Sorry. Cokehead."

"Fine. I see that. But you're missing the point. The point is, I have a perfectly good witness for the time of the murder, but there's no way in the world he's going to come forward and testify."

"It doesn't matter. They fix the time of death between twelve-thirty and one-thirty. So you could have killed him after you got home."

"Oh."

"Yeah. So that's the way it is. Now, before we go any further, do you have any more little surprises for me?"

"Well, sort of."

Steve sighed. "Okay. Let's have it."

"When I found the body I had a gram of coke on me. I was afraid I'd be arrested and searched, so I put it in an envelope and mailed it to myself. The mail hadn't come before the cops picked me up, but it must have come by now."

"So?"

"I keep an extra key to my apartment on the ledge over my door. There's a key to the mailbox in the drawer of my night table." She paused and then went on, ironically mimicking his earlier speech to her. "Now, I'm *not* advising you to get that letter before the police get it. That would be compounding a felony and conspiring to conceal a crime. So I'm *not* advising you to get that letter."

Steve looked at her. Some girl, he thought. She was stickin' it to him good. Despite her predicament, she was still scrapping. He had to admire her spunk, though he wasn't going to let *her* know that.

He frowned and rubbed his forehead. "What a nice little playmate you are," he said. "I haven't been working for you twenty-four hours, and you've got me running dope."

22

"STEVE. I'VE been trying to reach you. The cops picked up Sheila Benton."

"Yesterday's news, Mark. I'm calling from the lockup."

"You see your client?"

"Yeah. I saw her."

"What's her story?"

"She's innocent, what did you think it was?"

"No, I mean—"

"Forget it. You got anything for me?"

"Not from the police end. They got something and it's hot, but I can't get a line on it. But I've got something hot they don't have. At least I think they don't."

"Great. What?"

"All right. Now, this is just a tip, and the source will not be quoted, but about a month ago Greely was putting the squeeze on a guy named Louie Carboni."

"You're kidding."

"Not at all."

"I thought Greely had no record as a blackmailer."

"With the police, he doesn't."

"So how'd you get this?"

"I told you, the source will not be quoted."

"Just between you and me."

"I got an operative who's friends with a snitch. Ever since the murder, the snitch is going out of his mind 'cause he's got this bit of hot info on Greely that the cops would love to get their hands on, but he's scared to give it to 'em."

"Why?"

"Carboni's connected."

"No shit!"

"Yeah. So the snitch is scared shitless to talk to the cops for fear it might get back to the mob. So when my man promised him fifty bucks and he'd keep him out of it, the guy fell all over himself trying to cooperate."

"That's great."

"Isn't it. And the best part is, unless we blow it, there's no way this info is going to get to the cops."

"Terrific. You made a pass at Carboni yet?"

"No. I thought you'd want to handle it."

"I sure do. You got the address?"

"Sure."

Taylor gave it to him. An apartment on East 90th Street. Steve copied down the address and hung up the phone.

He was so pumped up by the prospect of getting a lead, that he stepped out into the street and started to hail a cab before he realized what he was doing. He was way the hell downtown. A cab ride to East 90th Street could just about break him.

Steve walked down to the Chambers Street station and caught the number six uptown. As he rumbled along, he couldn't help smiling. He wondered how many other lawyers on their way to interview a material witness in a murder case had ever taken the subway.

It was right after the train pulled out of the Grand Central stop that he remembered—tonight was the night he had that early dinner date with Judy Meyers. Damn. He'd have to call and cancel. Even if this lead on Carboni didn't take long, he still had to get back over to the West Side and get that letter out of Sheila's mailbox. And besides, Steve realized he just wasn't in the mood. There was just no way he could sit still for dinner.

Yeah, he'd have to call and cancel. Judy'd be pissed, but he couldn't help that now.

He got off the subway at 86th and Lex, and walked uptown to Carboni's address.

It was a third-floor walkup on East 90th Street in one of those buildings that some day someone would renovate and make a killing on, but which presently were dives.

Steve pushed the outer door open and went in. There were no buzzers or bells, so he figured the inner door would be unlocked too. It was. He pushed it open and went up the stairs.

Carboni lived in 3C. At least the number was on the door. In some places like this, the numbers weren't.

Steve banged on the door. There came the sound of footsteps, then the sound of the plate sliding away from the peephole and then back over it, and then the click of the bolt unlocking.

The door opened fast, so fast Steve had no time to react before the fist came crashing into his stomach. As he doubled over in pain, hands grabbed him and wrenched him around. He caught another hard fist in the stomach.

The last thing he felt was another, square in the face.

23

STEVE WINSLOW felt vague sensations. Hands. Lots of hands. Gripping him under the shoulders. Supporting him. Holding him up. Two pairs of hands. Two men, one on each side, raising him up, holding him between them. And stairs. Lots of stairs. Bumping down them between the two men, feet dragging on the steps.

Then light. Sunlight. Outside. In broad daylight, for Christ's sake, dragging across the sidewalk to the street and . . .

A car. The back seat of a car. Someone beside him, holding him up. Or just holding him. Holding him away from the door. Why? Because the car was not moving, stopped at a light. Now moving, and the hand on his arm relaxing somewhat. Moving, driving. How long? Stop and go. Then cruising, moving right along. Then slowing, twisting, turning. Then different sounds, different rhythms. Tires on gravel, not pavement. A driveway. Stopping.

Hands again. An open car door. Hands through the door, pulling, dragging, grabbing, supporting. On either side now, bumping up some short steps and through a door.

Plush carpet. Falling backwards. Onto the carpet? No. Something in his back. Soft. Comfortable. A chair.

And at last, a dim voice in the fog: "Freshen him up."

Movement around him. Footsteps. The clink of glass.

Then something cold on his forehead. Cold and wet. Water dripping down his face.

Then something thrust into his hand, and a voice, "Here. Drink this."

Hands raising the glass to his lips. The sudden smell. Brandy. Then the taste. Trickling down his throat. Warming him.

Steve's eyes blinked, cleared, focused.

It was a large living room. Richly furnished, as richly as Maxwell Baxter's. But with a difference. Maxwell Baxter's living room was rich but tasteful. This living room was just rich. It was gaudy, flashy. Aggressively rich.

A man sat in a chair opposite him. A large man, powerful. In his mid-fifties, perhaps. The man belonged in the room. He wore a huge gold watch and gold rings.

A woman sat on the arm of his chair. Mid-twenties. Voluptuous. She also matched the room. A prop. A showpiece. An expensive ornament.

The man held a brandy snifter identical to the one Steve held. He raised it in a gesture. Polite and gracious, the perfect host.

"Nice of you to drop in on us, Mr. Winslow," he said.

Steve straightened himself with an effort, and glanced around at the two men who stood on either side of his chair. He looked back at his host.

"Thanks for the invitation," he said.

The man smiled. "Don't mention it. You like the brandy?"

"Very good."

"My private stock. An excellent vintage."

Steve's head was beginning to clear enough to want to try to make some sense out of the situation. "You seem to know me," he said, "but I don't believe I've had the pleasure."

"Ah, excuse me," said the man. "I am Tony Zambelli."

He said it in the manner of one making a pronouncement, and Steve knew he should be impressed, but actually he had never heard the name before. But he knew enough to know that if he were a real, practicing lawyer, he *would* know the name. He also knew that the name itself did not matter—he knew who Zambelli *was*.

"My pleasure," he said.

Zambelli smiled. "My wife, Rita," he said, indicating the girl.

Steve nodded. Rita looked bored.

"The boys I believe you know," Zambelli said.

"We met. All right, what's the pitch?"

Zambelli smiled. "I like a man who gets right to the point. All right, Mr. Winslow. It has come to my attention that you are investigating a blackmailer named Robert Greely. I thought perhaps I could be of help."

"How thoughtful."

"You apparently are under the impression that Greely was blackmailing Louie here." Zambelli indicated the man standing at Steve's left.

Steve gave him a look. Louie never blinked.

"That, however," Zambelli went on, "is incorrect. Louie paid Greely the money, but he was merely the go-between. Greely was actually blackmailing me."

Steve looked at Zambelli in surprise. "Why are you telling me this?"

"Because under the circumstances I believe it will be to my advantage to make sure you have all the facts."

"I'm listening."

"Very well. Greely was a blackmailer. A few months ago he put the bite on me."

"Over what?"

Again, Zambelli gestured to the girl. "Rita is my second wife. We were married last month." He said it as if announcing he had purchased a stock.

"Congratulations."

"Thank you. We are very happy. Now then, a few months ago I was in the process of divorcing my first wife. There was naturally the question of a property settlement."

"I think I get the picture," Winslow said.

"Exactly. Greely got hold of some information which would have been worth several hundred thousand dollars to my ex-wife if she had gotten her hands on it. He wanted ten thousand dollars to keep it quiet. I gave it to him."

Steve smiled, taking the sting out of the words. "Come off it, Zambelli. That's not your style. You're not the type of guy to pay blackmail. You'd have rubbed him out first."

Zambelli seemed quite unruffled by the suggestion. "Mr. Winslow," he said. "I'm a businessman. It would have cost me more than ten thousand to have him killed. Therefore, I paid him off."

Steve shook his head. "Yes, but you know perfectly well that a blackmailer never quits. Ten grand was just the first bite. What was to stop Greely from boosting the ante?"

"In the first place, I checked him out. He was a very clever blackmailer. You probably know that he's never been arrested. That's because he never tried to bleed his marks. He'd take one bite and quit.

"In the second place, as soon as my divorce was settled, he lost his leverage."

For the first time, Zambelli's face got hard. "And in the third place, he wouldn't have dared. Now look, you and me, we're sitting here, we're talking blackmail. That's because Greely was a blackmailer, and that's how you got the story, so between you and me, that's fine, what do I care? But let me tell you. This was not blackmail. You are right, I would not pay blackmail. It happens that Greely is a guy who in his profession hears things and finds out things. He got this information. He brought it to me, through Louie, and I was grateful to have it and to know where it came from, because then I could dry up the source. So I gave him the ten grand. It was a reward, a thank you, for bringing it to me and no one else. It was payment for a job well done."

Zambelli waved his hand. "Now, that's neither here nor there. We can call it blackmail. And the police would certainly call it blackmail. But if you have to know why I paid, then you are right. I would not pay blackmail. I *would* rub him out first. But this was not blackmail, and that is why I paid."

Steve thought that over. "All right," he said. "Suppose I buy all that? Why is it to your advantage to have me know all about this?"

Zambelli was once more the smiling host. "Because I have no wish to be dragged into court. You're Sheila Benton's lawyer. You're perfectly capable of subpoenaing me and throwing me in the district attorney's face as a possible suspect. Now, I had nothing to do with the murder. That doesn't bother me. But I would find it particularly embarrassing to have the district attorney cross-examine me concerning my activities on the day in question."

"I would hate to cause you embarrassment."

"Then keep me out of it."

"You still haven't given me a reason why I should."

Zambelli took a drink of brandy. "As it happens," he said, "at the time of the murder I was engaged in a little game of cards."

Steve looked at him skeptically. "At twelve-thirty in the afternoon?"

"The game actually began the night before. Two of the players were wealthy corporate executives. Being heavy losers, they were reluctant to quit. So they phoned in sick, and the game continued."

"Did their luck improve?" Steve inquired with mock seriousness.

Zambelli matched his tone. "It did not."

Zambelli reached into his jacket pocket and pulled out a folded piece of paper. He extended it to Rita, who took it to Winslow, then returned to her seat. She managed to give the impression of a dog doing a trick.

"Here's a list of names," Zambelli said, "of the people involved in the poker game. The first two names are friends of mine. You'll find them most cooperative. The last two names are the corporate executives. They may be a trifle touchy."

"Touchy corporate executives are my specialty," Steve said. "But why should I do this for you? Even if this is true, you'd still make a dandy red herring."

Zambelli shook his head. "You can't gain anything by dragging me into court. All you'll do is prove that Greely was a blackmailer. The police know he's a blackmailer, but they can't prove it. So it's to your client's advantage to keep me out of it."

Steve thought that over. "Okay," he said. "I'll look into it. If this checks out, you've done me a favor."

Zambelli smiled broadly. "Sure," he said. "What are friends for?"

24

MAXWELL BAXTER paced his living room like a caged tiger. He still couldn't quite accept it. His niece was in jail, and he was powerless to do anything about it. Him. A man of power. A man with connections. A man with influence. And he could do nothing.

He'd gone to jail to see her and she hadn't told him a thing. Not a thing. Except to say that she had her own lawyer, and he could damn well pay him. Fat chance! That weirdo. That twerp.

And his own lawyers were powerless to help him. Marston, Marston, and Cramden had been besieging the D.A.'s office all day, but to no avail. She was arrested, it was an open-and-shut case, there was not the slightest possibility of bail. And that was that.

He could get no information, that was the infuriating thing. If the cops had an open-and-shut case, what was it? No one was talking. The lid had never been on so tight. Even a personal call to the commissioner had been fruitless. There simply was no information to be had.

Max shook his head. Jesus, what the hell were his attorneys doing? Or his detectives, for that matter? Should he call them again? How long had it been? He checked his watch. Ten minutes. Impossible. Only ten minutes?

The house phone rang. God, let it be news. He dove for it.

"Yes?"

The voice of the doorman said, "Mr. Baxter, there is a Mr. Winslow down here. He insists on seeing you."

Max was ready for any information at this point. "All right. Send him up."

The voice of the doorman was apologetic. "Yes, Mr. Baxter. I must tell you, the gentleman is somewhat disheveled and he smells of liquor."

"I see. It's all right. Send him up."

"Very well, Mr. Baxter."

Max hung up the phone and strolled out into the foyer. The elevator arrived, the door opened and Steve Winslow, as described, but very determined, emerged and strode up to him.

"All right, Uncle Max," he said. "Take out your checkbook."

Max prided himself on his self-control. It took a lot in this instance, but he merely raised his eyebrows, not his voice.

"What the devil do you mean barging in here in this fashion?" he said coolly. "You smell of liquor and you look as if you've been in a barroom brawl."

Steve wasn't about to take any shit. "Never mind that. Just take out your checkbook."

"Now see here—"

"Take out your fucking checkbook."

The elevator man, who had been reluctant to bring Steve up at all, now hovered expectantly.

Max waved him away. "That will be all, Frank," he said.

Frank somewhat reluctantly closed the door.

Max stood aside and gestured Steve into the living room. His manner was still cool and polite.

"And just why should I take out my checkbook?" he said as he ushered Steve in.

"You are going to write me a check."

Max smiled. "I think not."

Steve wheeled around to face him. "I'm tired of working for nothing. You are going to give me a twenty-five-thousand-dollar retainer."

Max stared at him. "Twenty-five thousand dollars! You must be drunk."

"Did you know that your niece took drugs?" Steve snapped the words out, slapped him in the face with them. "Well, she does. Cocaine, to be exact. When the police get their hands on that bit of information you can kiss her ass goodbye."

Max recoiled, genuinely shaken. "Mr. Winslow—"

"Not to mention the fact that she lied to the police about where she was at the time of the murder."

Max was still at sea. "She told you that?"

"She sure did," Steve said. "Which brings us to an interesting situation. Either I'm your niece's attorney or I'm not."

"Well, you're not."

Steve went on as if he hadn't heard the interruption. "If I *am* your niece's attorney, everything she told me is a privileged communication, and no power on earth can drag it out of me. If I'm *not* her attorney, the prosecution can put me on the stand and force me to tell everything I know."

Max stared at him. "But . . . but . . . they wouldn't know to put you on the stand."

"Wanna bet?" Steve said. "I'll bet you twenty-five thousand dollars that if I walk out that door without that check, inside of fifteen minutes the district attorney will get an anonymous tip to pick me up and shake me down."

Max stared at him, openmouthed. "Mr. Winslow," he said. "That's blackmail!"

Steve nodded in grim satisfaction. "Yeah," he said. "Ain't it?"

25

STEVE WINSLOW came out the front door of Baxter's building holding the check in his hand. He folded it, stuck it in his pocket and headed for Lexington Avenue.

He found a phone on the corner, dropped in a quarter and punched in the number.

"Hello," came the voice of the dispatcher.

"Charlie? It's Steve."

"Yeah?"

"You know yesterday I told you I was sick? Well, I got worse and died."

Steve hung up the phone, stepped out into the street and hailed a cab. He gave the cabbie Sheila Benton's address, then settled back in the seat as the cab headed uptown and through the park. It felt good to be riding in a cab instead of driving one. Steve pulled the check out of his pocket, unfolded it and looked at it again.

Yeah, it felt good.

The cab pulled up in front of Sheila Benton's apartment. Steve paid the fare and over-tipped, knowing how the cabbie felt.

He went up the front steps and into the foyer, looked through the slot in the mailbox. Sure enough, there was something inside. He sighed and headed up the stairs.

The key was over the door, right where Sheila had said. He took it down and fitted in into the lock, clicked the bolt back and opened the door.

Hands grabbed him, pulled him into the darkness, wrenched him around. Jesus, not again. He braced himself for the blow.

It never came. Instead, the lights clicked on, and Steve could see the two men who had pinned him against the wall. Cops. They jerked his arms down and twisted them behind him. He felt the cold metal and heard the click of the handcuffs.

The cops spun him around and he saw the figure of a third man who was seated on the couch. A solid, beefy cop, obviously in charge.

Sergeant Stams arose from the couch with a triumphant grin. His stolid, impassive look was just the face he wore for Lieutenant Farron. It was his second-in-command face, his good-soldier face. But Sergeant Stams wasn't the second-in-command here. This was his operation. He'd thought it up, he'd put it into operation, it had worked and now it was his moment to shine, to be as suave, as ironic, and as sarcastic as the rest of them.

"Well, well," he said. "I figured maybe Greely had an accomplice."

Steve stared at him. "Are you crazy? I'm Sheila Benton's attorney."

Stams looked at Steve's rumpled clothes. "Sure you are."

One of the cops who had been frisking Steve for a weapon held up the check. "Hey Sarge, look at this."

Sergeant Stams took the check and looked it over. A broad grin twisted his face. "Well, well. A check from Maxwell Baxter for twenty-five grand. That ought to clinch it."

Steve couldn't believe it. "I tell you, I'm Sheila's attorney. That check is my retainer."

Stams looked at him ironically. "Yeah. Sure. You really look like an attorney. Can't you come up with a better line than that?"

"I tell you—"

"Save it, buddy. You're going downtown."

Steve blinked. He took a deep breath and let it out again. He controlled himself with a great effort.

"All right," he said. "But under the circumstances, I feel compelled to ask you one question."

"Oh yeah?" Stams said. "What's that?"

Steve looked him right in the eye. "How would you like to kiss my ass?"

26

LIEUTENANT FARRON stood to one side as the guard unlocked the door of the holding cell and let Steve Winslow out.

"I'm terribly sorry, Mr. Winslow," he said.

"Yeah, sure," Steve said. "Are you familiar with the laws regarding false arrest?"

Lieutenant Farron guided Steve down the hall toward the main desk. "As a matter of fact, I am," he said. "The charge of false arrest can be defended if the officer in charge acted in good faith and had reasonable grounds to make the arrest."

"You considered that check sufficient grounds?"

"It did tend to tie you in with Greely."

"You ever hear of a blackmailer who took checks?" Steve said.

"I admit the situation is unfortunate."

They reached the front desk. Farron led Steve over to the coun-

ter where he had surrendered his personal possessions before being
locked up.

"Winslow," Farron told the cop at the desk. "Check him out."

The cops reached under the desk and brought out a manila
envelope.

"Sign here, Mr. Winslow."

Steve signed his name, opened the envelope and poured the
stuff out on the table. His wallet, his keys, some loose change, his
watch and Sheila Benton's apartment key.

"Where's the check?"

"I have it here," Farron said, taking it out of his pocket.

"Oh?"

"It was considered evidence and was examined as such."

"I see."

Steve folded the check and stuck it into his pocket.

"Now that you're convinced that I'm Sheila Benton's attorney,
do you have any objection if I inspect the scene of the crime?"

"Be my guest," Farron told him.

Steve jerked his thumb in the direction of the holding cell.

"Thanks," he said. "I just was."

Steve made his way out of the police station, hailed a cab and
took it straight back to Sheila Benton's apartment. He went up the
stairs, unlocked the door and went in. He switched on the light
and looked around. This time there was no one there.

He went over to the night table and opened the drawer. It was
full of junk. Pencils, tissues, eyeliner, change, papers, buttons,
string. He pawed through it, found the key. He held it up and
looked at it. It was a mailbox key, all right. He sighed and shook
his head.

He stuck the key into his pocket, with the feeling that just by
doing that he was taking a chance. He went to the door, opened it,
switched the light off and went out, locking the door behind him.
He did not replace the apartment key over the sill. Instead, it
joined the other one in his pocket.

He went down the stairs, not even glancing at the mailbox as he went through the foyer. He just kept on going out the door and down the front steps.

Outside, he paused for a moment, then strolled off toward Columbus Avenue.

He walked slowly around the block. As far as he could tell, no one was paying any attention to him. No one seemed to be paying any attention to the apartment house either. Of course, there was no way to be sure. He was worried about Lieutenant Farron and Sergeant Stams. Either one of them could be having the apartment watched. Farron because he was smart, smart enough to figure Steve might be up to something. And Stams because he was dumb, dumb enough to watch the apartment in the vain hope of vindicating himself from looking stupid, even though that was now a useless exercise.

It was a hell of a situation to be in. Just when he'd finally gotten his retainer, too. Steve chuckled. What had he said to Lieutenant Farron? "You ever hear of a blackmailer who took checks?" Well, the check *was* blackmail, wasn't it? His first retainer, and he'd had to blackmail someone to get it. There certainly were things they didn't teach you in law school.

He stopped outside the building. Okay, should he do it or not? Silly question. Of course he should. A lawyer's duty was to his client, even if that client held out on him and loused things up. Yeah, he had to do it. The only question was whether or not he would get caught. Well, he'd already been caught. The funny thing was, if Sergeant Stams had only been smart enough to have staked out the *building* instead of the apartment, he would have caught him red-handed.

Well, nothing ventured, nothing gained. Steve went up the front steps and into the foyer. He took the key out of his pocket, opened the mailbox and took out the letter. The envelope was hand addressed, with no return address on it. It seemed to have a small packet inside. He folded it, stuck it in his pocket.

He went out the front door and down the steps, trying hard to keep from looking around. He headed back to Columbus Avenue.

There was a garbage can on the corner. He would have loved to tear the letter open and ditch the coke, but he didn't dare. Instead, he walked out into the street and looked for a cab.

It was five minutes before one came. He flagged it down, hopped in and gave the driver his address.

In the relative privacy of the backseat, Steve tore open the envelope and took out the packet of coke. He stuck the envelope in one pocket, and the packet of coke in another. He immediately felt better. He could still get busted for possession, but his client was safe.

As safe as one can be when they're in jail charged with murder.

The cab pulled up in front of Steve's building. He paid off the cab, went up the front steps and opened the door.

Inside. Safe at last, unless they were waiting for him in his apartment, something he couldn't quite put past Sergeant Stams.

They weren't, however. The apartment was a holy mess, as he had left it, but there was no one there.

Steve locked and bolted the door. There, safe at last. Which, he realized, was a strange way to be feeling. This whole thing was making him paranoid. But then, how often did he get arrested on his way to pick up someone's drugs?

He sat on the couch, picked up the phone and called his answering service. There was one message from Judy Meyers: "Where are you?"

He sighed. Hell. He'd forgotten to call and cancel. This was the third time he'd stood her up, too. Only this time he had a legitimate excuse.

That thought made him realize the other two times he must not have had a legitimate excuse. Was he avoiding Judy Meyers? Not consciously. He hadn't really thought about it before.

He looked at the clock. 11:30. Where had the day gone? Well, not too late to call. He reached for the phone. Stopped. Shit. It *was* too late to call. Judy had an audition tomorrow morning. That's why they'd made an early dinner date. She'd be asleep now.

He suddenly realized how tired he was. What a day. He should be sleeping too. But first things first. Take care of business.

He went in to the bathroom and took the packet out of his pocket. It was a small brown envelope. He tore it open. Inside was a small plastic bag filled with a white powder. He tore the bag open, dumped the powder into the toilet, then threw the plastic bag and the brown envelope in too.

He flushed the toilet. It didn't flush. It gurgled encouragingly for a few moments, but then quieted. The ripples in the bowl smoothed out, and the water moved in a gentle circle. The envelope and plastic bag floated like ducks on a pond. The coke floated on the surface too—white pond scum.

He stood looking down at the bowl and chuckled. Well, a fitting end to the day, somehow. Sometimes the toilet worked and sometimes it didn't. He'd been after the super for weeks to fix the damn thing. Well, he couldn't call him now. "Yeah, it won't flush. Please ignore the cocaine floating in the water."

He moved the pile of old magazines and assorted junk off the tank of the toilet and took off the top. About five minutes of fiddling produced the desired effect. Water coursed down, and envelope, plastic bag and cocaine were flushed away. He kept watching to make sure they didn't pop up again. They didn't.

He emerged from the bathroom, bent down, untied his shoes and kicked them into the corner, then pulled off his jacket and tie and threw them over a chair. He stepped out of his pants and hung them on the doorknob. They missed, fell to the floor. He let them lay. Well, fold out the couch? Screw it. He was too tired. As usual.

He flung himself facedown on the couch and was instantly asleep.

27

"YOU SON of a bitch!"

To understate it, Sheila Benton was not happy. She was glaring daggers through the wire mesh screen in the visiting room.

Steve Winslow, on the other hand, was in rare good humor. He had gotten a good night's sleep. He had showered and shaved, and attended to his cuts and bruises. His jacket and tie were the same, but he had put on clean socks and underwear, a clean shirt and a clean pair of pants.

And he had money in the pockets.

"Nice talk," he said sardonically. "Why am I a son of a bitch?"

"You know why," Sheila said between clenched teeth. "You told Uncle Max I was taking drugs."

"He was here, then?"

"I'll say he was here! Do you know what you've done? Do you have any idea? You've probably fucked me out of my entire inheritance."

"Well, I wouldn't worry about it. You've got eleven years to work your way back into his good graces."

"Yeah! Great. Why the hell'd you have to tell him I was taking drugs?"

"I had to."

"Yeah. I know. He told me. You needed the money."

"That was only part of it. I had to get him to call off Marston, Marston, and Cramden before they bungled you into a first-degree-murder rap."

Sheila laughed sarcastically. "Oh, sure. Here you are, the great savior. What the hell makes you think they'd do any worse a job than you've been doing?"

He shrugged. "I don't know. But I'd sure like to hear what they would have said when you asked them to pick up your cocaine for you."

She had been preparing another angry retort, but that stopped her. "Oh. Did you get it?"

"Yeah. I got it."

She lowered her voice. "Do you have it on you?"

Steve looked at her in disbelief. "No, I do not 'have it on' me. I have enough trouble without walking around with drugs in my pockets. Did you know the police picked me up and frisked me last night?"

"That was before they knew who you were. Now that they think you're clean you'll be perfectly safe."

"Yeah. Sure. So now you'd like me to smuggle cocaine into jail for you."

"I didn't say that."

"You implied it. And you can forget it. All we need right now is for the cops to catch you with drugs."

Sheila smiled, and, once again, Steve had to admire her spunk. In spite of everything, she was playing with him. Teasing him.

"Oh, you're just so conservative," she said.

He shook his head, chuckled. "I'm glad to hear it. In the past two days I've had to resort to blackmail and possession of dope. It's nice to know that when I'm brought up before the bar association I'll have a character witness of your stature to assure them my conduct has always been one of strict legal decorum."

"See," she said. "You even sound like a stuffy old lawyer."

"Right, that's what I am. A stuffy old conservative lawyer. Now if you'd like to talk to a hip, free-thinking swinger, there's one out there waiting to see you just as soon as we're through."

"Oh?"

"Johnny."

"Oh."

"Yeah. Johnny's here to see you. He's here today, and I'll bet he was here yesterday, right?"

She looked at him. "Why?"

"Was he?"

"Yes. Of course he was."

"Ain't love grand," Steve said. Sheila started to make an angry retort, but he held up his hands. "No, no. No offense. I was just wondering about something."

She looked at him suspiciously. "What?"

"Well, what with you and Johnny being such good buddies and all, and him being here yesterday and again today to see you and all, I'm just wondering why it was you asked *me* to pick up your coke."

"Oh."

"Any answer will do."

She looked at him as if he were an idiot. "Isn't it obvious? You were here first. I couldn't let the cops find it, so I asked you. If Johnny'd been here first I'd have asked him."

Steve pursed his lips and nodded. "Good. Not true, but good."

Her eyes flickered. "What do you mean, 'not true'?"

"Well, let me give you my version of what happened," Steve said. "I think you're the type of girl who manipulates men for your own purposes. You always have been and you always will be. You do it by getting them involved with you. I don't mean necessarily physically involved, just involved. That's what you did with me. You had me pick up your coke so I'd be involved with you. So you'd feel you had a hold over me.

"That's one reason. There was another. You did it to save your pride. You had to tell me the window-shopping was a lie, so you had to tell me about buying the coke. You didn't like that. That put you on the defensive. It made you feel as if you were a little girl, and I was the grownup in charge. So what you did was, you put yourself back in charge by getting me to do your bidding."

"That's not true," Sheila said.

He shook his head. "It has to be. You know why? A minute ago you were asking me if I'd brought it with me. Well, you knew perfectly well I wouldn't. But if you'd really wanted some, if that was your main concern, aside from getting it away from the cops, well there's good old Johnny out there who would have been just stupid enough to smuggle it in here for you."

Sheila was about to make a reply, but Steve held up his hand to cut her off. "But forget that. You didn't really want that. You're not that stupid, and you're not as much of an airhead as you like to pretend to be. You just asked me if I had it on me so you could needle me about being too conservative. Because that's how you operate. That's how you deal with men. Kid 'em, tease 'em, needle 'em, keep 'em off their guard. And the thing is, that's stupid, 'cause you don't have to do that with me. I'm your lawyer. I'm on your side. I'm working for you. So you don't have to play that kind of game."

He expected a gruff answer. He didn't get one. She just looked at him. And there was something in that look, something guileful and crafty that told him that somehow his assessment of the situation was wrong.

"You're right. I don't," she said, and her manner reminded him of a cat playing with a mouse.

It didn't take long for him to learn why.

"Did you know," Sheila almost purred, "Uncle Max investigated you?"

Steve had known this was coming sooner or later. He just hadn't expected it now. He tried to keep a straight face.

"Oh?"

"Yeah, that's another reason he was so furious with me. He said I was insane to hire a lawyer I knew nothing about to handle a murder case. So he made it his business to find out."

Steve said nothing. He sat and waited.

"It seems you haven't always been a lawyer. You used to be an actor. The only trouble was, you couldn't get any work. You know why? Because you're a pain in the ass. Because you're too much trouble. You're like the actor in that movie—who was it?—Dustin Hoffman, who was such a pain in the ass no one would hire him so he had to dress up like a woman to get any work. You wouldn't take direction. You thought you knew everything. You fought with directors and writers. You had opinions about everything, and you didn't know how to shut up."

She paused and looked at him. "Who would have thought it of you?" she said.

"So," she went on, "you alienated everyone. You were determined not to take shit from anyone, so the result was you took shit from everyone. You were your own worst enemy, and you fucked yourself every chance you got.

"It got to a point where no one would work with you anymore. So you gave up. You quit acting, and you worked your way through law school. You just got out a year ago. You went to work for the law firm of Wilson and Doyle. You handled one case for them. They fired you. You haven't worked since."

She stopped talking and just looked at him.

He sighed. "I see."

"Is it true?"

"Yeah. It's true. They fired me. You wanna know why?"

"No, but I know you're dying to tell me."

"Shit."

"Go on. Tell me."

"Forget it."

"No. I'm sorry. Tell me."

"Okay." He leaned back in his chair and rubbed his face. "Well, it was my first case. A hit-and-run. An elderly man struck down at a crosswalk. The man accused of driving the car was our client. I wasn't handling the case. I was just assigned to get experience. My job was to coordinate information for the real lawyer. Mainly to answer the phone and fetch coffee. I wasn't supposed to *do* anything.

"Well, I found out the victim had regained consciousness and

the police were going to drag our client up to the hospital to see if
he could identify him. Well, you know what that means. Or
maybe you don't. But anyway, in a hit-and-run, nine times out of
ten the victim never even saw the car coming. At best, he just
caught a glimpse while trying to dive out of the way. But the
police go to him and tell him they got the guy who hit him, but
they want him to take a look to make sure. So when they drag the
guy in there the victim usually identifies him without even stopping to think about it. After that, your client doesn't stand a
chance."

He paused.

"So?"

"So, I got a guy about our client's age and description and
rushed him down to the hospital before the police got there. Sure
enough, the victim took one look at him and said, 'That's the guy.'
So, when the police showed up fifteen minutes later with our
client, the victim said, 'Naw, that can't be the guy. I just saw the
guy who hit me and it wasn't him.'"

She was looking at him with genuine interest. "So they fired
you?"

He shrugged. "The police were pretty mad. They came down
on Wilson and Doyle hard. Well, they should have backed me
up—what I'd done might have been sharp practice, but it was
perfectly legal. But they didn't want to stand the flack, so they
fired me. The irony is, because of what I'd done our client beat
the rap."

"Was he innocent?"

"How the hell should I know?" Steve said. "I'm a lawyer, not a
judge and jury. My job is to present my client's case in the best
possible light. I do everything I can to prove him innocent. The
prosecution does everything it can to prove him guilty. The jury
decides. The minute I start trying to decide if a client's innocent
or guilty I'm violating that client's right to a trial by jury."

Sheila, quietly undercutting him, said, "Was he guilty?"

"He . . . uh . . . yeah, he was guilty, guilty as hell," Steve said.
He leaned back in his chair and rubbed his forehead.

She sat watching him. She was intrigued. She'd scored with the question, "Was he guilty?" She'd really gotten to him. She'd expected to get to him with the news she knew he'd been fired, but she hadn't. It had bothered him, but not badly. Not like this. It was unexpected, and it was interesting.

"Did you know it?" she asked.

He looked at her. "Know what?"

"Did you know he was guilty?"

"What's the difference?"

"I'd like to know."

"Why?"

"Because you're my lawyer, and what happens to me depends on you, and I need to know how you work. Did you know he was guilty?"

He sighed. "I found out later. I didn't know at the time."

"What do you mean at the time?"

"When I did it. Pulled the stunt. I believed the story, what the other lawyers on the case told me. The guy was innocent, the cops had gotten the wrong man, and were trying to force an identification. It's an old line. Only I was the one who swallowed it."

"Would you have done it if you'd known?"

"Hell no." Steve rubbed his head. "But I was stupid. I read it wrong. I thought it was a case of an innocent man being wronged. It wasn't. It was a case of some rich son of a bitch hiring a bunch of high-priced lawyers to try to get himself out of a mess. And I helped. Like a damn fool, I helped. It's kind of funny, really. My one act as a lawyer, and what did it do? It got me fired, it let some rich bastard beat the rap, and it earned good old Wilson and Doyle a whopping big fee."

Sheila was looking at him closely. "You wouldn't have done it if you'd known he was guilty?"

"Didn't I just say that?"

"Yeah. You did. Are you telling me you wouldn't defend me if you thought I was guilty?"

"I wasn't telling you that, no."

"But you wouldn't, would you?"

"No."

"What would you do?"

"If I thought you were guilty? I'd withdraw from the case."

"Well," she said, sarcastically. "Isn't that just fine. Here you are, defending me, and any time things start to look a little black, you can just decide I'm guilty and walk away."

"That isn't going to happen."

"Oh? Why not?"

"Because you're innocent."

"Oh, you've decided that, have you? Of course you have, or you wouldn't have taken the case. Well, that's just great. And just why are you so sure I'm innocent?"

The needling was getting to him. "I'll tell you why," he snapped. "Because of what I told you before. Because you're a shrewd, calculating, manipulative woman. Because, whatever else you are, you're not dumb. Now, I wouldn't put it past you to have killed this guy—you might have done it—but not like that. It's too stupid. You kill him in your apartment with your knife after taking his blackmail letter to the police, and you haven't even thought up a decent story to tell. All you say is, "I don't know who he is, I don't know what he's doing here, I don't know who killed him." I mean, hell, you're either the stupidest murderer that ever lived, or else you're innocent."

"Oh, great," she said. "That's why you think I'm innocent. That I couldn't be that stupid. Not that you have any confidence in me."

"*Confidence* in you?" he said. "Hell, you change your story every time I talk to you. You really inspire confidence." Suddenly he felt very tired. "All right, that's the story. That's the way things are. Now you know the whole thing. And you know where we stand. So it's up to you. You want to fire me?"

She looked at him. "If I do, it means the end of your law practice, doesn't it?"

He smiled mirthlessly. "I *have* no law practice. At least I'll be twenty-five grand to the good."

"No you won't. Uncle Max will stop payment on the check."

He shook his head. "Don't kid yourself. I cashed that check the minute his bank opened this morning."

She smiled. "You know, you're not as dumb as you look."

28

MARK TAYLOR was just hanging up the phone when Steve Winslow walked in and tossed a wad of money on his desk.

"Here," he said. "Credit this to my account."

Taylor picked it up, snapped off the rubber band and riffled through it. He whistled.

"Say," he said. "You weren't shitting me about a big retainer."

"Would I lie to you?" Steve pulled up a chair and sat down. "So what's new?"

"Not much. The lid's still on tight. Most of the stuff I'm getting is the stuff that doesn't matter, the stuff the cops are feeding to the papers anyway."

"Such as?"

Taylor shrugged. "Character assassination, largely. They got a next-door neighbor, a Mrs. Rosenthal. She's got the apartment right next to Sheila Benton's. She's the snoopy-busybody-gossipy-old-lady type. Her story is that Sheila often had a young man up to her apartment, and that he often slept over."

"Shit."

"Yeah, it's bad publicity, but it's just gossip. They can't use it in the trial."

"Yes, they can," Steve said, wearily. "It goes to prove motivation. She has a trust fund she loses if she's involved in any scandal. This would be the scandal Greely was presumably blackmailing her about. It's totally relevant."

"I hadn't thought of that."

"The D.A. has. Give me the worst of it. Will she testify to one man, or many?"

"Apparently only one. As I understand it, Mrs. Rosenthal is somewhat disappointed at having to admit that."

"I'll bet. Has she identified him as John Dutton?"

"Oh sure. She's seen him in the hall, she's seen him going in and out. The way I get it, she's the type of woman who sits with her door open two inches on a safety chain, and *watches* who goes in and out."

Steve straightened in his chair. "What about the day of the murder?"

"What *about* it?"

"Did she see who went in and out?"

Taylor shook his head. "That's the thing. The murder took place in the early afternoon. Mrs. Rosenthal's main concern was who went in in the evening and who left in the morning."

"Yeah. It would be. So she I.D.'s Dutton as an overnight guest?"

"On several occasions."

"Great. What about Dutton? Are the police working on him?"

"They aren't *talking* to him, if that's what you mean. He was in Reno at the time of the murder, so they figure he's out of it. I'm sure they're digging around in his personal life. If so, they're gonna get what we got. The guy's a young hotshot stockbroker with the reputation of being a playboy. He may be divorcing his wife over Sheila Benton, but word is he's got one or two other little romances going on the side, and if the police dig deep enough they're sure to come up with them."

Steve shook his head. "Wonderful."

"It's not that bad, is it?"

"Well, it ain't good. You know how juries are. They judge a case half on its merits and half on whether they happen to like the defendant. The prosecution is going to play up John Dutton's divorce and cast Sheila in the role of a home wrecker. To counter that I have to create the picture of two young people caught in the grip of an overwhelming passion so great it defied all conventional boundaries, leaving them no choice but to follow the irre-

sistible impulse of an overwhelming love." Steve broke off the
mock oratory and said, dryly, "Johnny's trying for a piece of tail
on the side isn't going to help."

"This is true."

"What about Dutton, anyway?"

"What *about* him?"

"Any confirmation he actually went to Reno?"

Taylor stared at him. "You picked him up at the airport. His
ticket was used."

"Yeah, but anyone could have used it."

"You trying to prove *he* did it?"

"I will if I have to."

"But he's Sheila's boyfriend."

"Yeah. But he's not my client. She is. Just find out if he really
took that plane."

"Okay." Taylor scribbled on his pad.

"While you're at it, check the alibis of Maxwell Baxter, Teddy
Baxter and Phillip Baxter. Check Mrs. Rosenthal, too."

"You kidding?"

"No. Check her. If we pass her up, she'll turn out to be some
frustrated old spinster that Greely did out of her life savings.
Check her out."

"Okay. Anyone else?"

"Yeah. Tony Zambelli."

"*What?*"

"You know him?"

Taylor stared at him. "I don't *know* him. I know *of* him."

"Well, don't look so surprised. You told me Carboni was connected. Zambelli's the connection. It happens he had a perfectly
good motive for the murder. Check him out."

Taylor gawked. "Do the police know this?"

"No. And they mustn't find out. Be discreet about it."

"Jesus Fucking Christ." Taylor shook his head. "Look, Steve,
I'm working for you. I'll do anything I can. But Tony Zambelli?
Guys who check him out have a habit of not being seen again."

"Don't sweat it," Steve said. "Zambelli *wants* us to check him out." Steve took out the list of names and handed it to him. "This is a list of people who were allegedly playing cards with Zambelli at the time of the murder. It don't mean shit, 'cause if Zambelli did it, he wouldn't have done it himself, he'd have ordered it done. But check it out just the same. I don't think there's a chance in hell you can find out if Zambelli ordered the hit, but if you should stumble over that information in the course of your investigations, please don't throw it away."

Taylor looked at Steve with frightened eyes. "Anything else?"

"Yeah. There's a chance the police may have these names too."

"Oh yeah?"

"Yeah. The list was in my pocket when the cops picked me up and searched me last night."

"When they *what?*"

Steve grinned. "Oh, your detectives missed that too. Your pipeline into police headquarters isn't all it's cracked up to be."

Taylor was incredulous. "They arrested you?"

"A slight misunderstanding. I'm not surprised your boys missed it. Sergeant Stams thought he'd cracked the Benton case. I'm not surprised they played it very hush-hush."

"You're kidding."

"Not at all. The point is, the cops had access to that list, so they may be running it down too. Only they don't know what it is, so they won't know what questions to ask. In case your boys should stumble over them in the course of the investigation, they should try not to give 'em a hint. Particularly since Zambelli would take it to mean we had spilled the information to the cops, and probably wouldn't be pleased."

"Jesus Christ!"

"So? Anything else?"

Taylor laughed nervously. "Yes. Yeah, there is. I saved the best for last. I have a bombshell. At least I thought it was a bombshell. After that, it's gonna seem like a firecracker, but I got it."

"What?"

"Well, like I said, nothing's coming out of police headquarters except the shit they're feeding the papers. But one of my boys got lucky."

"How?"

"The cops brought in a woman. Cheap. Flashily dressed. Looked like a hooker bust. But she wasn't processed, she was taken upstairs. So my man tagged along on a hunch. Sure enough, they hustled her straight in to see Dirkson. She was there about an hour. When she left, it was quietly and by a side entrance.

"My man was waiting and tagged along. He followed her home and checked her out. Without her knowing about it, of course."

"So? Who is she?"

"Her name is Carla Finley."

"Why is she important?"

Taylor grinned. "She was Greely's girlfriend."

Steve's eyes widened. "No shit. And the police picked her up?"

"Picked her up and let her go again."

"She must have had a good story. What'd she tell 'em?"

"I have no idea."

"Can I see her?"

Taylor grinned. "You can see *all* of her."

29

CARLA FINLEY was lying nude on a slowly revolving table. Her knees were drawn up and her legs were spread wide. Her hands were reaching around the insides of her thighs to give a little assist just in case the position itself was not sufficient to be truly revealing. Her neck was craned up from the table, and she had a look on her face that was surely supposed to pass for unbridled lust.

Steve Winslow watched her through the window of his private

booth, one of the dozen or so such booths that ringed the performing area. Steve, unlike the half a dozen other men whose faces appeared in the various windows, was studying her face.

Carla was heavily made up, but, on close inspection, the powder and rouge could not hide the fact that the face behind it was worn, that this was a woman on her way out, not on her way up, if such expressions applied in her chosen profession. Her face was lined, but that was not the thing that really gave her away. It was her eyes. For despite the devilish gleam she was attempting to affect, there was another, more sincere look she was unable to keep out of them.

They were tired eyes.

Steve's minute was up, and the blind on his window began to close. He bent down, looking under it until it closed completely.

He fished in his pocket and pulled out another quarter, then dropped it in the slot.

The blind went up again. As it did, he could see that Carla was getting up from the revolving table. She stood, stretched, smiled and then began walking around the room, cupping her sagging breasts and smiling at the customers in the windows.

When she reached his window, he banged on the glass and pantomimed wanting to talk to her. She smiled knowingly, pointed toward the back of the shop, held up three fingers, and mouthed, "Booth three." Then she moved on to the next customer.

Steve watched until she finished her rounds and left the stage.

He left his booth and headed for the larger encounter booths in the back of the shop. A stout, perspiring Hispanic in a white t-shirt stopped him.

"Goin' to a booth?"

"Yeah."

"Gotta buy a token, buddy."

"I just want to talk to her."

"Course you do, buddy. But first you buy a token, see."

"Yeah. I see. How much?"

"Buck."

Steve pulled a dollar out of his pocket and gave it to the attendant. The attendant gave him a metal token.

"I'll need a receipt," Steve said.

The attendant stared at him. "You shittin' me?"

"No. I want a receipt."

"What for?"

"My expense account."

The attendant shook his head and laughed. "Now I heard everything."

The attendant moved off, still chuckling.

Steve shrugged, and moved toward the booths in the back.

There were four of them. They were two-person affairs, arranged so the customers saw a side view of both compartments. One compartment was for the girl, the other was for the customer.

Two of the booths were occupied by customers. In those booths, curtains were pulled over the windows, hiding the occupants from view.

The other two were waiting for customers. The curtains were open. The girls sat on stools and smiled at the prospective customers. The doors to the client's side of the booths were invitingly open.

The girl in booth three was Carla. She was wearing skimpy panties and bra, covered by a diaphanous something or other. She smiled at Steve as he approached. He smiled back, and entered the booth.

It was not unlike the booth he'd just been in. A window with a blind and a coin slot. The main difference was a telephone receiver hanging next to the window.

He closed the door and dropped his token in the slot. The blind went up, revealing Carla sitting on her stool. She picked up the phone receiver and gestured for him to do the same.

He picked up the phone.

"Hi, sugar," she purred. "What can I do for you?"

"I just want to talk."

She winked. "Sure you do, sugar. Why don't you tell me what kind of things you like?"

"Are you Carla Finley?"

Her smile froze, and her face got hard. "Hey, what is this?"

"Robert Greely."

"Who the hell are you?"

"Sheila Benton's lawyer."

She stared at him for a second. "Get the hell out of here."

"I will, but not just yet. I did pay for my time."

"The cops told me not to talk to you."

"You always do what the cops tell you?"

"In my business, you don't cross 'em."

Steve smiled. "And we don't tell 'em all we know, do we?"

She looked at him. "What do you mean?"

"I mean if you happened to tell me something, you wouldn't have to tell the cops you told me. And I certainly wouldn't tell 'em."

Her face twisted with anger, making the age lines more pronounced. "Listen, Mister, don't get chummy with me. Bob Greely is dead, and Sheila Benton killed him, and why the hell should I help you?"

"She didn't kill him," Steve said. "But someone else did. If you help the police convict her, you're just helping the real killer get away."

"Yeah. Sure. Tell me another one."

He looked at her for a while. "All right," he said. "Let me tell you something. You're going to talk. Now, we can do this the easy way or the hard way. The hard way is I put detectives on you day and night until I catch you in a compromising situation with some prominent, upright citizen who can't afford to let his name get dragged into this. Then I put the squeeze on him so hard he has to put the squeeze on you. It may not get me what I want to know, but it'll sure as hell put a dent in your social life."

He paused and let that sink in.

"That's the hard way," he said.

He reached in his pocket and pulled out a roll of bills.

"Now," he said, "which would you rather be? Blackmailed or bribed?"

30

STEVE WINSLOW sat on Maxwell Baxter's couch. Max had not offered him a drink this time, but if he had Steve might have accepted it. He was enjoying himself, and was very much at ease.

Max was not. He stood looking down at Steve with ill-concealed hostility.

"Well," he said, dryly. "What is it this time, more money?"

Steve smiled. "Uncle Max. You misjudge me."

"Not by much. I'll have you know I consulted my lawyers."

"Oh?"

"Yes. That was a lot of crap you fed me, about if I didn't give you a retainer the D.A. could put you on the stand. Sheila spoke to you in confidence as her attorney. Fees don't come into it. There's no way you could testify."

"I know," Steve said. "I was bluffing. I know the law. I just figured you didn't."

Max glared at him. "You're just lucky you cashed that check as quickly as you did."

"Oh yeah? Well, now I think *you're* bluffing. Let me ask you something. When did you consult your attorneys?"

"What's that got to do with it?"

Steve grinned. "It's got everything to do with it. Here you are, striding around, saying, 'Boy are you lucky you cashed that check in time.' I think that's bullshit. You want to have me believe that when you talked to your attorneys, it was too late to stop payment on that check. It never happened that way and you know it. You're not that kind of guy. You didn't wait till this morning to call your attorneys. You got 'em out of bed last night, and you told 'em the whole thing, and they told you what the law was. You could have stopped payment on the check, but you *didn't*. And you *wouldn't*. I could have that check in my pocket right now, and it would still be good, 'cause you have no intention of stopping payment on it."

Steve paused, put his feet up on the coffee table and relaxed into the couch. "You see," he said, "I have you by the balls. You don't want to admit it, and that's why you're making these hollow 'you're lucky you cashed it in time' remarks, but that happens to be the fact. Because, despite what your lawyers told you, which happens to be absolutely true, you can't get away from the underlying threat in what I told you. Because, if you didn't pay me, even if I couldn't testify, there would always be a way of leaking what I know to the district attorney. And the thing is, you don't know me well enough, and there's nothing you can find out about me to convince you one way or another as to whether I'd be unscrupulous enough to do that. And you just can't take the chance.

"So, like it or not, I'm Sheila Benton's attorney, and you just have to get used to the fact. So, if you would be so kind as to give a message to Marston, Marston, and Cramden the next time you talk to them, please tell them this—lay off my client. Butt out. Because if they don't, I am going to file a complaint with the Grievance Committee, charging them with tampering with a client and attempting to solicit her away from her attorney. And from what I know about the conservative, respectable firm of Marston, Marston, and Cramden, that is going to cause them to choke on their soup."

Maxwell Baxter had not been a man of wealth and power for many years without developing a tremendous amount of poise. He showed it now.

"I see," he said.

"But that's not what I came for," Steve said.

"Oh? What did you come for?"

"I thought perhaps we could talk over the case."

"I fail to see what we have to talk about."

"Well, for one thing, I just had a talk with Carla Finley. Nice girl. You should meet her."

"Who's Carla Finley."

"Your detectives haven't told you? She was a friend of the late Mr. Greely."

"So?"

"She tells a very interesting story. It seems about a week ago Greely was all excited over something. She didn't know what it was, but it was something big. He told her in a few weeks he'd have enough money to take her someplace. He told her she'd never have to work again."

"So?"

Steve shrugged. "So, the police theory on this case is cockeyed. They figure Greely knew something that would have cost Sheila her trust fund, so he was putting the bite on her."

"Obviously."

"But it doesn't add up. Sheila doesn't come into her money until she's thirty-five. No one's going to get rich blackmailing her. So, I said to myself, if I were a blackmailer, who in this case would I blackmail?"

"Hypothetically, of course," Max said ironically.

"And so I come to you."

Max considered that for a moment. "I see. And so you're going to claim that since Sheila had no money, Greely must have actually been blackmailing me. Therefore I killed him."

"It's a nice theory," Steve said. "It would at least punch a few holes in the prosecution's theory of the case."

Max shook his head. "Frankly, I don't think so. The police will claim that Sheila expected to get the money from me."

"Of course that's what they'll claim. And I'll have a devil of a time proving otherwise. But you and I both know that's bullshit.

You're Sheila's trustee. Can you really imagine her coming to you and saying, "There's a blackmailer who knows something about me that you wouldn't want to know. Unless you give him a lot of money he's going to tell you."

"That's absurd."

"Well then, you explain it to me so that it doesn't sound absurd."

"That's not the point," Max said, with a condescending smile. "The point is, your fine theory is full of holes. If Greely were blackmailing me, why would he bother with Sheila at all? You see what I mean? It's illogical."

Steve smiled back. "Yes, but that's not my problem. I don't have to *prove* my theory, I just have to advance it. Then the prosecution has to disprove it. Because they have to prove Sheila guilty beyond all reasonable doubt. Reasonable doubt, that's all I need."

Steve paused while Max thought that over.

"Well, there you are," Steve said. "You're the perfect red herring. I'll dangle you in front of the jury and claim you killed him. The prosecution will have to prove you didn't."

"That's ridiculous. By your own reasoning, there was no way Greely could blackmail me over the trust."

"That's right," Steve said. "I'll claim he was blackmailing you over the will."

Max was genuinely surprised. "The *will?*"

"That's right. If he knew something that could upset the will, you'd be in a position to lose everything. It'd be a dandy motive for murder."

"You're crazy," Max said, shaking his head. "The will was probated twenty years ago. It's good as gold. There's no way on earth he could have upset the will."

"Oh no?" Steve said with a smile. "Try this on for size. No person convicted of murder may profit by inheritance from his victim. Suppose you killed your father. Suppose Greely knew about it. His testimony could convict you, and convicting you would upset the will."

For once, Max lost his cool. His face reddened.

"Well you son of a bitch."

Steve shrugged. "Funny. That's what Sheila said."

31

IT WAS a third-floor walkup in a grungy brownstone east of Allen. No one seemed to be home. Steve Winslow had been pounding on the door to no response. He was just turning to go when the lock clicked back and the door opened, revealing a gaunt man with disheveled gray hair and bloodshot, sleepy eyes.

"Mr. Baxter?" Steve inquired.

"Yeah?"

"Steve Winslow. I'm Sheila Benton's attorney."

For the first time, there was a gleam of interest in those tired eyes.

"Oh. Come in. Come in."

Theodore Baxter stepped back and ushered Steve into a small, ill-furnished living room.

Baxter pointed to the couch. "Please sit down."

Steve sat. Baxter moved some papers off an old easy chair and sat too.

"Excuse me," he said. "But I was asleep. I work nights."

"I know. Castle Hotel. Night clerk."

"I see you do your homework."

"I try."

Baxter shook his head. "Terrible business, this thing with Sheila. I can't imagine her doing such a thing."

"I can't either."

"You think she's innocent?"

"Yes I do."

"And so do I. But, of course, it's not what we think, it's what a jury will think. So how can I help you?"

"I hoped you could clear up a few points for me."

"Certainly. Would you care for some coffee?"

"No thanks."

"Would you mind if I made some? I find it hard to function when I get up without coffee."

"Go right ahead."

Baxter got up, ducked into his kitchen alcove and put a pot of water on the stove.

Steve waited patiently while Baxter clattered around in the kitchen, opening cabinets and drawers.

"Sure you won't have some?" Baxter called. "It's only instant, but it's not that bad."

"No thanks. I've had my daily quota."

Baxter emerged from the kitchen, holding a cracked coffee mug. He sat down and took a sip. A bit of color seemed to return to his cheeks. He looked up at Steve.

"I presume that Max has told you all about me?"

"I believe he mentioned you, yes."

"I'm sure he did," Baxter said. He sighed. "I don't suppose I can make you see it from my point of view. My dear brother Max is a pompous, self-righteous, patronizing, moralistic snob."

"I don't find that hard to see."

Baxter took another sip. "My father was the same way. Even more so, if that's possible. At any rate, he was the stingiest man in the world. Except when it came to my sister. Alice, Sheila's mother. He lavished all his love and affection on her. And money. Max and I got nothing. Well, Max was younger, and he didn't find the situation quite so galling. He was quite a stick-in-the-mud even then. But I was the poor son of a rich man, and I couldn't stand it. I was desperate to get away and get some money of my own so that I could break out of the situation.

"Well, you know what happened. I met some men who had a

scheme to make some money, big money. It was a crooked scheme. I was arrested. I served two years in prison. When I got out, my father and my sister were dead, and Max was in control.

"So now I'm a night clerk in a second-rate hotel, and Max is God Almighty."

Baxter paused and took another sip of coffee. "I know this isn't what you came here to ask me, but when someone's been talking with Max I like to have equal time."

"I can understand that."

"So, what did you want to know?"

"To begin with, what time was it when you and Phillip left Max's apartment?"

"Eleven twenty-five."

"You sure?"

"Absolutely. We had to get to Port Authority to catch the eleven forty-five to Boston. We just made it."

"How did you get there?"

"By cab."

"Did you see Phillip off on the bus?"

"No, I hopped out at Forty-second Street and took the subway downtown. But Phillip called me from Boston that night. He said he'd just made it."

"Phillip's there now?"

"Yes. Harvard Law School. School is the one thing Max is willing to shell out for."

"Okay. Tell me about your father."

Baxter looked up in surprise. "What about my father?"

"Any chance his death wasn't an accident?"

"What on earth are you talking about?"

"Any chance he was murdered?"

"*Murdered.*"

"Yes."

Baxter shook his head. "Not a chance in the world. He had cancer. His doctors gave him six months. He actually lasted nine."

"Uh huh. What about Sheila's father?"

"What *about* him?"

"Any chance he's still alive?"

Baxter's eyes narrowed. "What do you mean?"

"I think you know what I mean."

Baxter thought that over. "You mean is Sheila illegitimate?"

"That's one possibility. Another is that her parents were married, and then they divorced or separated. Her mother found it easier just to let Sheila think her father was dead."

"Why is it important?"

"If Sheila's father is living, he might be in a position to contest your father's will and upset Sheila's trust."

"How? I'm Phillip's father and a blood relative and I have no control over Phillip's trust."

Steve nodded. "Yes, but your case is different. You were specifically disinherited in the will. The will makes no provision at all for Sheila's father. Thus her trust may be open to attack. If the trust is upset, the will's upset, because the trust is a provision of the will."

Baxter thought that over. "I see. Well, the answer is, I don't know. I never met Sheila's father. None of us ever did. Alice was in California at the time. She wrote us that she was married. To a Samuel Benton. Then she wrote that her husband had been killed in a plane crash. When she came back East, Sheila was three."

Steve got up. "Okay. Thanks. That's what I wanted to know."

Baxter followed him to the door.

"Mr. Winslow?"

"Yes."

"I don't know exactly what you're driving at, but it seems as if somehow you suspect Max of something."

"Well?"

Baxter looked at him with those sad, tired eyes.

"Well, it may not sound very brotherly, but if you could pin something on him, I'd be very grateful."

32

DISTRICT ATTORNEY Harry Dirkson was worried.

Steve Winslow. He'd never heard of Steve Winslow. And a check into Winslow's background had told him why. The guy'd only been a lawyer for one year. He'd worked for one firm for two weeks and that had been it. He hadn't worked since. And now, here he was in a murder case.

Dirkson didn't like it. Sure, if the guy was as green as all that, he should be Dirkson's meat. Dirkson should cut him up in court. But still.

He was an unknown quantity. That was what Dirkson didn't like. The other, more seasoned lawyers could be a pain in the ass, but at least Dirkson knew them. He could deal with them. He was onto their tricks, and knew how to counter them. But this guy—Dirkson just didn't know.

Well, take his current situation. Having been forced into the decision to charge the girl, Dirkson was eager to go to trial. Because the longer this dragged on, the longer he was caught between his duty as prosecutor on the one hand, and Maxwell Baxter's influence on the other. Already he had had a painful phone call from the commissioner. The commissioner, though in essence backing him all the way, was, in reality, in between every other line demanding to know what the hell he thought he was doing. And it could only get worse.

Yeah, Dirkson was eager to get to trial. And the thing was, he knew that if any other attorney was on the case, he'd be throwing roadblocks in his path right and left. He'd be storming his office with writs of habeas corpus, and orders to show cause, and demands for bail hearings, and what have you. All of which was a bother, but all of which he could deal with.

But Winslow wasn't doing that. And even though Dirkson didn't want it done, it bothered him that Winslow wasn't. What was Winslow's game? Was he just dumb, or what? Christ, he hadn't even met the guy. He had reports of Winslow showing up at the jail to interview his client, and, of course, that bit about him getting arrested, which a shamefaced Sergeant Stams had been unable to hush up. The reports were that the guy looked like some long-haired hippie freak. Well, that didn't mean anything— he'd clean himself up for court.

But who *was* he?

Yeah, that was the question.

The guy appeared to have Maxwell Baxter's support—he had his twenty-five-thousand-dollar retainer check—so he must have something going for him.

But what?

The phone buzzed.

Dirkson scooped it up. "Yes?"

"A Mr. Steve Winslow on the line," Reese said.

"I'll take it." Dirkson sighed. Well, that was a relief. Finally. Business as usual. He pushed the button. "Dirkson, here."

"Yes, Mr. Dirkson. This is Steve Winslow. I'm attorney for Sheila Benton."

"I know. I'd been expecting to hear from you."

"Yes. I've been busy. I'd just like to know how you intend to proceed."

Dirkson frowned. God, this guy was green. No demands. No assertions.

"Well," Dirkson said, feeling he was doing the man's job for him. "With regard to bail—"

"I'm not asking for bail."

"What?"

"It's a capital crime and the evidence you have is fairly conclusive. I see no hope of reasonable bail. I won't contest it. But under those circumstances, I must insist on my client's right to a speedy trial."

Dirkson blinked. Any other attorney would have got the client out on bail and stalled forever.

"I see," Dirkson said. Though he didn't.

"How do you plan to proceed? Preliminary hearing or grand jury indictment?"

"I'm going before the grand jury," Dirkson said.

"Fine," Steve said. "Indict her and let's go to court. I'll waive all matters of time, and stipulate away all red tape. Indict her and set the trial date."

"Fine."

"See you in court," Steve said, and hung up.

Dirkson hung up too. He felt slightly nauseous. What the hell was going on? And why did he feel so uneasy about it? He'd wanted the guy to call him—the guy had called him. He'd wanted a speedy court date—the guy had given it to him.

Dirkson had just gotten everything he wanted.

And he didn't like it at all.

33

STEVE WINSLOW slumped into one of Mark Taylor's overstuffed clients' chairs and rubbed his eyes. "Okay," he said. "Here's the rundown. The grand jury's indicted Sheila Benton for murder. You can go over the transcripts all you want, but you won't find anything we don't already know. The D.A. gave the grand jury just enough to indict, nothing more. Any little surprises he has for me are gonna remain surprises until he springs them on me in front of the jury. Meanwhile, she is remanded to custody without bail."

"As expected," Taylor said.

Steve nodded. "Right. Okay. Let me tell you what I want you to work on, then you can tell me what you've got."

Taylor grabbed a notepad. "Shoot."

"You got any connections in California?"

"Yeah. I know a guy with an agency in L.A. Why?"

"Samuel Benton."

"Who?"

"Sheila Benton's father."

"What about him? He's dead, isn't he?"

"That's what I want to find out. According to the best information I have, Samuel Benton married Alice Baxter in California shortly before Sheila was born. How shortly I don't know, but I wouldn't necessarily go back a full nine months. Sheila's twenty-four now, you can do the math for yourself.

"Now, the story is he was killed in a plane crash before Sheila was born. That shouldn't be hard to trace. Find out about it. I want to know for sure whether Samuel Benton is dead or alive."

Taylor was staring at him. "What's the idea, Steve?"

"All right," Steve said. "Let's look at this case objectively. To begin with, let's assume Sheila is innocent."

"I thought you said objectively."

Steve looked at him sharply. "Don't you think she is?"

Taylor looked uncomfortable. "Look, Steve, you're my client. I'm partisan. I'm on your side. I give service. But—"

"All right. Fine. Then just bear with me. Assume that Sheila is innocent."

"Okay."

"Then how does any of this make sense?"

"That's the problem. It doesn't."

"I know. But it has to. So here's how I figure. If Sheila is innocent, then everything that's happened to her is part of a deliberate frame-up. And the question is *why*. And the answer is Sheila. Not Greely. Not blackmail. Sheila. Someone has framed Sheila because of who she *is*. And who is she? She's Maxwell Baxter's niece. An heiress. The beneficiary of the Baxter trust. Now, if Sheila Benton's father is alive, he would be in a position to upset that trust. And that opens up a lot of possibilities."

Taylor's nod was not enthusiastic. "Yeah, I guess so."

"Look, I'm going up in front of a jury. The prosecution has to prove her guilty beyond all reasonable doubt. Reasonable doubt, that's all I need."

"Yeah."

"So get going on the California end."

"Will do. You ready for the rundown?"

Steve sighed. "Yeah. Let's have it."

Taylor turned back a few pages in his notebook. "Here we are. Phillip Baxter, John Dutton, Carla Finley, and Tony Zambelli have complete alibis for the time of the murder. Stella Rosenthal, Maxwell Baxter and Teddy Baxter do not."

Steve frowned. "Teddy Baxter. Why is that name familiar?"

Taylor grinned. "The anchorman on the 'Mary Tyler Moore Show.'"

"Oh yeah. He must be the life of the Castle Hotel. Okay, let's have 'em."

"Phillip Baxter was on the bus to Boston. The evidence there is circumstantial. The bus driver doesn't remember him, but then you wouldn't expect him to. Phillip's father says he was on his way to the bus, and Phillip checked into his dorm at Harvard that night."

"Okay. Next."

"John Dutton was in Reno at the time. I checked his reservation on the plane. His ticket was used."

"Yeah, but is there any chance someone else used it?"

"None at all. One of the stewardesses remembered him. She

identified his picture. He was handing her a line and trying to date her up for later that evening."

"Great, just great. Next."

"Before we move on, I got some more on John Dutton."

"What?"

"Well, there's a little discrepancy. According to his secretary, he was staying at the Wilshire Hotel. However, the Wilshire has no record of him staying there."

"Really . . ."

"Yeah, but before you get all excited, I think there's an explanation. We know Johnny's a playboy, and there's every reason to believe he had something lined up in Reno he didn't want anyone to know about."

"Yeah, that checks," Steve said. "No, it doesn't either. If he had some girl waiting for him, what the hell would he be doing trying to date up the stewardess?"

Taylor shrugged. "Probably just running his game. It seems to be a compulsion with him. Anyway, I don't think it's any big deal. The stewardess he was hitting on saw a young woman run up and hug him when he got off the plane, so that's probably all there was to it."

"I suppose so."

"Plus we have the confirmation that he did meet with his wife's attorneys while he was out there."

"All right, all right, I give up," Steve said. "If he met with the attorneys . . . Hey, wait a minute."

"What?"

"What about his wife? Did he meet with her too?"

"I don't know."

"Find out, willya?"

Taylor looked puzzled. "Why? I mean, if the attorneys confirm the meeting."

"They confirm him. What about her?"

"Her?"

"Yeah. Dutton's wife."

Taylor looked at him. "Are you kidding?"

"No. I'm not kidding. What I've been looking for all along is someone who hates Sheila Benton, who would have reason to want to frame her. I can't think of anyone with a better reason than the present Mrs. John Dutton."

Taylor shook his head. "I really think you're grasping at straws."

"I gotta grasp at something. What's his wife's name?"

Taylor consulted the pad. "Inez Dutton."

"Fine. Check her out. Who's next?"

"Carla Finley."

"Ah, yes. Let's not forget Carla Finley. What about her."

Taylor grinned. "Carla Finley happens to have the best alibi of all. At the time of the murder, she was seen by at least fifty people. Naturally, none of them would be very eager to testify, even if they could be found."

Steve grinned. "I'll bet. Next."

"Zambelli, as he said, was involved in a poker game at the time. There again, no one is particularly anxious to testify."

"Which proves nothing. If he hit him, he'd have hired it out. Who's next?"

Taylor wheeled around and put his feet up on his desk. "Now we come to the have-nots. Mrs. Rosenthal, the next-door neighbor, claims she was at the supermarket at the time."

"For the whole hour?"

"So she says. She points to an eighty-nine-dollar, forty-seven-cent cash-register receipt and a stocked refrigerator and pantry as confirmation."

"Wait a minute. How could she carry that much stuff?"

"She didn't. She had it delivered. The delivery boy brought it around two-thirty that afternoon."

"That sounds about right. But wait a minute. Wouldn't he have run into the cops, then?"

"He did. Mrs. Rosenthal was out in the hallway giving the cops an earful when he arrived. At first the cops weren't going to let him through, but then Mrs. Rosenthal raised merry hell about her frozen foods melting, and billing the cops for it, and suing the city, and finally they gave in just to shut her up."

"So . . . her alibi is purely circumstantial."

Taylor sighed. "Yes it is. Now, I know you asked me to do this, so I did it, and I have to tell you, if there's any connection between Mrs. Rosenthal and Robert Greely, I can't find it. And just between you and me, alibi or no alibi, I'd be willing to bet you my agency she didn't do it. Mrs. Rosenthal isn't the type of woman who would have known Robert Greely. Mrs. Rosenthal is the type of woman who accounts for the large number of bachelors in this country. In short, Mrs. Rosenthal is an obnoxious, gossipy, interfering, nosy pain in the ass."

"All right," Steve said, relenting. "Next."

Taylor glanced at the sheet. "Teddy Baxter says he was at home. Whether he was is anybody's guess. As a widower living alone, he has no corroborating witness."

"Too bad."

"Uncle Max has the same problem. The elevator man doesn't remember seeing him go out, but of course there's a back entrance, and a man on his way to a murder might be inclined to use it."

"He certainly might. I'd give anything to be able to prove that he did."

"You'd really like to pin it on him, wouldn't you?"

"I certainly would."

"I don't blame you. With him convicted of murder, you could knock out the trust, get Sheila a few cool million, and cut yourself a nice slice of the pie."

"Yeah. But that's not why I want to do it."

Taylor looked at him. "Oh? Well then, why?"

Steve shrugged. "I don't know. He just really pisses me off."

34

FOR ONCE, Sheila Benton was subdued. She was doing her best to keep up a good front, but her perky facade was so transparent Steve Winslow could see right through it. She was really scared.

"Well," she said, "how bad is it?"

"You want information or reassurance?"

"Information."

"Well, the way it looks right now, the only way I could make any money on this case would be to bet on the prosecution."

"That's not funny."

"No, it isn't."

"The trial really starts tomorrow?"

"Well, not the trial itself. Jury selection will probably take a couple of days. But we have to be in court, if that's what you mean."

"Couldn't you have gotten a continuance?"

"Why would you want one? The longer we stall, the longer you have to stay in jail."

"I don't see why you couldn't have pushed for bail."

"Well, it probably wouldn't have done any good. And the thing is, I have a big problem there. See, one of the main points in our defense is that you have no money, and therefore no one could have been blackmailing you. If I pushed for bail, I'd be in the position of arguing that on the one hand, you had enough collateral to post bail, but on the other, not enough to pay blackmail. That would seriously weaken our position."

"What do you mean 'our'? I'm the one in jail."

"This is true. I feel it's only fair to tell you, if you'd let Uncle Max handle this, Marston, Marston, and Cramden probably *could* have arranged bail."

"What? Why?"

"They're a highly reputable and conservative firm. Their assurances carry weight. Besides, you'd have Uncle Max and his millions behind you. It wouldn't even be a question of a bail bond, then. Uncle Max would post cash bail for you."

Sheila bit her lip. "I see."

"But there's other reasons for not getting a continuance. I want to rush this thing to trial before the D.A. finds out about your little habit of sticking drugs up your nose."

Sheila started to protest, but stopped. It just wasn't in her today. Instead she looked searchingly into his face.

"You don't like me, do you?" she said.

Steve laughed. "Hey, come on."

Sheila kept looking at him. "No, it's true, isn't it? You don't like me. You think I'm just a rich bitch. And you don't like me."

Sheila looked down. Sighed. Looked up at him again. "Do you know what it's like to be me? I don't mean here, now, in jail. I mean me in general. Would you like to know what it's like to be me?"

Steve felt like saying, "No, but I know you're dying to tell me," but realized that would be terribly cruel. He said nothing.

"Well, it's hard," Sheila said. "It's very hard. Rich bitch? Well, I am, but I'm not. When I'm thirty-five I'll be a rich bitch, but right now I'm not. I have all of the disadvantages, and none of the advantages.

"I'm young, and I'm pretty, and I'm fun, and men like me. They love me. They go nuts about me. But always in the background there's Uncle Max's millions, and I can never be sure. Is it me? Do they like me for me?

"And I have no money. None at all. I live like a pauper. I get by. And you know how I get by? Men. I live off men. That's what Uncle Max has done to me. That's what he's reduced me to. If I wanna go out to dinner, I have to find some man to take me. And if I do, I never know if he's taking me because he likes me, or because he's trying to hit on me, or because of Max. Is he thinking of spending money on me as a long-term investment? I can never be sure."

She paused, and a new look came into her eyes, and for a moment Steve wondered what it was. Then he got it. Defensive. She'd had no problem with what she'd said so far, but for what she was about to say she was taking a defensive stand.

"Except for Johnny," she said. "I love him. We're in love. I don't know if you can understand that. But he loves me. Just for me. Not for the money. He doesn't need the money. He's young, and brilliant, and he makes all the money he needs. He takes care of me."

She paused again. Steve said nothing. Waited.

"All right, there's the coke. I guess I should stop it. All right, I *know* I should stop it. It's just that Johnny was so perfect, so right, you know. It didn't seem that bad. I mean if Johnny did it, how could it be wrong? And I was in love and I went along, and you can't understand that. To you I'm just a cokehead. As far as you're concerned, I *deserve* to be in jail. That's what you think, isn't it?"

"What do you care what I think? You don't like me, anyway."

Sheila's body tingled when he said that. It was a strange sensation. Something new. Something unexpected. And something very unsettling. She shivered slightly, and the sensation passed.

"Right," she said, mustering up some of the old spunk. "I don't like you and you don't like me. But we're stuck with each other, so what the hell are we gonna do now?"

Steve smiled. "We're gonna go to court."

Sheila felt another sensation, and this one was entirely unpleasant. Her face lost a little color.

"Yeah," she said.

"Hey," Steve said. "It's not gonna be that bad. What you're having now is stage fright. Opening-night jitters. When you get in the courtroom you'll be fine. Just remember, you don't have to do anything. You just have to be there. I'm the one who's gonna do all the work. All you have to do is sit there and look innocent."

"How the hell do you look innocent?"

"I don't know."

"Then how the hell am I supposed to do it?"

"All right, then. Just try not to look guilty."

"Oh, hey," she said, sarcastically. "Great advice. Thanks. And just what do I do when you put me on the stand?"

Steve took a breath. "Look," he said. "Let me tell you a little bit about our plan of attack. Right now, our best strategy is to sit back and try to poke holes in the prosecution's case. There's bound to be some, and we can find 'em. The money thing, for instance. How could you be blackmailed if you have no money? See what I mean? The prosecution has to prove you guilty beyond a reasonable doubt. Always remember that. All we have to do is raise a reasonable doubt."

Sheila was looking at him suspiciously. "Wait a minute. Are you trying to tell me you're *not* going to put me on the stand?"

"All right, look, we have a big problem here. You told your story to the police. And you lied. If you change your story, you have to admit you lied. Unless you have a damn good explanation, that's suicide, and you don't have one.

"If you stick with your story, you're sticking with a lie. And if the D.A. catches you in a lie in front of the jury, you're done.

"So the answer is no. I can't afford to put you on the stand."

"But why not? They can't prove I wasn't window-shopping. Why, I can remember every store I went to."

"I bet you can. Unfortunately, there are other little matters, which you can't explain."

"Like what?"

"Your uncle gave you a hundred bucks. How much money did you have when you were arrested?"

"About eleven dollars."

"Sure, cause you spent the hundred on cocaine. Well, the D.A. is gonna wanna know where that hundred dollars went."

"Can't I say I bought something for my apartment?"

"You don't *own* anything worth a hundred dollars. That's just the type of lie I'm talking about. They'd catch you in it right away. They'd want to know what you bought and where, and they'd check the stores for the sales records."

Sheila bit her lip. She thought a moment. Then she got a gleam in her eye. It was the old fire. The old spunk. Steve was glad to see it.

For a moment.

"All right," she said. "I'll say I gave it to you for a retainer."

"Whoa! Back up!" Steve said. "Now you're asking me to commit perjury."

"Well, why not? You're a lawyer, aren't you? If anybody knows how to commit perjury, you ought to."

"Well forget it. I'm not putting myself on the witness stand. In the first place, it's questionable ethics for an attorney to testify in behalf of his client, even when he's telling the truth. In the second place, the jury would never believe me anyway."

Sheila put on a pout. "All right, be that way. But let me tell you something. If you can't beat the prosecution's case, you'll have to put me on the stand. And when the D.A. asks me what happened to the money, I'm gonna tell him I gave it to you. Then if you try to prove that I didn't, it's gonna make you look like one hell of a lawyer, isn't it?"

Steve looked at her. Sighed. She was back in form, all right.

35

STEVE WINSLOW sat in the barbershop, waiting his turn and thinking about the case. The old man in the chair near the window looked about done. Then a quick clip, and he could get out of there and hunt up a clothing store and buy a suit off the rack—no time for alterations, thank god he was average build—and go home and hit the law books.

The case. The goddamn case. His first, his one and only case. Tomorrow he'd be in court.

Jesus.

Steve thought about what he'd told Sheila Benton. Stage fright. Opening-night jitters. Well, he had 'em all right. God was he nervous.

Nothing to worry about, he told himself. It's just another play. You're an actor, and it's a play. Think of the courtroom as a stage set. That's all it is. Just a bit of courtroom drama.

Then it hit him. A cold chill ran down his spine. It was a play all right. *A play he hadn't rehearsed. A play in which he didn't know the lines.* The actor's nightmare come to life.

Steve felt a moment of panic. It was immediately replaced by something else. Anger. Anger at himself. Selfish bastard, he thought. So concerned about how *he* was going to look, what impression *he* was going to make in the court. A young girl's future was at stake. A silly, irresponsible girl, perhaps, but still, one that deserved better. It was his job to defend her, and damn it, he had to be up to the task.

But what a task. To convince twelve people that Sheila Benton didn't kill Robert Greely. Steve wondered if there were twelve people in all of New York City that didn't believe Sheila Benton had killed Robert Greely.

There was a pile of old magazines and newspapers on the table next to him. On top was a copy of the New York Post. "BAXTER NIECE INDICTED" screamed the headline. "Baxter niece," that was the thing. This wasn't the Sheila Benton case. It wasn't the Robert Greely case. It was the Baxter case, and the media wasn't going to let anyone forget it. Maxwell Baxter's niece killed someone, that was the message the media was putting out loud and clear, and the public was lapping it up. People always loved to see someone big, and rich, and powerful in trouble. An heiress with a multimillion-dollar trust fund killed someone. That's what everyone believed. Even Mark Taylor. So how the hell was he gonna make anyone think different?

Sitting there in the barber shop, Steve thought back to the first time he'd ever dealt with a lawyer. The first and last time he'd ever been up against one. Steve remembered him well. That smug, oily son of a bitch, smiling and nodding and explaining to the arbitrator at the hearing just through what legal loophole, on what technicality the State of New Jersey would be able to get out of paying the grant money awarded by the Arts Council. Money on the promise of which Steve had organized and performed a tour of children's theater to the New Jersey public schools. Money that was owed to six actors, including himself, who had subsidized the program themselves by drawing no salary for the three months of the tour, and who were now all hopelessly in debt. Steve had been the one who'd had to argue with the lawyer, since he'd been in charge of the tour and felt responsible. "What about the actors?" he'd argued. "They gave their services on the promise of that money. The work has been performed and has to be paid."

"On *your* promise of the money," the lawyer had answered. "On your mistaken belief that the money would be forthcoming. If you acted in ignorance of the law we can be sorry for you, but we can't be held accountable."

Steve had been stymied. He couldn't argue the case on legal grounds. He couldn't cite some legal precedent that could have swung the decision. He could only argue the case on what was fair and just. On the grounds that just because a loophole was there didn't mean the state had to take advantage of it. That the state should feel compelled to do what was right.

The state did not agree.

And Steve had wound up paying off the other five actors himself, in some cases, in spite of their protests.

It had taken him four years.

Later, when he had finally given up all hope of ever making it as an actor, the incident with the Arts Council was not the only reason he decided on law school.

But it sure didn't hurt.

Steve thought about that now, thought about how he felt standing in that hearing room, listening to the lawyer talk. The feeling of helplessness, the feeling of being totally at sea.

The feeling of being outclassed.

He knew the law now. Or thought he did. But he'd never been in a courtroom before.

He wondered if he'd feel that way tomorrow.

Snap out of it, he told himself. It's just a play, and the jury is just an audience. A small audience, to be sure, but still an audience. And like any audience, their emotions could be swayed. They could be moved to laughter, to tears, to sympathy, to anger, to regret. It was just a question of dynamics. Whatever the prosecution was doing, do the opposite. Change the pace. Break the mood.

Give them a show.

The old man in the chair by the window got up. The barber snapped the apron, shaking off the hair.

"Next," he called.

Steve got up and walked over.

"Changed my mind," he said, and walked out the door.

He flagged a cab and took it home to study, to prepare himself for court. He stayed up till two in the morning, poring over his books. But he didn't read his law books.

He read his Erle Stanley Gardners.

36

DISTRICT ATTORNEY Harry Dirkson glanced nervously around the courtroom. It was packed. The defendant and her attorney weren't even in court yet, but it seemed as if everyone else in New York City was. People were elbowing each other for every inch of available space. It was a zoo. A media circus.

Dirkson was jumpy, and for good reason. Steve Winslow. He hadn't even met the guy yet. That was unprecedented, at this stage in a murder trial. He'd talked to him on the phone, and the guy had sounded perfectly rational. Too rational. Dirkson smiled, as lines from a movie flitted through his head: "It's quiet out there. Too quiet." Right. The settlers in the fort wondering where the Indians are. Funny, but that's how he felt. This Winslow wasn't making any waves. Great, but why? What was his game? That was Dirkson's great fear. The fear of the unknown.

Yeah, Dirkson was scared. Scared enough that he didn't want to go through with the trial, but he had no choice. This was one case he couldn't pass off on any assistant D.A. He'd have taken too much flak for it. The press would have crucified him. No, this was one he had to handle himself.

And he needed a conviction. He needed it desperately. But he wasn't even thinking about that now. His only concern was getting out unscathed. With all the media coverage, with all the publicity focused on this trial, he couldn't afford to make any mistakes. Above all, he could not let himself appear foolish.

Which could very easily happen in a circus like this. Jesus, he thought, look at the clowns in the audience. Why was it that so many of the people who came to trials turned out to belong to the lunatic fringe? The zanies. The crazies. Jesus, look at that guy coming down the aisle now—some long-haired hippie who's so stoned out he thinks it's still the sixties. Why do they let them in here? Why don't they screen them out and . . . Wait a minute. He's coming through the gate. Why isn't the bailiff stopping him? Is everyone asleep here? Is no one doing his job? Can't they see some clown just wandered into—*Oh my god.*

Steve Winslow walked over to the defense table. So. Sheila Benton wasn't here yet. But they'd be bringing her out soon. He should sit down. Was this his chair and that hers, or vice versa? He'd never done this before. No, this was his chair on the end, near the middle of the courtroom. He was the one who had to get up and down. She just had to sit there and look innocent. Great advice he'd given her. He wondered if other attorneys had given their clients the same advice. "Try to look innocent." Words of wisdom.

Steve looked over at the jury box, empty now, but soon to be filled with prospective jurors. And up at the judge's bench, imposing, regal. And at the witness stand, where he would do battle, where he would have to shine.

Last he looked over at the prosecution table. And there he was. The pudgy, bald man in the custom-tailored suit that was failing to do its job of hiding his excess weight had to be Harry Dirkson. The Dirk himself, as the attorneys at Wilson and Doyle used to refer to him. Jesus, Steve thought. The guy doesn't look like that much. Can he really deserve his reputation as a demon cross-examiner? As he thought that, Dirkson looked at him and their eyes met. Steve nodded and smiled.

Dirkson stared at him. Oh Jesus, he thought. He's a clown. A goddamn clown. It's a circus and he's the clown, and there goes my political career.

The door at the side of the courtroom opened, and the bailiff ushered in a police officer, a matron and the defendant, Sheila Benton. The bailiff led her to the defense table.

Sheila stopped, stared, then slid into her seat next to Steve.

"Jesus Christ," she said. "What's the matter, couldn't you afford a suit?"

"Shhh. Don't worry about it."

"How the hell do you expect to make an impression on the jury dressed like that?"

"I'm not trying to make an impression on the jury. I'm trying to get you acquitted."

"You've got a funny way of showing it."

"Shhh."

"Please rise," ordered the bailiff.

Steve and Sheila got to their feet. She was still staring at him, but he was looking at Judge Preston Crandell, who had just entered and was taking his seat at the bench. Crandell, with thirty years on the bench, had a reputation as a hard, no-nonsense judge. In New York City, famous for its turn-'em-loose judges, Crandell was an exception—a judge who would convict if at all possible. A prosecutor's judge.

Crandell banged the gavel.

"Court is now in session," announced the bailiff. "The People of the State of New York versus Sheila Benton. The Honorable Preston Crandell presiding."

Judge Crandell turned to Harry Dirkson. "Is the prosecution ready?"

"Ready, Your Honor."

Crandell turned to Steve Winslow. He appeared to hesitate a second and raise an eyebrow before inquiring, "Is the defense ready?"

Dirkson was afraid Winslow would say something smart, do something clownish, but he merely said, "Ready, Your Honor."

Crandell turned to the bailiff. "Bring in the first jurors."

During jury selection, some of Harry Dirkson's fears evaporated. Far from being flamboyant, the defense attorney seemed quiet and subdued. He asked only easy, general questions of the prospective jurors, regarding their ability to be impartial and fair, and seemed to take their answers at face value. Things went so smoothly, in fact, that the jury was impaneled that morning, and following the noon recess, Judge Crandell commenced the trial.

"Does the prosecution wish to make an opening statement?" he inquired of Dirkson.

Dirkson rose to his feet. "The prosecution does, Your Honor."

Dirkson had expected the jury selection to have taken several days. However, he was a shrewd prosecutor who took nothing for granted, and thus his opening speech was well prepared. This was his moment to shine, and he was fully prepared to do so. He felt that old kick, that old surge of adrenaline, and he actually felt good as he strode out into the middle of the courtroom.

"Your Honor. Ladies and gentlemen of the jury," he began. "The prosecution intends to prove, that on the seventh day of June of this year, the defendant, Sheila Benton, did, premeditatedly and with malice aforethought, murder one Robert Greely. We intend to prove that Sheila Benton is an heiress with a trust fund worth several million dollars. The trust is in the control of her uncle, Maxwell Baxter, until Miss Benton reaches the age of thirty-five, at which time he is to turn over the principal to her. However, there is a provision in the trust which states that if Sheila Benton is involved in any scandal that would bring disrepute on the family name, the entire trust is forfeit, and the money goes to charity. We intend to prove that Sheila Benton was engaged in an affair with a married man, one John Dutton. We intend to prove that Robert Greely learned of the affair, and demanded blackmail for his silence. Threatened with exposure, and unable to raise the sum of money Greely demanded, Sheila Benton lured him up to her apartment and killed him.

"We shall prove all of these things by competent evidence, and we shall expect a verdict of guilty at your hands."

Dirkson smiled at the jury, went back and sat down.

Steve was impressed. It was an effective opening statement, short and to the point, stating what Dirkson expected to prove, but showing none of his hand. Steve realized the jury was impressed too. He had been watching them during Dirkson's speech. They had listened intently. Some had even nodded. And now, all of them were looking at the defendant, a sure sign that the prosecution had scored.

"Does the defense wish to make an opening statement?" asked Judge Crandell.

Steve looked up. The judge clearly expected a negative response. It would be unusual for the defense to make an opening statement at this time. The usual practice would be to reserve the opening statement until the prosecution had rested and the defense began putting on its case.

But Dirkson's opening statement had done its damage. The jury had already turned against the defendant. Okay, Steve thought. Break the mood.

He rose to his feet. "The defense does, Your Honor."

He stepped out into the middle of the courtroom. All eyes were on him, all heads turned to watch this strange-looking man, to hear what he had to say.

"Your Honor," Steve said, in his best stage voice. "Ladies and gentlemen of the jury."

He paused theatrically, looked around the courtroom. Then he shrugged his shoulders, smiled slightly and, in a smaller voice with just a hint of Brooklyn twang, said, "She didn't do it."

Steve walked back to his seat and sat down.

A ripple of amusement ran through the courtroom. It was a delayed reaction, as the people slowly realized that was his entire opening statement.

Steve watched the jurors. Some smiled. Some looked at each other.

The mood Dirkson had created was gone.

Steve looked around the courtroom at the reaction, and in that moment, all his opening-night jitters were gone. He was in a fight, and he loved it.

But Dirkson's world had just collapsed. It was his worst nightmare. My god, he thought, he *is* a clown.

37

AS HIS first witness, Dirkson called the coroner, Dr. Marvin Fenton. Fenton, a bald, pudgy man with a slightly pompous bearing, stated his name and occupation.

"Now," Dirkson said, "directing your attention to the afternoon of June seventh of this year, were you summoned to apartment 2B of an apartment house at 193 West 97th Street?"

"I was."

"And what did you find there."

"I discovered the body of a man."

"Was he alive?"

"He was dead."

"Did you determine the cause of death?"

"I did. Death had been caused by a large carving knife, which had been stabbed into the back of the victim. The blade had entered the back just below the left shoulder blade, and angled down until it penetrated the victim's heart."

"That was the only cause of death?"

"It was."

"There were no contributing factors? No bruises or contusions of any kind?"

"No, sir."

"No presence of any drug in the body?"

"No, sir."

"The knife was the sole cause of death?"

"Yes, sir."

"Was the knife still in the body?"

"It was."

"Would you know that knife if you saw it again?"

"Yes. I scratched my initials on the handle of the knife."

Dirkson smiled his approval. He walked over to the prosecution table, where his assistant handed him a paper bag. With something of a flourish, he produced a carving knife.

"Doctor," he said, striding back to the witness stand. "I hand you a knife and ask you if you have ever seen it before?"

Dr. Fenton took the knife and examined it.

"Yes, sir. This is the knife I found in the body of the victim."

Dirkson took back the knife and approached the judge's bench.

"Your Honor, I asked that this knife be marked for identification as People's Exhibit number one."

"No objection," Steve said.

"So ordered," said Judge Crandell.

Dirkson handed the knife to the court clerk to be marked. He turned back to the witness.

"Now then, Dr. Fenton. Did you determine the time of death?"

"Yes, sir. I did. The decedent met his death on June seventh between the hours of twelve-thirty and one-thirty P.M."

"Thank you, Doctor," Dirkson said with a smile. He turned to the defense table. "Your witness."

Steve frowned. It was a damn clever way of presenting the evidence. The coroner was undoubtedly armed with a barrage of expert medical testimony to back up his determination of the time of death. But Dirkson hadn't asked for it. He was going to let Steve bring it out himself and crucify his own client.

Steve got up and went over to the clerk. "Could I see the exhibit, please? Thank you."

Steve took the knife and approached the witness. He smiled, and began his cross-examination almost conversationally.

"Dr. Fenton, you identify the knife by the initials you scratched on the handle?"

"Yes. I do."

"What tool did you use?"

Fenton frowned, wondering what he was getting at. "A small etching tool I carry for that purpose."

"Well, Doctor, if you scratched your initials into the handle of the knife with an etching tool, how can you be sure that the pressure you put on the knife didn't alter its position in the body and cause more extensive wounds than would otherwise have shown up in your autopsy?"

Dr. Fenton was indignant. "I did no such thing. I never said I scratched my initials on the knife while it was still in the body."

Steve feigned surprise. "Oh? So when you scratched your initials on the knife it had been removed from the body?"

"It had."

"Did you remove the knife from the body?"

"Ummm. No, sir. I did not. My assistant, Dr. Blake, removed it."

"And what did he do with the knife?"

"Ummmm. Well . . ."

"Yes?"

"Well, Sergeant Stams wanted to fingerprint the knife, so he turned it over to him."

"I see. So it was Sergeant Stams who gave you back the knife?"

Dr. Fenton shifted in his seat. "Well, no, actually it was Lieutenant Farron who returned it to me."

"Ah. So it was Lieutenant Farron who gave you back the knife. And where were you at the time?"

"In my laboratory at the city morgue."

"And it was at Lieutenant Farron's request that you scratched your initials on the handle of the knife, wasn't it?"

"Yes."

"Then how do you know that the knife Lieutenant Farron handed you was the same knife you found in the body?"

"I recognized it."

"How? You hadn't scratched your initials on it yet."

"I recognized it by the blood."

"Anyone can put blood on a knife. What was there about the knife itself that enabled you to distinguish it from the hundreds of other knives of the same make and model as that found in the body?"

"It looked like the same knife."

"I daresay it did. Now then, Doctor, if I were to produce evidence that on the afternoon of the seventh Lieutenant Farron purchased a knife similar to the one you have identified as People's Exhibit number one, is there anything in your testimony that would prove that this was not that knife?"

Dirkson was on his feet. "Your Honor, I object. Counsel is indulging in the wildest fantasy. I defy him to produce such testimony."

"It is a hypothetical question only, Your Honor," Steve said, "for the purpose of impeachment."

Judge Crandell nodded. "It is an impeaching question. The objection is overruled. Witness will answer the question."

Dirkson slowly sat down.

Steve turned back to the witness.

Dr. Fenton sighed. "No, sir, there is not," he said wearily.

"And you can't identify this knife as being the one you found in the body?"

"No. I cannot."

"Thank you." Steve turned to the judge. "Your Honor, I move that the doctor's testimony as to the knife, People's Exhibit number one, being the fatal weapon, be stricken from the record."

"Granted," said Judge Crandell. "It will go out. The jurors will disregard Dr. Fenton's testimony concerning the murder weapon."

Dirkson was back on his feet. "Your Honor, this comes as something of a surprise. I had intended to introduce the knife into evidence at this time as the murder weapon."

Judge Crandell shook his head. "Not unless you can connect it up."

"I understand. If I might have a short recess to locate the necessary witnesses?"

Judge Crandell glanced at the clock. "Court will stand in recess for half an hour."

The judge banged his gavel. Court broke up.

Steve Winslow turned to Sheila Benton. Already the officer and the matron had appeared at her side.

"Chin up, kid," he said.

She had time to flash a twisted smile before they led her away.

38

MARK TAYLOR pushed his way through the crowd in the courtroom.

"Steve!" he called out.

Steve turned and saw him coming through the gate.

"What is it, Mark?"

"I just heard from our correspondent in California."

"And?"

"There's no record of a marriage license issued to an Alice Baxter and Samuel Benton. There is no record of a death certificate on Samuel Benton. *And* there is no record of a birth certificate issued for Sheila Benton or a Sheila Baxter."

Steve stroked his chin. "So maybe she was illegitimate."

"Maybe. And maybe this Samuel Benton didn't die after all." Taylor smiled. "That's assuming he ever existed in the first place."

"Let's assume he did. Try finding him, Mark. Give him top priority. I don't care about anything else in the case, but I want that man."

"I've got men working on it now. Listen, what's this about the knife not being the fatal weapon?"

Steve waved it away. "Forget it. That's bullshit."

"You mean it *is* the fatal weapon?"

"Of course it is. The prosecution will connect it up as soon as the recess is over."

"Then why make such a fuss about it?"

"Just misdirection."

"Misdirection?"

"Yeah. You know, like the way a magician fools his audience by focusing their attention on his right hand while he's doing something with his left. The important part of the coroner's testimony isn't the murder weapon, it's the time element. The D.A. laid a trap for me by only asking the doctor when Greely was killed, and not asking his reasons. He wanted me to cross-examine him as to how he determined the time of death. Then the doctor would come out with volumes of medical testimony, all of which would have pointed up the fact that Greely was killed at just the time Sheila was in the apartment. Every question I asked would only prejudice the jury against her. So I'm ignoring the time element and concentrating on the murder weapon."

"Great. But when the prosecution connects it up, won't it look as if you've lost a point?"

Steve smiled grimly. "Listen," he said. "I'm going to lose a lot more of them before this is over."

39

WHEN COURT reconvened, Dirkson called Dr. Morton Blake to the stand.

"Your name?" Dirkson asked.

"Dr. Morton Blake."

"What is your occupation?"

"I am deputy coroner."

"Directing your attention to the seventh of June, were you called to 193 West 89th Street, apartment 2B, to examine a body?"

"I was."

"And did you examine the knife in the back of the body?"

Steve Winslow rose to his feet. "Your Honor, the prosecutor is leading the witness. All these questions are leading and suggestive."

"These are preliminary questions, Your Honor," Dirkson said, irritably.

"I think they are," Judge Crandell said. "Nevertheless, try not to lead the witness. The objection is sustained. Please rephrase your question."

Nettled, Dirkson turned to the witness and said sarcastically, "Did you notice anything sticking in the back of the decedent that struck you as unusual?"

Dr. Blake smiled. "Yes, sir. A knife."

"Did you do anything to that knife?"

"Yes, sir. I removed it from the body."

"And then what did you do with it?"

"Well, the police wanted to test it for fingerprints, so—"

"That's not the question," Dirkson interrupted quickly, hoping to stave off another objection. "You know you can't testify as to what the police wanted. The question is, what did *you* do with it?"

"I gave it to Sergeant Stams."

"And where were you when you gave it to him?"

"Right there. At the scene of the crime."

"And did you see what Sergeant Stams did with the knife?"

"Yes, sir. He put it in a plastic evidence bag and wrote his name on it."

"Thank you, Doctor," Dirkson said. He turned to the defense table. "Your witness."

With a broad grin, Steve announced, "No questions."

Dirkson frowned. After Steve's cross-examination of the coroner, Dirkson had expected him to tear into Dr. Blake.

"The witness is excused," said Judge Crandell. "Call your next witness."

"Call Sergeant Stams," Dirkson said.

Sergeant Stams, on the stand, said, "Yes, sir, I received the knife from Dr. Blake."

"And what did you do with it?"

"I was very careful not to disturb any fingerprints that might be on the knife," Stams said self-righteously.

Dirkson was about to interrupt, but Stams let that matter drop, and got back to the point.

"I placed the knife in a plastic evidence bag and wrote my name on it."

"And then what did you do with it?"

"I took it to the police lab."

"And what did you do with it there?"

"I gave it to Reginald Steele to be fingerprinted."

"Thank you. That's all."

"No questions," Steve announced cheerfully.

Dirkson gave him a look. "Call Reginald Steele."

Reginald Steele took the stand and testified that he was an expert technician employed in the police lab.

"That is correct," Steele said. "I received the knife from Sergeant Stams."

"And what did you do with it?"

"I removed it from the evidence bag and tested it for fingerprints."

"I see," Dirkson said. "Now then, I am not asking you about any fingerprints you may have found at this time. I am merely trying to account for the whereabouts of the knife. With that understanding, please tell us what you did."

"Yes, sir. I developed latent fingerprints on the knife, and turned it over to my assistant to photograph them."

"And who is your assistant?"

"Samuel Beame."

"Your witness."

"No questions," Steve announced, with the same broad grin.

With a sinking feeling, Dirkson suddenly realized what was going on. That grin. That damned, infuriating grin. It was infectious, and people in the courtroom were catching it. With each successive witness, the atmosphere in the courtroom was getting lighter. In a murder trial, for Christ's sake. Dirkson couldn't believe it.

And yet, he realized, there was no help for it. He had to keep on with what he was doing, even though he knew he was playing right into that clown's hands.

"Call Samuel Beame," he said, and out of the corner of his eye he could see some of the spectators smiling, and some of the jurors looking at each other.

"Yes, sir," Samuel Beame testified. "I received the knife from Reginald Steele."

"And what did you do with it?"

"I photographed the fingerprints on the knife."

"Fine. I'm not asking you about those fingerprints at this time. But the fact is you photographed them?"

"Yes, sir."

"And then what did you do with the knife?"

"I returned it to Reginald Steele."

"That's all."

"No questions," Steve said, grinning.

Dirkson knew it was coming. He'd been in the courtroom often enough to be able to read audiences just the way an actor would. And there was no mistaking the expectant hush of the crowd. But he had no choice.

"Recall Reginald Steele," he said.

That's when it hit. The first audible chuckles. Judge Crandell immediately banged them silent with his gavel, but Dirkson knew the dam had broken, and from here on the reaction could only grow.

"That is correct," Reginald Steele said. "I received the knife back from my assistant, Samuel Beame."

"And what did you do with it then?"

Steele seemed unhappy about his answer, which only made

things worse. "I gave it to Sergeant Schneider to deliver to Sergeant Stams."

"Thank you. That's all."

Steve grinned. "No questions."

Dirkson sighed. "Call Sergeant Schneider."

As Dirkson had expected, it was worse. The chuckles were louder this time. Even some of the jurors were grinning. Christ, even the *defendant* was grinning.

Sergeant Schneider turned out to be one of those bullnecked cops who look and talk as if they had the I.Q. of a tree stump, which didn't help.

"Yeah, I got the knife," he said.

"Where did you get it?"

"Steele gave it to me."

"And what did he tell you to do with it?"

"Give it to Sergeant Stams."

"So what did you do with it?"

Schneider helped Dirkson out by staring at him as if he were an idiot. "Gave it to Sergeant Stams."

"Thank you. That's all."

"No questions," Steve announced happily.

"Recall Sergeant Stams." Dirkson announced. He got it in quickly, before the audience could build up the anticipation to it. It was a good strategy. It got chuckles, but not proportionally bigger than the last.

Sergeant Stams looked unhappy as he took the stand. It was apparent to everyone that he didn't want to be there, and that he was giving his testimony very grudgingly. Which, of course, only heightened the mood.

"Yes, sir, that's right," he said. "I received the knife back from Sergeant Schneider."

"And what did you do with it?" Dirkson asked.

Sergeant Stams looked trapped. He hesitated, looked around and then blurted, "I gave it to you, sir."

Laughter rocked the courtroom. The spectators laughed. The jurors laughed. Everyone except the police and the prosecution was terribly amused.

Judge Crandell banged for silence, but even he seemed to be suppressing a smile.

Harry Dirkson stood, stonyfaced, and waited for it to be over. There was nothing else for him to do.

When the courtroom was quiet again, he said dryly, "Thank you, Sergeant. And what did I do with the knife?"

"You gave it to Lieutenant Farron, sir."

"In your presence?"

"Yes, sir."

"That's all," Dirkson said, wearily.

Steve was on his feet. "Your Honor, I have no questions of this witness. I would also like to say at this time that the defense has no wish to embarrass the prosecutor by forcing him to take the stand. Therefore, we will stipulate that Harry Dirkson, if called upon to testify, would state that he received the knife in question from Sergeant Stams and that he gave it to Lieutenant Farron."

Dirkson accepted the stipulation with bad grace. No attempt to embarrass him indeed, he thought. And then, having done so, the guy had the gall to play the good guy by making the stipulation. But there was nothing Dirkson could do but accept it.

Dirkson called Lieutenant Farron to the stand.

"Yes, sir," Farron testified. "You gave me the knife."

"And what did you do with it?"

"I delivered it to Dr. Fenton."

"That's all."

"No questions," Steve said.

"Recall Dr. Fenton."

"That is correct," Dr. Fenton testified. "I received the knife from Lieutenant Farron."

"And it was then, and in his presence, that you scratched your initials on the handle?"

"Yes, sir."

Dirkson turned wearily to Judge Crandell. "I now ask that the knife be received in evidence as the murder weapon."

"No objection, Your Honor," Steve said brightly.

Dirkson, who had expected a long argument, stared at the defense counsel in exasperation and disbelief.

Judge Crandell came to his aid. "So ordered," he said. "It is now well past the hour of adjournment. Court stands adjourned until tomorrow morning at ten o'clock."

40

JUDY MEYERS propped herself up on one elbow and looked at Steve Winslow. Judy, twenty-nine, married, divorced, an actress who waited tables more often than not, probably knew Steve as well as anyone, which, she was well aware, wasn't really saying much.

Steve was lying in bed next to her, staring at the ceiling. They had just had sex, if one could call it that. His mind had obviously been miles away.

"You're scared stiff, aren't you," Judy said.

Steve might not have heard her. He appeared to be counting the cracks in the ceiling.

"Or perhaps 'stiff' isn't the right choice of words," Judy said.

Even this got no response.

Judy got up, padded naked into the kitchen, got a bottle of cognac, and filled two snifters. She came back into the bedroom and shoved one of them into Winslow's hands.

"Here. Drink this."

"What is it?"

"Ah. The man lives," Judy said. "Never mind. Just drink it."

Mechanically, Steve raised the glass to his lips and took a sip. Judy sat on the bed, watching him.

"You know," she said. "I haven't seen you in over a month."

"I told you where I was."

"That night, yeah. The other times, I don't know. You had some excuses that were so plausible I can't even remember them. I doubt if you can, either."

He said nothing.

"And we wouldn't have even had a date at all if I hadn't run into you at that audition last month."

"I've been working nights."

"You were working nights before. And you were staying here three, maybe four nights a week. That's why you stopped. You got scared. You thought it was becoming too permanent. You didn't want to be tied down."

He opened his mouth to say something, but she cut him off.

"No, don't argue. That's it. You don't want to be tied down. And that's stupid, because I don't want to be tied down either. Despite what you think."

She took a sip of brandy. "You may not see me for a while, anyway. I got a callback for a national tour of *The Foreigner*. If I get it, I'm gone."

"Break a leg."

"Thanks." She took another sip. "My guess is you came here tonight because you're upset about something, and you thought you could take your mind off of it. But it didn't work, did it?"

Steve sighed, rubbed his head. "No. It didn't."

"So what's the problem? You got a murder trial. Aside from a Broadway lead, I thought that was what you always wanted."

"So did I."

"So what's wrong?"

He took a sip of the brandy, then scrunched up to a sitting position. He twirled the cognac around in the glass, and watched it swirl.

"When I passed the bar and Wilson and Doyle hired me I was all gung ho. I was really excited, you know. It was a new career.

Something important. Something worthwhile. When they fired me it was hard to take. I did everything I could to get another job. And it was like the fucking acting thing again, only worse. I made the rounds. I went to every goddamn law firm in the city. And I couldn't get hired. 'We'll call you.' The same old line. And they never did. Cause it was the talk of the industry. I was the guy who'd fucked up conservative, respectable Wilson and Doyle. Maybe I could have gotten a job assisting some ambulance chaser or something, but I didn't want that. I studied criminal law, for Christ's sake. So I did nothing. I went back to making the rounds again. I drove a cab and had an answering service, only now I was an out-of-work actor *and* lawyer. And it was a slow year." He smiled. "I got extra work in three movies and one murder case."

"I know," Judy said. "That's what I don't understand. You got a murder case, for Christ's sake. You should be dancing on the ceiling."

"Yeah."

"So what's wrong?"

He took a sip. "I guess every young attorney has the fantasy of going into court and conducting brilliant cross-examinations and getting his client off."

"So?"

He shrugged. "So here I am. I've finally gotten into court and I don't know what to do."

"Wait a minute. From what you told me, it sounds like you did pretty well today."

He waved it away. "That was just jerking off. It didn't prove anything. And I don't know what to do. All of the facts in the case are against my client. I can conduct all the brilliant cross-examination I want, and the facts will still be the facts. And she's going to be convicted—there's nothing I can do about it. And I don't even think it's me. I don't think *any* lawyer could do anything about it. But that doesn't help."

"Well, maybe she's guilty."

"Maybe. But I think she's innocent."

"Well, that's half the battle, isn't it?"

Steve sighed. "That's what they tell you in law school. Actually, it's a crock of shit. If your client's guilty, at least you know what the facts are, and you can make up a story to account for them. If your client's innocent, you don't know what the fuck is going on."

The phone rang. Judy picked it up. "Hello? . . . Yeah, what time? . . . Okay. Great. Goodbye." She hung up the phone.

"Another audition?"

"Yeah. Commercial."

"Break a leg."

She looked at him. "You know what the trouble with you is?"

He sighed. "Shit."

"I know. You don't want to hear it. Listen. You know the character in *Arms and the Man*? Captain Bluntschli?"

"I played Bluntschli in summer stock."

"Yeah? I played Raina. At Long Wharf. So you know. Bluntschli was this supercool, superprofessional soldier. They were all in awe of him. Is he a man or is he a machine? That's the tag line, right? 'What a man. Is he a man?' And he's just cool, crisp, efficient. Not a nerve in his body. And then, in the end, when he's accounting for himself, he admits that he's a man who all his life has spoiled his chances through an incurably romantic disposition. And they're floored, because that's the last way they would think of him. And then he explains himself—I did this when a man of sense would have done that—and it's true."

Judy smiled. 'And that's you. That's who you are. An incurable romantic. No, don't argue. I know you don't think so. You see yourself as this practical, no-nonsense guy, cutting through the bullshit. Well, maybe you are. But the *reason* you are is because behind it all you're the romantic hero, the white knight on the charger, slaying dragons and saving damsels in distress."

Steve laughed. "Jesus Christ. This is what I came here for? Two-bit amateur psychoanalysis?"

"No." She smiled. "I know what you came here for. Now this particular damsel in distress. I saw her picture in the paper. She's pretty."

Steve looked at her. "Are you implying something?"

"Why? Is there something to imply?"

"Are you kidding? She's just a kid."

"Right. Of twenty-four. Whereas I am a worn-out old hag of twenty-nine."

He laughed. "Right. Over the hill. Washed up. Soon to be playing old-lady-character parts."

He tickled her. She giggled, twisted away.

"Stop that."

"No, devil woman. You are in the clutches of the incurable-romantic tickling machine."

She twisted away again, laughing and spilling brandy.

The phone rang.

"Time. Saved by the bell," Judy said. She leaned over and grabbed the phone. "Hello."

She listened, then turned to him with a slightly puzzled expression on her face. "It's for you."

"Oh. That'll be Mark Taylor. I gave him this number."

"Oh." She handed him the phone.

"Hello, Mark. What's up?"

"We can't get a line on Sam Benton. He never served in the military. He never filed a tax return. He never drove a car."

"Well, he was born, wasn't he?"

"Not according to vital statistics. So in all probability, Sam Benton isn't his right name."

"Shit. What about Alice Baxter?"

"We're trying to run her down. The trail's pretty cold. It's been twenty-five years, you know."

"Yeah, yeah, I know." Steve hung up the phone. His momentary kidding mood was gone.

Judy looked at him. "Bad news?"

"That's the only kind I get," he said.

41

WHEN COURT reconvened the next morning, Dirkson called Carla Finley to the stand.

Sheila Benton leaned over to Steve Winslow, and whispered, "Who's she?"

"Greely's girlfriend," Steve whispered back.

"Oh."

Sheila was surprised. She had been so caught up in her own predicament, that it had never occurred to her the dead man was a person too, with a life of his own, and friends, and girlfriends. She watched Carla Finley with some interest.

Steve watched Carla Finley with some interest too. It was hard to believe that this woman walking down the aisle and taking the witness stand was the same woman he had seen in the peep show. Her hair was pulled back from her forehead and tied in a sedate bun. She was dressed in conservative, black mourning attire. But the main difference was her eyes. The eyes that in the peep show had seemed so bright, so alert, so challenging, the eyes that held the come-hither look, were now discreetly downcast. The effect was to transform a porn queen into a bereaved widow.

In Steve's opinion, she had been brilliantly coached.

Carla Finley took the stand, and, in soft, halting tones, guided by Dirkson's skillful questioning, stated that she had known the deceased, Robert Greely, in his lifetime, that she had gone to the morgue to identify a dead body, and that the dead man was the man whom she had known as Robert Greely.

"That's all," Dirkson said.

Carla Finley got up to leave the stand.

Steve rose to his feet. "I have a few questions on cross-examination," he said. He crossed to the witness stand. "Now. Miss Finley, you say you recognized the body as that of Robert Greely?"

"Yes."

"How long had you known Mr. Greely?"

"About five years."

"Did you meet him through your work?"

Dirkson was on his feet. "Objection, Your Honor. This witness was called for a limited purpose, that of identifying the body. Let counsel confine his questions to that. These matters he is touching on are incompetent, irrelevant and immaterial."

Judge Crandell leaned over the bench. "I think the objection is well taken. The witness was called for a limited purpose."

"Yes, Your Honor," Steve said. "Identifying the body. Which is what I'm going into. Surely the accuracy of her identification of the dead man will depend on how well she knew him. Which is what I'm going into."

Judge Crandell narrowed his eyes. "You're questioning the matter of identity?"

"I don't know, Your Honor, because I haven't asked my questions yet. But I certainly intend to ask them. So far, all we have in evidence here is the fact this witness claims the dead man was Robert Greely. I certainly intend to find out on what grounds she bases her claim."

"Very well. The witness will answer the question."

"The question," Steve said, "was did you meet him through your work?"

"Yes."

"What were you wearing at the time?"

"Objection, Your Honor," Dirkson said. "Incompetent, irrelevant, and immaterial."

"Sustained," Judge Crandell ruled.

"May I be heard, Your Honor?"

Judge Crandell shook his head. "The question is clearly improper."

"Very well." Steve turned back to the witness. "Then let me ask you this—were you wearing *anything* at the time you met Robert Greely?"

Dirkson was on his feet shouting. "Your Honor! Your Honor! Objection. I charge the asking of that question as misconduct. Your Honor has already ruled."

"Mr. Winslow," Judge Crandell said sternly. "I believe the prosecutor is correct. Your question borders seriously on misconduct. I may have to find you in contempt of court. Before I do, do you have any explanation to make for asking such a question?"

"I do, Your Honor."

"Then would you please explain?"

"Certainly, Your Honor. I am trying to find out the basis for Miss Finley's identification of the dead man. She has testified that she met him through her employment. It happens that Miss Finley is employed as a nude dancer in a peep show on Forty-second Street. I am attempting to find out if Mr. Greely was merely a customer in that establishment, for surely the identification of someone who was a longtime friend of the decedent will be more forceful than that of a nude model who knew him only as a customer who used to ogle her naked body in a peep show."

Dirkson was on his feet to object, but Carla Finley beat him to it. "You son of a bitch!" she shrieked from the witness stand. Her demure manner was completely gone and her eyes were blazing.

The court burst into an uproar. It took Judge Crandell five bangs of the gavel to quiet it.

"That will do," Judge Crandell said. "Mr. Prosecutor, please be quiet. I will handle this. Now then, Mr. Winslow," Crandell went on, "have you any reason at all, however remote, why I should not consider the statement you have just made contempt of court?"

"Certainly, Your Honor."

Crandell gawked at him. "You do?"

"Yes, Your Honor. I made that statement in response to a direct question by you, asking me to explain my reasons for asking the witness if she was wearing anything at the time she met Robert Greely. I had no choice but to make it, since the question was a directive from the court. In fact, had I *not* made that statement, I would be in contempt of court.

"If I am in error, I would like to apologize to the court and to the prosecutor. And as far as the question itself goes, I will not pursue this any further, I will withdraw it. And I have no further questions of this witness."

Dirkson started to say something, thought better of it and held his tongue.

Crandell glared down at Winslow, trying to think of the proper rebuke. None came to mind.

"Very well," Crandell said. "I am holding the matters of misconduct and contempt of court under advisement. I shall rule on them at a future time. For the time being, the question is withdrawn. The witness is excused."

Steve bowed to the judge and returned to his table. As he sat down, Sheila leaned over and said, "Why did you do that?"

"What do you mean?"

"That didn't accomplish anything. That poor woman. What difference does it make what she does for a living? She loved that man and she's upset. Why did you have to do that?"

"The prosecutor was trying to play on the sympathies of the jury. So they dress her in black and play her up as the bereaved. I had to counteract that. I did it."

"It wasn't right."

"Your displeasure is noted."

Judge Crandell banged his gavel somewhat irritably. "Call your next witness."

Dirkson recalled Reginald Steele. This time the prosecutor took pains to qualify him as an expert, asking for his education, training and experience as a police technician.

Steele gave them with some pleasure. He was a tall, thin man with a sort of squashed-in-looking face, that still managed to have that aloof quality of some expert technicians. He had been somewhat uncomfortable during the knife-identification sequence, but in giving his qualifications he was smug.

"Now Mr. Steele," Dirkson said, after he had qualified the witness, "you testified that you developed fingerprints on the murder weapon, People's Exhibit number one?"

"Yes, sir."

"And did you subsequently identify those prints?"

"I did."

"Whose prints were they?"

"The prints of the defendant, Sheila Benton."

Dirkson nodded at Winslow. "Cross-examine."

Steve got to his feet, crossed to the witness and smiled.

"You say you found the fingerprints of the defendant on the knife, Mr. Steele?"

"That is correct."

"I notice the district attorney didn't ask you if you found anyone else's fingerprints on the knife."

Reginald Steele said nothing.

"Can't you answer that, Mr. Steele?"

"No I can't."

"Why not?"

Steele smiled. "Because it isn't a question."

Laughter greeted this sally. Dirkson let the jury see his broad grin.

Steve smiled back at the witness. "You're right. It isn't. So let me ask you some questions. *Did* you find the fingerprints of anyone else on the knife?"

"No. I did not."

"You found only the fingerprints of the defendant?"

"That's right."

"How many fingerprints did you find?"

"I found four legible fingerprints. That is, four prints that were clear enough to classify and identify."

"And what prints were they?"

"I found the print of the defendant's right thumb, right index finger, right middle finger, and right ring finger."

"I see. Did these four prints, taken together, indicate the position of the hand gripping the knife?"

"Yes they did. The four prints indicated that the defendant had held the knife in a firm grip."

Steve nodded his head. "Well, that's mighty interesting, Mr. Steele. But you didn't consider that particularly important, did you?"

"Of course I did."

"You didn't mention it on direct examination."

"I wasn't asked."

"I noticed that. Now let me ask you this. Did you *know* you weren't going to be asked on direct examination?"

Dirkson was on his feet. "Objection, Your Honor. How could the witness know what he was going to be asked on direct examination? Counsel is asking for a conclusion from the witness."

"The witness would know if he had been *told* what he was going to be asked. So I would like to ask you, Mr. Steele, if you and District Attorney Dirkson discussed the manner in which you would give your testimony."

"Your Honor, Your Honor," Dirkson cried. "This is beyond all bounds. Naturally a prosecutor does not go into court blind. I discuss with the witnesses what their testimony will be. But that discussion has no bearing on the case, and counsel has no right to inquire into it."

"It's always proper to show bias," Steve said.

"What bias?" Dirkson said impatiently. "This is an expert technician giving expert testimony. The fingerprints belong to Sheila Benton. The facts are the facts. Nothing can alter them."

"The facts may be the facts, but the manner in which they are

presented, as counsel well knows, may have a bearing on the out-
come of this trial. Now, Your Honor, it is my contention that this
witness had an understanding with the district attorney that it
would be more damaging to the defendant's case to have the
details about the fingerprint evidence—that the only prints on the
knife were those of the defendant, and that the four prints indicated where the knife had been held in a firm grip—brought out
by me on cross-examination, rather than by the district attorney
on direct examination. It is my contention that because of this
understanding, Mr. Steele deliberately refrained from mentioning
these points on direct examination, and that his doing so is an
indication of his bias."

Dirkson was ready with an argument, but Judge Crandell cut
in. "I think it is more an indication of the skill of the prosecutor
than the bias of the witness. What you are describing, Mr. Winslow, is rather elemental courtroom strategy. Now if you really
wish to pursue the matter under the guise of establishing bias, I
suppose you have the right to do so, but I must warn you I feel
you are beating a dead horse."

Steve smiled. "I think we can let the matter drop, Your Honor.
Let's move on to something else. Mr. Steele, in addition to developing the prints on the knife, you also developed fingerprints in
the defendant's apartment, did you not?"

"I did."

"Did you examine a knife rack affixed to the wall of the
defendant's kitchen?"

"Yes, sir. I did."

"How many knives were in the rack?"

"I believe there were three."

"But there were spaces in the rack for four, were there not?"

"I can't be sure how many spaces there were in the rack."

"Yes, but there was one empty space in the rack, was there not?
What I'm getting at is, regardless of how many knives there were
in the rack, there was space for one more."

"That is correct."

"And aside from the size and shape, were the knives similar in style and design to the murder knife?"

"Yes, sir. They were."

"And did you examine these knives for fingerprints?"

"I did."

"And did you find any?"

"Yes, sir."

"On all the knives?"

"Yes, sir. I believe so."

"And whose fingerprints were they?"

"The fingerprints of the defendant."

"So, if I understand your testimony correctly, there were at least four knives in the apartment, including the murder knife, and all of them had the defendant's fingerprints on them."

"Yes, sir. That is correct."

"So assuming the murder weapon was a knife from the rack, you would have considered it unusual if it had *not* had the defendant's fingerprints on it."

Dirkson leapt to his feet. "Objection, Your Honor! The question is argumentative, assuming facts not in evidence, and calls for a conclusion on the part of the witness."

"I'll withdraw the question," Steve said. "Now, Mr. Steele, I believe you took photographs of the prints on the murder weapon."

"I directed such pictures to be taken. My assistant was the one who actually took them."

"Would you produce them, please?"

"Your Honor," Dirkson said. "Those photographs are a part of the prosecution's case. I intend to introduce them into evidence at a later time."

"And I'd like to introduce them now," Steve said. "Because I intend to cross-examine this witness on them. Now I could simply delay my cross-examination and recall Mr. Steele at a later time, but in the interest of expediency I don't see why we can't introduce them now."

"But Mr. Steele didn't take the pictures."

"Well, the defense will stipulate that his assistant did, and that the pictures you are producing are those pictures that he took."

"I prefer to put on my own case in my own way, Your Honor."

"I understand," Crandell said. "But the stipulation would save time. And I take it there is no dispute as to the accuracy of the pictures."

"No, Your Honor. Very well, I stipulate the pictures may be produced in evidence."

The pictures were produced and marked by the clerk, People's Exhibit number two, A through K.

Steve examined the pictures. He chose one, and approached the witness.

"Now, Mr. Steele, I hand you a photo, People's Exhibit number two-D, and ask you what it shows."

Steele examined the photo. "That is a picture of the handle of the knife. The large print that you see is the imprint of the defendant's thumb. The smaller prints, which are only partly visible on the bottom edge of the handle, are the defendant's first, middle and ring fingers."

"I hand you another photo, People's Exhibit two-E."

"That is another angle on the knife handle, showing the prints of the fingers more clearly."

"Very good," Steve said. He crossed to the defense table, reached in his briefcase and took out a roll of masking tape, then crossed to the clerk and picked up the knife. He crossed back again to the witness.

"Now, Mr. Steele, I hand you the knife, People's Exhibit number 1, and this roll of masking tape, and I ask you to take this tape, and referring to the photographs, mark on the knife handle where the defendant's fingerprints are."

"Mark them how?"

"Here's a pen. Just affix a piece of tape to the handle where each print is, and sketch in the direction of the finger."

The witness took the masking tape and affixed four short strips to the knife handle. Then he took the pen and drew in the fingers.

Steve took the knife and looked at it. "Thank you, Mr. Steele. Now let me ask you this. Having examined the fingerprint evidence in this case, have you reached an expert opinion as to the guilt or innocence of the defendant?"

Dirkson started to stand up, then slowly sat down again. He couldn't quite believe this was happening, but he wasn't about to stop it.

"I have," Steele said, grimly.

"And what is your expert opinion?"

Judge Crandell leaned forward. "One moment, here. Before the witness answers the question. Mr. Winslow, although it is not my position to presume what this witness's answer may be, I must point out to you that the answer that you are calling for might be one that is highly detrimental to your client. I have no wish to let the record of this trial be blemished in any way so that it could be claimed that the defendant did not have adequate representation. So I ask you to reconsider your question."

"I'm sorry, Your Honor. I don't wish to do that."

Judge Crandell's lips clamped together. "Very well. Miss Benton."

Sheila, startled at being addressed, said, "What?"

"Have you heard what your attorney asked the witness?"

"Ah, yes."

"Call me Your Honor."

"Yes, Your Honor."

"Do you object to what your attorney is doing?"

Sheila looked sideways up at Steve. He looked down at her. His face was neutral, like that of a poker player running a bluff. She couldn't read it at all.

She looked back at the judge. "No, Your Honor."

Judge Crandell looked greatly displeased. "Very well," he said. "The witness will answer the question. Court reporter will read the question."

The reporter pawed through his paper tapes. "Question: 'Having examined the fingerprint evidence in this case, have you reached an expert opinion as to the guilt or innocence of the defendant?' Answer: 'I have.' Question: 'And what is your expert opinion?'"

Steele took a breath. "It is my expert opinion," he said, "that the defendant, Sheila Benton, stabbed the decedent, Robert Greely, with the knife."

A gasp went up from the audience in the courtroom, followed by a loud murmur.

District Attorney Dirkson grinned broadly.

Judge Crandell frowned, and banged for silence.

Steve smiled and held up his hand.

"Thank you very much, Mr. Steele. Now then, you have testified that in your expert opinion, Sheila Benton stabbed Robert Greely with this knife. You base your opinion on her fingerprints, which you have marked on the handle of the knife with masking tape and pen. Now, I am going to ask you to take hold of the handle of the knife in your right hand, and place your fingers in the positions of the prints which you have marked on the handle."

Steele took the knife and positioned it in his hand, lining up the finger marks.

Steve looked at him and smiled. "That's what I thought, Mr. Steele."

Steele looked at him. "What?"

"When you put your hand on the knife in the position you claim the defendant held it, you're holding it like a sword, out in front of you. Your thumb is on the part of the handle closest to the blade of the knife, and your fingers are curled around the handle behind it. Now is that not the position in which you would hold the knife to carve a roast?"

"Objection," Dirkson said. "What the witness would do is incompetent, irrelevant and immaterial."

"I'll withdraw the question, and ask another. You testified that in your expert opinion Sheila Benton stabbed the victim while holding the knife in the manner in which you are now holding it. In your expert opinion, is it possible to stab someone in the back while holding a knife like that?"

"It is."

"Is it?" Steve said. "Stand up, please."

"I beg your pardon?"

"Stand up."

"May I ask the purpose of this?" Dirkson said.

"This witness has testified that my client stabbed the decedent with this knife. I intend to test his recollection, and his qualifications."

Reginald Steele looked up at Judge Crandell for guidance.

"Counsel is within his rights," Crandell said. "The witness will stand up."

Steele rose.

"Come down here," Steve said. "Yes. That's right. Right down here with me."

The witness did as he was instructed.

"You are now holding the knife in the manner in which you say the fingerprints indicate the defendant held it?"

"That's right."

"Fine." Steve turned his back to the witness. "Stab me in the back."

There was a moment of stunned silence, then gasps of shock, and a murmur of voices ran through the courtroom. Dirkson lunged to his feet. "Objection!" he blurted.

Steve pitched his voice above the din. "Stab me in the back," he repeated.

The courtroom was in an uproar. Dirkson was trying to shout over the noise.

Crandell banged the gavel. "Order! Order!" he roared.

The courtroom quieted. Crandell glared down from his bench. "Please be advised that this is a courtroom, not a sideshow. If we cannot have order, I will have the spectators removed. Is that clear?"

Crandell's eyes swept the room. No one moved.

"Now," Crandell said. "Mr. Prosecutor, if you have an objection, please state it."

"Yes, Your Honor," Dirkson said. "Counsel for the defense has asked this witness to stab him in the back. I maintain that this is not proper cross-examination. It is a stunt, a theatrical exercise, and is totally out of place in a courtroom. I assign it as misconduct."

Judge Crandell frowned. "This is the second time this morning the charge of misconduct has been raised."

"May I be heard, Your Honor?" Steve said.

"You may."

"Your Honor, this witness is an expert technician in the employ of the police department. He has testified that in his expert opinion, the fingerprint evidence that he found on the knife indicates that the defendant killed Robert Greely. That testimony is an utter falsehood, founded only upon this witness's bias in favor of the prosecution, and made only with the intention of prejudicing the jury against the defendant. I intend to make the witness retract that testimony, and I am going to cross-examine him on it until he does so, even if it takes all afternoon.

"The witness has stated that Sheila Benton held the knife in the manner in which he is now holding it, and stabbed the decedent. That is utter nonsense. The medical evidence indicates that the blow was struck by someone stabbing the knife *down* into the back of the victim. I have asked this witness to stab me in the back, holding the knife the way he says Sheila Benton held it. *He can't do it.* He can't do it, and he's a good four inches taller than she is. He can't do it because he's holding the handle like a sword, with his thumb in the position on the handle closest to the blade, and the fingers behind it. Whereas, to have inflicted the fatal blow, it is clear the assailant must have held the knife the other way, with the thumb toward the end of the handle, and the fingers closer to the middle of the knife, so that the knife could be stabbed down.

"These are clear and incontrovertible facts, which would be admitted by any witness that was not prejudiced in favor of the prosecution, and I intend to make this witness admit them if it takes all day."

"Your Honor," Dirkson said. "Counsel has no right to argue the case at this time."

"Exactly," Crandell said irritably. "Mr. Dirkson, no further argument is needed at this time. Nor from you, Mr. Winslow. The Court is going to make a ruling. But first the Court is going to charge the jury." Judge Crandell turned to the jury and addressed them. "I want the jurors to understand that the remarks of the defense attorney are not in evidence, and you should give them no weight. He was arguing why he should be allowed to question the witness on the point. His arguments on the point, the contentions that he has made, are his and his alone, and do not constitute evidence. The only thing you are allowed to consider as evidence in this case is the body of pertinent questions that are asked, and the answers they elicit." Crandell turned back to the attorneys. "The Court is now going to rule. The Court is going to rule," Crandell said, with a trace of an ironic smile, "that it is not incumbent upon this witness to stab the defense attorney in the back. In other words, the objection is sustained. However, Mr. Winslow is quite correct in his contention that he be allowed to cross-examine the witness on the statement that he made, and the Court is going to allow any reasonable amount of pertinent questions on that subject. Now, Mr. Winslow, aside from asking to be done bodily harm, you are free to question the witness."

"Thank you, Your Honor," Steve said. "Mr. Steele, if you would care to sit down."

Steele returned to the witness stand.

Steve stalked him, as a cat might stalk a mouse.

"Now, Mr. Steele, you have testified that in your opinion Sheila Benton stabbed Robert Greely, holding the knife in the manner you indicated?"

"Objection," said Dirkson. "Already asked and answered."

"I think it was," Crandell said, "but it would also seem to be merely preliminary. Could we attempt to dispense with overly technical objections?"

"Yes, Your Honor," Dirkson said with poor grace.

"Answer the question," Steve said.

"Yes," Steele said. "That's what I said."

"Sheila Benton stabbed Robert Greely with that knife?"

"Yes."

"Holding it in her hand?"

"Yes."

"In the manner you indicated?"

"Yes."

"Do you know how tall Sheila Benton is?"

"No, I do not."

"Is she six feet tall?"

"I don't know."

"You don't? You're an expert technician. You're trained to notice details. Do you mean to tell me you can't tell if Sheila Benton is six feet tall?"

"Objection. Argumentative," Dirkson said.

"Sustained."

Steve turned to the defense table. "Sheila Benton. Stand up.". Sheila stood.

"Now, Mr. Steele, I want you to look at the defendant and tell me if she is over or under six feet tall."

"Your Honor," Dirkson said. "I hate to keep objecting, in view of your admonition, but this is totally irrelevant and calls for a conclusion on the part of the witness."

"It does not, Your Honor," Steve said. "It goes to his qualifications as an expert, and it goes to show bias."

Judge Crandell looked down at him. "Bias?"

"Yes, Your Honor. The witness is a veteran observer. Surely he can look at a girl and tell if she is six feet tall or not. However, he knows what I am getting at, so he doesn't want to say that she's less than six feet tall. His refusal to say so is an indication of his bias."

Judge Crandell smiled. "The argument is adroitly framed, if somewhat farfetched. However, the question could be construed as a test of his qualifications. The objection is overruled. The witness will answer the question."

"Is the defendant over or under six feet tall?" Winslow asked.

"I'm not sure," Steele said.

"Thank you for a fair and impartial answer," Steve said, sarcastically. "Now, Mr. Steele, I'm not going to bother having the defendant come up here and stand next to you, I think I'll just let the jury judge your statement on its own."

"Objection, Your Honor."

"Sustained. Mr. Winslow, such remarks are uncalled for."

"I apologize, Your Honor," Steve said. He turned back to the witness. "Now, Mr. Steele, let me ask you this. Did you examine the vital statistics of the decedent?"

"I did."

"And how tall was *he?*"

"If he can remember, Your Honor," Dirkson put in.

Judge Crandell frowned. "Yes, if he can remember, Mr. Prosecutor. But in the event that he *cannot* remember, I am going to suggest that he be withdrawn from the stand until the evidence can be supplied by someone who *can* remember. I would like to point out that we are conducting a murder trial here, not a battle of wits between attorneys. The defense attorney is attempting to make a point here, which he has every right to do, and which the jury has every right to hear, and I would like to see the matter proceed without so many legal roadblocks."

Dirkson slowly sat down. Judge Crandell's rebuke had come like a slap in the face. For one sick, fleeting moment, he could feel the case slipping away from him.

"Can you recall?" Steve asked.

"Yes," Steele said, grudgingly. "Robert Greely was five feet, eleven inches."

"Five feet, eleven inches? Despite your reluctance to admit the defendant is under six feet tall, I think the jurors all saw her when she stood up and can judge for themselves, so—"

"One moment, Your Honor," Dirkson said, struggling to his feet. "I am sorry to interrupt in light of what Your Honor just said, but—"

"No need to apologize," Crandell said. "I think we both know the difference between technical objections and valid ones. Mr.

Winslow, I would not like it if it seemed that you intended to take advantage of my statement so as to make improper questions to which the prosecutor has been made reluctant to object."

"Yes, Your Honor."

"In any event, your summation was improper. The objection will be sustained. Please rephrase the question."

"Yes, Your Honor. Mr. Steele, you still maintain Sheila Benton stabbed Robert Greely with the knife?"

"I do."

"To do so, wouldn't she have to have been hanging from the ceiling?"

"Objection."

"Sustained."

Steve smiled. "Very well. Let me put it to you this way. You claim Sheila Benton held the knife in the manner you indicated, and stabbed Robert Greely. Would you kindly turn to the jury and tell them, in your expert opinion, just *how* she was able to do it, just how she was able to plunge the knife into his back so that it would end up in the position in which it was found by the medical examiner?"

Reginald Steele turned to the jury. "It is quite simple," he said. "The victim could have been seated at the time. Or he could have been bent over. He could have dropped something on the floor. When he bent over to pick it up, the defendant could have stabbed the knife into his back."

Steve stared at the witness. "That is your *expert* opinion?"

"It is."

"Is there any evidence whatsoever that the decedent was seated at the time he was stabbed?"

"Not to my knowledge."

"Or that he was bent over?"

"No."

"Or that he dropped anything on the floor?"

"No."

"You are testifying then to surmises?"

"You asked for them."

"I asked you to justify your expert opinion. Are you telling me the only way you can justify it is with unfounded surmises?"

"That is an unfair assessment of the situation. Any theory is founded on surmises. To characterize them as unfounded is indulging in semantics."

"But the fact remains, that you do not have one shred of evidence to back up your surmises?"

"That is true."

"The surmises upon which you base your expert opinion?"

"That is another inaccurate assessment of the situation. My expert opinion is not based on surmises."

"What is it based on?"

"Analysis of the evidence."

"And the evidence in this case is the fingerprints on the knife, the fingerprints that indicate that Sheila Benton held it in the position I would characterize as being like a sword?"

"That is correct."

"And on that evidence you base your claim, your expert opinion, that Sheila Benton murdered Robert Greely?"

"I do."

Steve strode to the defense table. He picked up a paper bag. He reached in and pulled out a rolling pin. He strode back to the witness.

"Mr. Steele, you claim you searched the defendant's apartment for evidence."

"I did."

"I hand you a rolling pin, and ask you if you ever saw it before."

"May I ask the purpose of this testimony?" Dirkson said.

"The witness testified that he inspected the defendant's apartment. I'm certainly entitled to test his recollection as to what he found."

The witness took the rolling pin and turned it over in his hands.

"I can't recognize it well enough to identify it. There was a similar one in Sheila Benton's apartment."

"Thank you,' Steve said. He took the rolling pin back from the witness. "Now then, you and I have both handled the rolling pin. If you were to examine this rolling pin, could you develop the fingerprints on it and tell me which were yours and which were mine?"

"Your Honor," Dirkson said. "I object on the grounds that this is incompetent, irrelevant and immaterial."

"I'm merely cross-examining him on his qualifications as a fingerprint expert," Steve said.

"Objection overruled."

"Yes. I could do that," Steele said.

"You could find my fingerprints?"

"Yes."

"And you could find yours?"

"Yes."

"On the rolling pin?"

"Yes."

"And," Steve said, "if I should produce a dead body whose head had been bashed in by that rolling pin, would you say that since your fingerprints were on it, you were guilty of the murder?"

Dirkson lunged to his feet. "Your Honor! I object! This is the most—"

Crandell's gavel cut him off. "Objection sustained. The question is clearly improper."

Steve Winslow, having made his point, smiled at the jury. "No further questions," he said. He went back to the defense table and sat down.

Judge Crandell announced that it had reached the hour of noon recess. As the guard and matron converged on Sheila Benton, she was looking up at Steve with newfound respect.

"You son of a bitch," she murmured.

42

DIRKSON CAME out firing right after the noon recess. The morning had been a disaster for him—Winslow had scored points and swung the sympathy of the jury—but now it was his moment to shine. There was no way Winslow could know the surprises Dirkson had in store for him. It was time to let him have it with both barrels.

Dirkson called Lieutenant Farron. He felt better just seeing him take the stand. After the bad impression made by the evasive Reginald Steele, Lieutenant Farron seemed to exude confidence.

"Now, Lieutenant Farron," Dirkson said. "Are you acquainted with the defendant, Sheila Benton?"

"I am."

"When did you first meet her?"

"On June sixth of this year."

"The day before the murder?"

"That is correct."

"Would you explain the circumstances of that meeting?"

"Yes. Miss Benton called the police and then came to the station. She first talked to Sergeant Stams, who brought her to my office."

"And what did she want?"

"She claimed that she had received an anonymous letter and an anonymous phone call."

"And did she show you the anonymous letter?"

"Yes, sir. She gave it to me."

"And could you describe the letter?"

"It consisted of words cut from a newspaper and pasted on a sheet of paper to form a message."

"And do you recall the message?"

"Yes, sir. It said: 'I know all about you.'"

"I hand you a letter and ask you if you have ever seen it before."

Lieutenant Farron took the letter and looked it over. "Yes, sir. That is the letter I referred to. The one the defendant gave me."

Dirkson took the letter back from Farron. "I ask that this letter be marked for identification as People's Exhibit number three."

"No objection."

"So ordered."

Dirkson handed the letter to the clerk and turned back to Farron. "Now then, Lieutenant. Did you examine the envelope in which the letter was received?"

Steve straightened in his chair. A warning light had come on. The *envelope*. Sheila hadn't mentioned the envelope, and he hadn't even asked.

"Yes, sir," Lieutenant Farron said.

"Can you describe the envelope?"

"It was addressed to the defendant. The address had been typed. There was no return address."

"But the address of the defendant had been typed on a typewriter?"

"Yes, sir."

Steve leaned over to Sheila. "Is that true?" he whispered. "Was the envelope typed?"

"Yes," she whispered back. "Why? What's the matter? Does it make a difference?"

"We'll talk about it later. Right now, just keep smiling and don't let the jury see it makes any difference."

Steve kept smiling, but his world was collapsing. *Does it make a difference?* Well, just a little, he thought ironically. He knew typing was as distinctive as handwriting. Which meant they could prove which typewriter had typed the envelope. Which meant they could tie the letter to Greely.

Dirkson had walked to the prosecution table and picked up an envelope. He crossed back to the witness.

"I hand you an envelope and ask you if you have ever seen it before."

"Yes, sir. That's the envelope the defendant gave me. The one she said the letter came in."

"How do you identify it?"

"By my initials, which I marked on it at the time."

"I ask that the envelope be marked for identification as People's Exhibit number four."

"No objection."

"So ordered."

"Now then, Lieutenant. Did you make a search of the decedent's apartment?"

"Yes, sir. I did."

"Did you find anything that you considered significant?"

"Yes, sir. I found a Smith-Corona portable typewriter."

Dirkson produced a typewriter from a bag on the prosecution table. "Is this the typewriter to which you now refer?"

"Yes, sir. It is."

"I ask that the typewriter be marked for identification as People's Exhibit—uh, what are we up to now?—number five."

"No objection."

"So ordered."

Dirkson watched while the clerk marked the typewriter for identification. He looked over at the defense table. Winslow was still sitting calmly, with that maddening smile on his face. All right, damn him, Dirkson thought. Time to turn the tables on him. Let's let him get angry. Let's let *him* start objecting. Let's wipe that smug smile off his face.

"Now then, Lieutenant," Dirkson said. "Did you make any tests to determine whether the envelope, People's Exhibit number four had been typed on the typewriter, People's Exhibit number five?"

Farron was surprised by the question. Dirkson hadn't intended to ask him that. It had been understood that the handwriting expert was going to give that testimony.

"I did," Farron said.

"And had the envelope been typed on that machine?"

"It had."

Judge Crandell frowned, and looked at Steve Winslow. Steve just sat smiling. He might not even have heard the question. Judge Crandell leaned forward.

"One moment here," Crandall said. "Would the court reporter read back that last question and answer?"

The court reporter looked at the tape. "Question: 'And had the envelope been typed on that machine?' Answer: 'It had.'"

Judge Crandell looked expectantly at Steve, who said nothing.

Crandell cleared his throat. "I do not wish to presume upon the responsibilities of the defense counsel, but in order to keep the record straight, I must point out that that last question clearly calls for a conclusion on the part of the witness for which no proper foundation has been laid. Lieutenant Farron is a police officer, but he has not been qualified as a handwriting expert."

Steve smiled. "I think the point is well taken, Your Honor."

Judge Crandell stared at him.

"In that case, Your Honor," Dirkson said, "I ask that the witness be temporarily withdrawn so that Stanley Forrester, an eminent handwriting expert, can take the stand."

"There's no need for that," Steve said casually. "I will stipulate that Mr. Forrester would testify that the envelope, People's Exhibit number four, was typed on the typewriter, People's Exhibit number five."

Judge Crandell looked at him incredulously. "Mr. Winslow, how can you possibly make such a stipulation? The prosecution hasn't even stated what it expects to prove by this witness."

"Why else would they call him, Your Honor?" Steve said. "I

think it's perfectly clear to everyone that the envelope was typed on the machine. I'll stipulate that it was."

Judge Crandell was annoyed by his attitude. "Well, I don't intend to have the matter disposed of in this manner. Mr. Forrester will take the stand."

Lieutenant Farron stepped down from the stand, and Stanley Forrester was sworn in.

"Yes," Forrester said. "There is no question. The envelope was typed on the machine, People's Exhibit number five."

"Cross-examine," Dirkson said.

Steve yawned. "No questions."

"I now ask that People's Exhibits numbers three, four and five be received in evidence."

"No objection."

"So ordered. Now, Lieutenant Farron was on the stand for direct examination. Would Lieutenant Farron please return to the stand?"

Sheila Benton leaned over to Steve. "I need to talk to you," she said between clenched teeth.

"Later."

"No. Now."

"Not in front of the jury."

"Then ask for a recess."

He saw the look on her face, and he didn't want the jury to see it. Strategically, it was a bad time to request a recess, but he had no choice. He stood up.

"Your Honor," he said. "Some of the recent testimony has covered matters of which the prosecution has been aware for some time, but which have come as a surprise to the defense. I find I need to confer with my client. If I could ask for a brief recess."

Dirkson rose to his feet. "No objection, Your Honor. I'm sure counsel and his client have a lot to talk over."

Judge Crandell, irritated by Dirkson's manner, considered a rebuke, but thought better of it. "Very well," he said. "Court stands in recess for half an hour."

As court broke up, reporters surrounded a grinning Dirkson, while guards led Steve Winslow and Sheila Benton out a side door. They were marched down to a small visiting room and left alone.

Sheila watched the guard close the door. The second it was closed, she wheeled on Steve. "All right," she asked angrily. "What the fuck do you think you're doing?"

"Trying to save your neck."

"Yeah, sure. What the hell happened to you?"

"What do you mean?"

"This morning you were going great. You were terrific. You had 'em all on the run. This afternoon you're a washout. What happened?"

Steve smiled. "Are you telling me you're dissatisfied with the way I'm handling your case?"

She stared at him. "Dissatisfied? No. Of course not. Why should I be dissatisfied? You run around court bowing and smiling like a fucking moron. You don't know when to object. The judge has to run your case for you. And then, when the prosecution puts on an important witness who ties me right in with the murder, you don't even cross-examine. Years from now, after I'm convicted of this crime, people will say 'Sheila Benton? I remember her. She was the girl with the asshole lawyer.'"

"Finished?"

"I'm just getting started! Who the hell do you think you are, Perry fucking Mason?"

Steve's eyes faltered. It was an accurate shot. He looked at her and smiled. "No," he said. "There's a difference."

"What?"

"Perry Mason knew what he was doing."

Sheila stared at him. "Are you telling me you *don't?*"

He nodded. "That's right. I don't. At least, not in the way you mean. You see, the thing about Perry Mason was he didn't just try to get his client acquitted. He always tried to find the guilty party, to prove who actually did it. And the hard thing to realize is, that's not the way it works." Steve smiled and shook his head. "No one is going to break down on the witness stand and confess to this crime. That's the thing you gotta understand. In all probability, we will *never* find out who really killed Robert Greely, or why. Now, that may be hard to take, but that's how it is. So when I tell you I don't know what I'm doing, what I mean is, I don't have any ultimate goal, any secret plan. I don't know who did it, and I don't expect to be able to find out who did it. All I can do is try to blunt the testimony of the prosecution's witnesses, and try to put your case in the best possible light. And in doing that, win over the jurors. 'Cause that's what it's gonna come down to—whether or not the jurors like us. That's really it. It's a popularity contest. Or a beauty contest. We score some points on the talent competition, and they crown you Miss Innocent Defendant. You see what I mean?"

"Yes," Sheila said. "I see what you mean. And I'm telling you, how you're going about it stinks."

"Oh?"

"Yeah. Didn't you think that letter was important?"

"It's damned important. It gives the prosecution the link they need to establish your motive. It's the most damaging evidence the prosecution's put on so far."

"And so you just sit calmly and watch them do it?"

"Look. The envelope was typed on that machine. That's a fact. Nothing I can do is going to alter that fact."

"You could at least try. Or did you take one look at that handwriting expert and realize he was too much for you?"

"I couldn't have shaken his testimony, if that's what you mean. All I would have accomplished would have been to make the jury think we felt the point was important." Steve took a deep breath, and let it out again. "Look. This is a case in which all the facts are against you. There's no getting away from them. I can't even put you on the stand to deny them, because you've told so many lies to the police that you can't stand up to cross-examination. So all I can do is sit back and punch holes in the prosecution's case. But

I've got to do it selectively. When the prosecution introduces evidence that is incontestable, I have to pass it off as if it weren't important. It does you more harm than good to have me make a big stink about something and lose. Our only chance is to treat the damaging facts as if they weren't particularly important."

"I don't agree with you."

"Then get another lawyer."

"I can't get another lawyer. You know that perfectly well."

"Ask your uncle to hire you a lawyer. I'll step out of the case."

She looked at him in surprise. "Why should you do that? That's what my uncle's been trying to get you to do all along."

"That's what *he* wanted me to do. But if you're convicted, I don't want it on my conscience that *you* wanted another lawyer."

Sheila frowned. She looked down, thought that over. She looked up at him again.

"Tell me. Do you really think what you're doing will work?"

Steve had been controlling himself for some time. Now he finally snapped. "How the hell should I know?" he said in exasperation. "I've never been in a fucking courtroom before."

They stood there, looking at each other.

43

HARRY DIRKSON wanted his headline. That was the thing he thought about during the thirty-minute recess. For Harry Dirkson was no babe in the woods. He was a veteran trial lawyer, and he knew all the ropes. And one thing he knew was, the common belief that cases aren't tried in the papers was bullshit. Sure, jurors were instructed not to read the papers, but many of them did. And even those who didn't couldn't walk down the street without seeing the newspaper headlines, at least the ones in the Post and the Daily News.

So Dirkson wanted his headline. And the thing was, when the day started, he'd thought he had it. "BLACKMAIL NOTE TIED TO GREELY." That was the headline. It had to be. A dramatic and damning bit of evidence that had caught the defense as well as the public by surprise. It was a natural.

Except for one thing. Reginald Steele. Goddamn Reginald Steele and his fingerprint evidence. Steele had made a hell of an impression on the stand. Too smug. Too assured. And that point Winslow had brought up, about how the knife must have been held. Steele hadn't handled that well at all.

It didn't bother Dirkson that Winslow's point had been quite valid, that it was almost inconceivable that the girl could have stabbed him holding the knife that way. Diakson was sure she was guilty, so things like that were annoyances, rather than anything to worry about or think about. The only real difference it made, as far as Dirkson was concerned, was whether he would get his newspaper headline.

That was the problem. Dirkson thought he had it. He thought the evidence about the typewriter was enough. But in the back of his mind was a horrible image he couldn't get rid of. And it was this: a photograph of a hand holding a kitchen knife, with the headline above it, "LIKE A SWORD?"

Dirkson stewed about it the whole recess. And in the end, what he decided was, he couldn't take the chance. The evidence of the handwriting expert was good, but not good enough. Not with the way the defense had sluffed over it, and paid no attention to it. It hadn't been built up enough.

Dirkson had to be sure. So he would do it. He would shoot his wad. He would use the evidence he'd planned to hold for the next day, for *tomorrow's* headline. He would use it today. Which meant rethinking his plan. Timing it. Ending with it, a grand finale.

When court reconvened, Lieutenant Farron resumed the stand.

"Now, Lieutenant," Judge Crandell said. "You are still under oath. The district attorney was questioning you on direct examination."

Dirkson rose, approached the witness stand. "Just a few more questions, Lieutenant. Now, you have testified that the defendant gave you this letter, People's Exhibit number three?"

"Yes, sir."

"Did she make any statement to you at the time concerning the letter?"

"Yes, sir. She said she thought it was a blackmail letter. I asked her if she was a likely target for blackmail, and she told me she wasn't because she had no money of her own and she had never done anything that anyone could blackmail her for."

"I see. And it was due to this statement on the part of the defendant that you decided that the matter didn't warrant investigation?"

Steve rose. "Your Honor, I object. We are here to try a woman for murder, not to whitewash the police department's sloppy investigative techniques."

Dirkson was furious. "Your Honor, that's not an objection. That's a gratuitous attack on the police department."

Steve equaled his tone. "And your question was a gratuitous defense of a police blunder."

Judge Crandell banged the gavel. "Gentlemen, gentlemen. Could we have some semblance of order here? Now, as far as the so-called objection goes, one point at least is well taken. We are supposedly conducting an investigation into a murder. Could we attempt to confine ourselves to that?"

Dirkson smiled. "Very well, Your Honor. I withdraw the question, and I have no further questions of the witness."

Lieutenant Farron was surprised. He had expected Dirkson to question him at some length, and he had no way of knowing of Dirkson's change in strategy.

"No questions," Steve said.

Dirkson smiled. He had been afraid Winslow might cross-examine Lieutenant Farron at some length, which might have spoiled his timing. But now he had all the time he needed for what he wanted to do. By not cross-examining, Winslow was playing right into his hands.

It had been understood by Dirkson's trial assistants that he would next call the cab driver to establish the time Sheila Benton returned to her apartment, so they were caught flat-footed when he instead called Sergeant Stams, and there was some delay getting him into the courtroom. The Sergeant was produced, however, and he took the stand.

"Sergeant Stams," Dirkson said, "on the afternoon of June seventh did you receive a telephone call?"

"I did."

"From whom?"

"From the defendant, Sheila Benton."

"How did you know it was the defendant?"

"I recognized her voice. Lieutenant Farron and I had talked with her the day before."

"I see. And what time did you receive the call?"

"At one thirty-five."

"And what did the defendant say?"

"She said that a man had been murdered in her apartment."

"And did you subsequently go to that apartment?"

"I did."

"What did you find?"

"The body of a man."

"The man who has subsequently been identified as Robert Greely?"

"That's right."

"Did you make a search of the victim's clothing?"

"I did."

"And what did you find?"

"A key."

"A key?"

"Yes."

"I hand you a key and ask you if this is the key you removed from the body?"

Sergeant Stams took the key and looked it over. "Yes, sir. That's the key."

"I ask that this key be marked for identification as People's Exhibit number six."

"No objection."

"So ordered."

"Now then, Sergeant, did you make any attempt to locate the lock that this key fitted?"

"I did."

"And what did you find?"

"The key was to the front door of the defendant's apartment."

There was an audible reaction from the spectators in the courtroom. And from Sheila Benton. She gasped, and her face contorted.

And the attention of the jurors shifted from the witness and focused on her.

Steve Winslow kept his composure and betrayed no emotion. But he'd been hit with two body blows. First, hearing the devastating information about the key. And second, seeing the focus of the jurors' attention shift to the defendant. It was a sign he could read clear as day.

A sign they'd made up their minds.

It was a delicious moment for Dirkson, and he did his best to prolong it. "Excuse me, Sergeant. Let me be sure I understand this. You say the key fit the door to Sheila Benton's apartment?"

Judge Crandell looked expectantly at Steve. The question had already been asked and answered, and Dirkson was clearly milking the situation. But Steve was silent. He knew better than to make a fuss at this point.

"That's right," Sergeant Stams said.

"It would open the door to her apartment?"

"That's right."

"You tested it yourself?"

"I did."

"And the key opened the door?"

"It did."

"The door to Sheila Benton's apartment?"

"That's right."

"Cross-examine," Dirkson said triumphantly.

Steve looked at the witness. He couldn't let this go by unchallenged. Not after the reaction of the jury. And particularly not after the reaction of the defendant. He had to do something to blunt the testimony. He got to his feet.

"Sergeant Stams," he said. "You say you found this key in the decedent's pocket?"

"Yes."

"Was it on a key ring?"

"It was not."

"In a key case?"

"No."

"Were there other keys with it?"

"There were not."

"Was the key attached to anything?"

"No."

"You're saying it was loose in his pocket?"

"That's right."

"Which pocket, by the way?"

"His right-front pants pocket."

"What else was there in that pocket?"

"Nothing."

"Nothing? Nothing at all?"

"I don't know how you can have a nothing without having a nothing at all."

This brought smiles from some of the spectators, but Steve paid no attention.

"You're saying the pocket was empty except for the key?"

"That's right."

"What about his other pockets?"

"They were empty too."

Steve stopped and looked at the witness. "Wait a minute. I want to be sure I understand this. You're saying there was *nothing* in *any* of his pockets except for the key?"

"That's right."

"Did you find anything belonging to the decedent in the defendant's apartment?"

"Objection, Your Honor," Dirkson said. "That calls for a conclusion from the witness. How would he know what belonged to the decedent?"

"I'll rephrase the question, Your Honor. Sergeant Stams, according to your testimony, the decedent's wallet was not on the body?"

"That's right."

"Did you find a wallet bearing identification of the decedent in the defendant's apartment?"

"No."

"The decedent had no keys, other than the one you have identified. No key to his *own* apartment?"

"No."

"Did you find a key to the decedent's apartment anywhere in the defendant's apartment?"

"No."

"Sergeant Stams, did you make a search of the *decedent's* apartment?"

"I did."

"Did you find his wallet?"

"I did not."

"Did you find the key to his apartment?"

"No."

"Yet neither of these objects was on the body of the decedent when you searched it?"

"That's right."

"Sergeant Stams, is it then your opinion that after Robert Greely was killed, the body was searched?"

"Objection, Your Honor. Assuming facts not in evidence and calling for a conclusion on the part of the witness."

"He's a police officer, Your Honor," Steve said.

"He's not a clairvoyant, Your Honor," Dirkson countered.

"The objection is sustained," Crandell ruled.

Steve figured he'd thrown up enough of a smoke screen. "No further questions," he said.

Dirkson was pleased. There was plenty of time left, and Dirkson figured he'd need it. His next witness was not going to be easy.

"Call Saul Callen," he said.

Saul Callen was a cantankerous old curmudgeon, quarrelsome and argumentative. He settled himself on the witness stand, and peered down at Dirkson through ancient-looking bifocals.

"Your name?" Dirkson said.

"You just called me by name," the witness said.

"For the record, give your name," Dirkson said.

"Saul Callen."

"Occupation?"

"Locksmith."

"You have a store on Broadway and Ninety-fifth?"

"I do."

"I hand you a key, marked People's Exhibit number six, and ask you if you have ever seen it before."

"I don't know."

"You haven't even looked at it."

"That's right."

"Would you look at it, please?"

"All right. I've looked at it."

"And have you ever seen it before?"

"I don't know."

"Have you seen a key like it?"

"Like it? I've seen a million keys like it."

"Can you tell me anything about it?"

"It's fairly new. It's been recently made."

"Do you recognize the blank?"

"It's a standard blank."

"Do you have blanks like it in your shop?"

"Every locksmith has blanks like it."

"Then you might have made this key?"

"Sure. And I might have been elected president, but I don't recall it."

"Directing your attention to June sixth, did a gentleman come into your shop and ask you to make a key?"

"If one hadn't, I wouldn't be in business."

"I beg your pardon?"

"Dozens of people come into my shop every day and ask me to make keys. If only one person came in a day, I couldn't operate. Do you know what my rent is?"

"Mr. Callen, I think you know what I'm getting at. Did the police ask you to go to the morgue to identify a dead body?"

Callen snorted. "I'll say they did. I lost half a day's work."

"And did you identify the body?"

"I don't know what you mean by identify."

"Had you seen the man before?"

"As I told the police, I thought I had."

"And where had you seen him?"

"In my shop."

"And when would that have been?"

"I told this to the police."

"And now I'd like you to tell me. When did you see him?"

"I can't be sure. Either the fifth or the sixth."

"Of June?"

"What do you think, November? Yes, of June."

"To the best of your recollection the man was in your shop on the fifth or sixth of June?"

"That's right."

"And what did he want?"

"He wanted me to make a copy of a key."

There was a reaction from the spectators. Dirkson glanced around. Newspaper reporters were scribbling furiously.

Dirkson smiled. "I'd like to pin this down. Did you make this copy from a wax impression or from another key?"

"From another key."

"And the man who came into your shop and gave you the key and asked you to make a copy was the man you identified at the morgue?"

"That's right."

"And what was the name of the man you identified?"

"Robert Greely."

"Cross-examine."

Dirkson turned and walked back to his seat. As far as he was concerned, his work for the afternoon was over. Winslow would really tear into this one. The guy hadn't identified the key. His identification of Greely was shaky at best, and those bifocals the guy wore made it look as if he could hardly see. Winslow would tear him apart.

Dirkson looked over at Winslow. Winslow appeared bored. He waved his hand. "No questions, Your Honor."

That announcement drew a bigger reaction than Callen's testimony about the key. Dirkson frowned.

"The witness is excused," Judge Crandell said. "Call your next witness."

Dirkson looked at the clock. He still had a good half hour left before adjournment. After the testimony about the key, any witness he put on would be an anticlimax. He didn't want that. So what could he do?

Then it came to him. All right. Go for the kill. Tie it down. If Winslow was going to let him do it, why not? Give 'em the motivation too, and tie it all together.

Dirkson stood up. "Call Maxwell Baxter."

An excited murmur ran through the courtroom. Maxwell Baxter! This was the name. This was the one they'd all come to see. And it was happening now. Necks craned to watch the aloof, distinguished millionaire as he walked to the stand.

Inside the gate, Maxwell Baxter stopped to look over at his niece. The effect that look created in the minds of the jurors could not have been a good one in terms of the defense. It was the look a stern parent might give a particularly naughty and unruly child.

Maxwell Baxter met Steve Winslow's eyes. The look Max gave Steve was one of pure contempt. Steve merely smiled.

Max took the stand and was sworn in. Dirkson approached the bench.

"Your Honor," he said. "This is a hostile witness. He is the uncle of the defendant, and he has refused to answer any questions put to him by the police or the prosecution. Therefore I may need to ask leading questions."

"I will reserve that ruling until it becomes necessary," Judge Crandell said.

Dirkson turned to the witness. "You are Maxwell Baxter, the uncle of the defendant?"

Max stared at Dirkson as one might stare at a particularly loathsome bug. "I am."

"You are, I believe, her trustee?"

"That is correct."

"Is hers a large trust?"

"That depends what you mean by large."

"What is the amount of the trust?"

"I'm sure I don't know."

"And yet you are the trustee?"

"That is correct."

"And yet you state you don't know the amount of the trust?"

"That is correct."

"Why don't you know the amount of the trust?"

"A large portion of the trust is in stocks, which constantly fluctuate. It would take an accountant to tell you what they're worth."

Dirkson looked at Judge Crandell in helpless exasperation.

"Very well," Judge Crandell said. "You have your ruling."

Dirkson turned back to Maxwell Baxter. "Mr. Baxter, is Sheila Benton's trust worth more than a million dollars?"

"It is."

There was a reaction from the spectators.

"Is it worth several million dollars?"

"What do you mean by several?"

"You tell me. How many millions would you say the trust is worth?"

"I'm sure I couldn't say."

"More than five?"

"Yes."

"More than ten?"

"Yes."

"More than twenty?"

"I'm not sure."

"Mr. Baxter, are you telling me that the amount of Sheila Benton's trust is somewhere close to twenty million dollars?"

"I'm not telling you anything. I'm answering your questions."

"Yes, you are. Let me ask you another one. As trustee, you are familiar with the provisions of the trust, are you not?"

"Yes."

"And is not one of the provisions to the effect that if Sheila is involved in any scandal that would damage the family name, the trust is declared void and the money goes to charity?"

"Yes. That is true."

That produced another reacton in the courtroom. However, Dirkson stood there and looked all around the room, and particularly at the jurors, just to be sure they all got the point, before he announced, "Your witness."

Steve rose to his feet. As opposed to the ponderous dramatic air of Dirkson, he was bright and breezy as he smiled and approached the witness.

"Yes, Mr. Baxter," he said. "And whose discretion is it whether Sheila's behavior is scandalous enough to warrant terminating the trust?"

"The decision is mine, as trustee."

"Yours alone?"

"Mine alone."

"And if someone had proven to you that Sheila was involved in an extramarital relationship, would you have considered that sufficient grounds for terminating the trust?"

"Certainly not," Max said. "I consider that provision in the trust particularly idiotic. I would always interpret it as leniently as possible."

Steve smiled. "No further questions."

Dirkson rose to his feet. He also was smiling. He could have objected to Winslow's question, but he had a counterattack of his own planned.

"I have some redirect, Your Honor. Mr. Baxter, did your niece, Sheila Benton, *know* that you wouldn't terminate the trust if she became involved in a scandal?"

Max glanced at the defense table, expecting an objection, but Steve just sat there. Max turned to the judge. "I think that's an improper question, Your Honor."

"There being no objection from the defense, you are required to answer."

"I can't answer for what my niece may or may not have known," Max said, evasively.

"Let me put it this way. Did you ever *tell* your niece that you wouldn't terminate the trust under those circumstances?"

Again Max looked at Steve and got no response. "I fail to see how what I may or may not have told my niece is relevant," he said to the judge.

"It is up to the court to decide what is relevant, Mr. Baxter," Judge Crandell said. "In the absence of an objection from the defense, you will answer the question."

"Then I will have to say that I can't remember."

"You can't remember telling your niece?" Dirkson asked.

"No."

"Then you probably did not."

"I can't remember," Max said.

"Then let me put it this way. Was there *in your own mind* the intention *not* to tell your niece that you didn't intend to break the trust, because by letting her think that you would break the trust you could control her actions?"

Maxwell Baxter, who had been well coached by his attorneys as to the type of objections he could expect Steve Winslow to make in his behalf, and who was thoroughly frustrated at not hearing them, now came out with them himself. "That is a wild allegation on your part," he blustered angrily, "assuming facts not in evidence, calling for a conclusion on my part, and inquiring into matters that are incompetent, irrelevant and immaterial."

Judge Crandell banged the gavel. "Mr. Baxter," he said sternly. "Another such outburst and I'll hold you in contempt of court. Must I remind you that you are not a lawyer?"

"I'm sorry, Your Honor," Max said. "But someone has to function as a lawyer around here, and my niece's inexperienced attorney is just sitting there letting the prosecution get away with these objectionable questions."

Steve Winslow got slowly to his feet, smiled and said calmly, with elaborate condescension, "Your Honor, I haven't been objecting because I don't want the jury to get the impression that Sheila has anything to hide. I think it would damage her case to do so. I assumed that Mr. Baxter was an intelligent man, capable of taking care of himself. If, however, he would like me to come to *his* rescue at the expense of his niece's best interests, I'll endeavor to do so."

Judge Crandell's gavel silenced Max's angry retort. "That will do," Crandell said. "The objection, if any, is overruled. The witness will answer the question."

"Did you intend *not* to tell your niece?" Dirkson asked.

Max, defeated and furious, looked around the courtroom. "No," he said. "I didn't intend to tell her."

Again the courtroom broke into a low murmur.

Dirkson smiled. "No further questions."

"Any recross-examination?" Judge Crandell asked.

Steve Winslow rose. "Yes, Your Honor." He strode up to the witness stand, smiled at Max, and said, "Mr. Baxter, do you like me?"

There was stunned reaction in the courtroom. No one could quite believe he had asked that.

Dirkson recovered first and struggled to his feet. "Your Honor, I object. Of all the absurd—"

Crandell banged the gavel. "That will do. If you have an objection, state it in legal terms."

"Incompetent, irrelevant and immaterial," Dirkson said.

"It's always relevant to show bias, Your Honor," Steve said.

Dirkson, still upset, said, "What bias? This is the defendant's uncle. He's biased *for* her."

"He may be biased for her, Your Honor," Steve said. "But he may also be biased against me. And since that bias might affect his testimony, I have a legal right to establish it."

"Objection overruled," Judge Crandell said. "Witness will answer the question."

Max looked up at the judge. "You want me to answer?" he asked grimly.

"Yes," Crandell said. "The court reporter will read the question."

The court reporter flipped through the tape. "Question: 'Mr. Baxter,' he read, 'do you like me?'"

Max looked around the courtroom, then straight at Steve Winslow. Steve smiled at him, a bright, broad smile.

Max's face purpled. "I think you're an incompetent jackass!" he said.

There was a huge reaction from the courtroom. Steve Winslow took no notice. He smiled, bowed and said politely, "Thank you. No further questions."

Judge Crandell banged for silence, excused the witness and announced that it had reached the hour of adjournment.

District Attorney Dirkson hardly heard. Despite the victories he had scored all day long, he had a hollow feeling in his stomach, and he could not keep his eyes from wandering to the back of the courtroom, to the sight that was making him feel queasy, the sight of the newspaper reporters, scribbling gleefully.

44

STEVE WINSLOW sat in the dingy coffee shop near the courthouse, moodily pushing the scrambled eggs around his plate.

Mark Taylor, a folded newspaper under his arm, came in the front door, looked around, spotted Steve and came over.

"Ham, eggs and coffee," Taylor called to the waitress as he slid into the seat. "Well, good morning."

"What's good about it?" Steve said.

"I know what you mean," Taylor said. He unfolded the paper and laid it on the table facing Steve. It was the New York *Post*. The headline read: "BAXTER: YOU'RE AN INCOMPETENT JACKASS!"

Steve glanced at it. "Yeah. I saw it."

"You also made the page-six cartoon."

Taylor flipped the paper open. The cartoon was a drawing of a jury. A small taxicab sat in front of the jury box. Out of the window of the cab, on a rubber neck, came a large caricature of Steve's face, framed by shaggy long hair. The caption on the cartoon read: "YOUR HONOR, I OBJECT!"

"Great," Steve said.

The waitress set a cup of coffee in front of Taylor. He dumped in cream and sugar, took a sip, sighed and said, "You'll pardon me for saying so, but it seems to me you've been going out of your way to make yourself look like an asshole."

Steve nodded. "I know. But I have to do something. The prosecution hit me with two body blows yesterday. The typewriter and the key. The key is the worst. Greely had the original to copy. The inference is that Sheila gave it to him."

"What does she say about it?"

Steve shook his head. "The same thing she's always said. She never met Robert Greely and she has no idea where he could have gotten that key."

"But they can't *prove* she gave it to him, can they?"

"They don't have to. It's bad enough in itself. The guy had the key to her apartment. And she claims she never met him."

Taylor nodded. "It's bad, isn't it?"

"It's the worst." Steve pointed to the paper. "This could read: "BENTON KEY FOUND IN GREELY POCKET." As it is, the story about the key is buried on page twelve."

Taylor thought that over. "Not bad for an asshole."

Steve shook his head. "Something has to break. Shit, haven't you got anything from California?"

"Nothing. The trail's cold. I'm beginning to think there may be nothing to get. I mean, just because Alice Baxter said she had a baby in California doesn't mean she did. Sheila could have been born in another state. She could have been born under another name. There's a lot of possibilities. Now, I have to tell you, frankly, I got more men working out there on the coast than you can afford, and I still got nothing. Which may mean that there's nothing to get."

The waitress brought Taylor's ham and eggs. He picked up a fork and dug in.

Steve looked dispiritedly at his own food. "The thing is, I need something fast. The prosecution's gonna rest its case today or tomorrow, the way things are going. And what the hell am I gonna do then?"

"Your client's gonna have to tell one hell of a convincing story."

Steve sighed. "She can't."

Taylor looked at him. "What?"

"She can't tell her story. I can't even put her on the stand."

"You're kidding."

"I'm not."

Taylor looked at him sideways. "Why? Cause she's guilty?"

Steve shook his head. "No. Cause she's innocent."

Taylor stared at him. "What?"

"She's innocent. That's the problem. She didn't do it. She's innocent, and she doesn't know shit. A man she never saw before was murdered in her apartment with her knife and with her apartment key in his pocket. She knows nothing about it. So what the hell can she say?"

"Just that."

"Great. And who's gonna believe it. Do you believe it?"

Taylor's eyes shifted.

"There you are," Steve said. "And the other thing is, she lied to the police in her statement." Taylor raised his eyebrows. "Oh, not about Greely, not about the murder. But about other things, unimportant things, really, like where she was and what she was doing before she found the body. But it doesn't matter, because all they have to do is catch her in one lie, any lie, about any small insignificant thing, and with the way the rest of the facts are in this case, she's dead meat. And look at her. She's young, naive in a lot of ways. You think she could stand up to cross-examination? You think Dirkson wouldn't rip her apart?" He shook his head. "No. There's no way I can put her on the stand."

"So what can you do?"

"That's the thing. If I don't have something by the time the prosecution rests its case, the only thing I can think of is, I'm gonna have to go after Zambelli."

Taylor looked up in alarm. "You're not serious?"

"I have to do something."

"You do something like that you're gonna wind up dead."

"I can't think about that. I have to think about my client. If you don't want me to go after Zambelli, come up with something else. What about Dutton's wife? You get anything there?"

"I got about two hundred and fifty dollars in operatives' fees confirming the fact that she was in Reno the whole day."

"Great."

Taylor's beeper went on. He switched it off.

"Gotta call the office. Maybe we got something."

"Yeah, sure."

Taylor got up and went to the pay phone at the front of the shop. Steve sat and made patterns on the plate with his eggs.

Taylor was animated when he came back from the phone. *"They got it,"* he said. "Actually they got it late last night, but there's a three-hour time difference so they didn't call because it was after midnight back here. They called first thing this morning. I mean, it's not even seven o'clock out there now, and—"

"Yeah, yeah, fine," Steve said impatiently. "What have they got?"

"We found the hospital where Sheila was born."

"You're kidding. Where?"

"A small town about a hundred miles north of L.A. Alice Baxter checked in under the name of Mary Brown. But it's a positive I.D., right down to the little baby footprints."

"And the father?"

"Listed as Sam Brown. We're looking for him, of course."

"All right. Now we're getting somewhere."

"Yeah finally," Taylor said. "We would have had the location sooner but we had the date wrong."

Steve looked at him. "We what?"

"We had the date wrong. You gave me November twelfth as Sheila's birthday. She's older than that. She was actually born on June fifth."

Steve sat bolt upright in his chair. "Jesus Christ!"

"What?"

"Call them back," Steve said excitedly. "Call your men back. Tell them to drop the investigation, dig a hole and crawl into it. Call everybody on the West Coast off."

Taylor frowned. "What's the big deal? You mean because Sheila's birthday's earlier she comes into her trust sooner, and—"

"No, damn it. Don't you see? June fifth is five months after

Alice Benton left New York. So she didn't go off to California and meet someone. She went out there to have the baby."

"What's the difference?"

"The difference is the father was someone from around here."

"So?"

"Think about it. Suppose Sheila's father were just a casual trifler for her mother's affections. Suppose after Alice Baxter left town he forgot about her, never even thought about her again. And suppose about a month ago, he just happened to see something in the paper about Maxwell Baxter—there's things about Baxter in the paper all the time."

"Yeah. So?"

"So, suppose this particular article just happened to mention Sheila Benton, twenty-four-year-old daughter of Maxwell Baxter's sister, Alice Baxter."

Now it was Taylor's turn to sit bolt upright in his seat. "You mean he'd figure he'd hit the jackpot and he'd go calling on his long-lost daughter?"

"You're damn right he would. And then a lot of things could happen." Steve looked worried. "If she weren't happy to see him, he might even wind up with a knife in his back."

45

STEVE WINSLOW went up the front steps of the courthouse, just as he had every morning since the trial had begun. Only today there was a difference. Every other day he had gone up the steps alone and unnoticed. Today he was besieged by reporters.

That should have been gratifying for a young attorney conducting his first trial. It should have been but it wasn't. Because Steve knew why the reporters were there, and it wasn't because of his brilliant courtroom technique. It was because of the role he had forced himself to play to try to take the heat off his client and focus the attention of the jury on himself. It was because of the image he had created, the image that was reflected in the newspaper cartoon.

It was because they saw him as a clown.

And if there were any doubt in his mind that that was what they thought, their questions dispelled it.

"How about a statement, Mr. Winslow?"

"Is it true Maxwell Baxter tried to fire you?"

"Is it true you've never been in court before?"

"Is it true you drive a cab?"

Steve pushed by them without comment and entered the courthouse. He was later than usual due to his meeting with Mark Taylor, and when he entered the courtroom he discovered Sheila Benton was already there and was looking around anxiously for him. As their eyes met, it seemed to him he could see the relief washing over her face, as if she were a drowning person who had just grabbed a life preserver. He slid in next to her at the table.

"Where the hell have you been?" she asked.

"Working."

"Working on what?"

"Tell you later."

Judge Crandell entered, called court to order, and Maxwell Baxter resumed his place on the stand.

After the fireworks of the day before, there was an aura of expectancy among the spectators, particularly when they saw Maxwell Baxter on the stand. But Dirkson disappointed them. Today was not his day for surprises, today was his day for crisp efficiency, and point by point he methodically laid out the facts that would show that Sheila Benton had had the opportunity to commit the crime.

"Mr. Baxter," he began. "Going back to the day of the murder, your niece called on you that morning, did she not?"

"Yes."

"Why did she call on you?"

"I'm her uncle."

"I daresay you are. The point is, she wanted to borrow some money, did she not?"

"Uh, yes, she did."

"One hundred dollars?"

"Yes."

"And you gave it to her?"

"Yes, I did."

"In cash?"

"Yes."

"And what time did your niece leave?"

"I have no recollection."

"Well, let's get at it another way. Was there anyone else in your apartment when your niece arrived that morning?"

"Yes. My brother Teddy, and his son, Phillip."

"Who left first?"

"My brother and his son."

"And Sheila remained behind?"

"Yes."

"How long after your brother left did Sheila leave?"

"I tell you I can't remember."

"More than fifteen minutes?"

"It might have been."

"More than half an hour?"

"I can't remember."

"Surely you remember generally. Did she stay to lunch? Did you offer her coffee or tea? Did you sit and chat?"

"I tell you I—"

"Or," Dirkson said, boring in, "did she leave as soon as you gave her the money?"

"Sir," Max said angrily, "I consider that remark—"

Dirkson raised his voice. "Did she take the money and leave, yes or no?"

Baxter glared at him and took a breath. "Yes, she did."

"Then she couldn't have been in your apartment more than fifteen minutes after your brother left, could she?"

"I suppose not," Max said grudgingly.

"No further questions," Dirkson said.

With that, the focus of the crowd shifted to Steve Winslow, in the hope of more fireworks, a hope that was dashed when he declined to cross-examine.

Dirkson's announcement that Theodore Baxter would be his next witness raised further expectations—another Baxter, another man of wealth and power—expectations that were immediately shattered by Teddy Baxter's entrance. His appearance labeled him for what he was: a poor relation.

His testimony was routine too, as Dirkson tried to pin down the time element.

"No sir," Teddy Baxter said. "I don't remember what time it was when we left."

"Perhaps I can refresh your memory. Your son, Phillip, had to catch a bus, did he not?"

"Yes he did."

"The eleven forty-five to Boston out of Port Authority?"

"Yes."

"And did he catch that bus?"

Steve knew the answer to the question was inadmissable— Teddy hadn't seen Phillip actually catch the bus, so his answer had to be a conclusion based on hearsay—but he also knew from Mark Taylor's investigation that Phillip *had* caught the bus, so he didn't bother to object.

"Yes, he did," Teddy Baxter said.

"No further questions," Dirkson said.

Steve didn't bother to cross-examine.

Dirkson called the cab driver who'd taken Sheila back to her apartment. He testified that he'd picked up Sheila Benton at the corner of Fifth Avenue and Fifty-third Street at five minutes after one and dropped her off in front of her apartment at one-twenty. He made a good impression on the jury, as Steve had known he would. Handsome and cocky, he so obviously considered himself a stud that his identification of Sheila Benton was unshakable. There was no way anyone was going to believe he could have missed her.

Steve could have challenged him on the time element, however. Five after one, and one-twenty were bound to be approximations —the guy's trip sheet wouldn't be accurate to the minute, and he would have a hard time maintaining that it was. But Steve saw no point in it. The prosecution could maintain that Sheila had killed him earlier and then dashed out to Fifth Avenue to build up an alibi by taking the cab back, or they could claim she killed him as soon as she got home and just before she called the police. A few minutes either way wouldn't make any difference.

Steve didn't bother to cross-examine.

The next witness, Stella Rosenthal, was more interesting just because she was a character. Middle-aged, lean, angular, with thick spectacles perched on a long pointed nose, she was a living caricature of a snoop.

Mrs. Rosenthal testified that she lived in the apartment next to Sheila Benton.

"That's right," she said, in a snippy, clipped voice. "Right next door."

"And what is the relation of the front doors of the two apartments? That is, can you see Sheila Benton's front door from your front door?"

"No way you could miss it. The doors are catty-corner to each other."

"Catty-corner? By that do you mean at right angles?"

"By that I mean catty-corner. Don't you know what catty-corner is?"

"Well, I—"

"I mean like this," Mrs. Rosenthal said, touching her left elbow with the fingers of her right hand, and forming a right angle.

"That's fine, Mrs. Rosenthal," Dirkson said, with a smile to the jury, "but your arms are not in evidence here."

"I beg your pardon?"

"What I mean is, the court reporter cannot record the manner in which you are holding your arms. So for the record, we need to state that you are holding one arm at right angles to the other arm."

"That's right. Catty-corner."

Dirkson smiled at the jury, and got several answering smiles. Dirkson was playing this witness just right. He was inviting them to share his amusement with her. By doing so he was extending to them a most welcome invitation—the invitation to feel superior.

"Yes. Catty-corner," Dirkson said. "So if your door were open just a crack, it would be possible to see who went in and out of Sheila Benton's apartment?"

"Well, I suppose it would. But I wouldn't want to have you think I spend all my time peeking out the crack in my door."

Dirkson stole a look at the jury, and noted with satisfaction that to the best if his judgment, every single one of them was convinced that that was *exactly* how Mrs. Rosenthal spent her time.

"Of course not," Dirkson said. "All I'm getting at is on the few occasions when your door was open you would be in a postion to notice who came and went."

"Well, of course."

"So let me ask you. Did Sheila Benton have any frequent visitors?"

"She had one."

"And who was that?"

"A young man," Mrs. Rosenthal said. Her tone made it sound as if she had said, "A child molester."

"And would you recognize this man if you saw him again?"

"You know I would. You showed me his picture, didn't you?"

"Yes, I did," Dirkson said. "But the jury doesn't know that. So if you could just tell them. Would you recognize the man?"

"Yes, I would. I recognized his picture, didn't I?"

"Yes you did. And can you tell me the name of the man whose picture you identified?"

"Yes, I can. His name is John Dutton."

"I see. This John Dutton called on the defendant on several occasions?"

"That's right."

"Did he ever call on her at night?"

"Of course. That's when he called on her."

"And on those occasions when he called on her, could you hear what was going on in the apartment next door?"

"Well . . ."

"Well? Could you?"

"Well, the walls are paper-thin."

"So you could hear?"

"Well, yes."

"And could you tell us, please, just what you heard going on in Sheila Benton's apartment on those occasions when John Dutton called on her?"

Mrs. Rosenthal's lips clamped together in a straight line. She drew herself up indignantly. "I most certainly could not," she snapped.

There was a roar of laughter. Dirkson turned and let the jury and the spectators see his broad grin. He waited until the laughter had subsided then announced smugly, "No further questions."

Steve Winslow got to his feet. There was not much he could do about her testimony. The damage had been done. But he still had a job to do. His job was to win back as much ground as possible with the jury, ground that he had lost through Dirkson's performance with Mrs. Rosenthal. And basically, there was only one way to do that.

He needed to get a laugh.

"Now, Mrs. Rosenthal," he said. "You say you saw John Dutton call on the defendant on several occasions?"

"That's right."

"Mostly at night?"

"Yes."

"And you were able to hear what was going on?"

"Yes."

"Because the walls of the apartment are so thin, I think you said?"

"That's right. Paper-thin."

"Tell me, did this disturb you?"

"What do you mean?"

"Well, did the things you heard ever keep you up at night?"

Dirkson started to rise, but thought better of it. If the defense was asking for this, let them.

"I'll say they did," Mrs. Rosenthal said.

"Did they disturb your sleep?"

"They most certainly did. I mean, how's a body to get to sleep with that sort of thing going on? And until such hours of the night, too."

"I see. So this must have been quite annoying to you."

"It certainly was."

"Tell me, did you ever speak to the defendant about it?"

"No."

"No? Why not, if it was such a disturbance?"

"Well, it's not the sort of thing polite people discuss."

"Maybe not. But there are ways of handling everything. Surely you could have just complained about the noise?"

"Perhaps."

"But you didn't?"

"No."

"Why not?"

"Well . . ."

"Tell me, do you *ever* speak to the defendant?"

"Well, no, I guess not."

"You're next-door neighbors."

"Yes."

"But you don't speak to her?"

"No."

"Why not?"

"Well, I hate to say this, but you're asking for it. She's just not the sort of person I would want to talk to. I mean, a young woman like that, fooling around with a married man."

"Oh? That's how you felt about her?"

"I'm afraid it is."

"Then you knew John Dutton was married?"

"Yes."

"How did you know that?"

"District Attorney Harry Dirkson told me so."

"I'm sure he did," Steve said with a smile. "But that was after the murder, wasn't it? You said the reason you didn't want to talk to her was because you knew she was fooling around with a married man, didn't you?"

"Yes."

"Then you must have known John Dutton was married then?"

"Well . . ."

"Did you?"

"Well, yes, I did."

"I see. And how did you know he was married?"

Mrs. Rosenthal's eyes shifted, and Steve knew he'd hit something. "Well . . ."

"Yes?"

"Well," Mrs. Rosenthal said. "You have to understand, this was quite an annoyance to me. And, of course, with all this going on next to me I wanted to be sure everything was all right. I mean, if there was going to be a young man in my building all the time, I wanted to know who he was."

"That's most understandable. So what did you do?"

"Well, I saw them getting into his car one day. One of those little sports cars, you know?"

"Yes. And?"

"Well," Mrs. Rosenthal said grudgingly. "I wrote down the license number."

"I see." Steve was now grinning just as broadly as Dirkson had. "And then what did you do?"

"Well . . . I have a cousin who works at motor vehicles."

"I see. So you asked your cousin to look up the license number?"

"Yes."

"And you found the car was registered to John Dutton?"

"Yes."

"And then you checked with the marriage bureau and found out that John Dutton was married?"

Mrs. Rosenthal glared at him.

"Did you?"

"Yes, I did," she said angrily.

"All because you wanted to know who this man was in case you ran into him in the hallway sometime?"

"Well, what's wrong with that?" Mrs. Rosenthal said testily. "Good gracious, I would think if you had someone in your building all the time you'd want to know who he was."

"I'm sure I would," Steve said. He stole a look at the jury, just as Dirkson had done. "I don't know if I'd go to such lengths to find out, but I'm sure I'd like to know."

Steve stood, smiling at the witness. Mrs. Rosenthal sat, glaring back.

"Now then," Steve said. "You say you've seen John Dutton enter the defendant's apartment on many occasions. Tell me, did you ever see the decedent, Robert Greely, entering the defendant's apartment?"

"No I did not."

"Or leaving her apartment?"

"No."

"Not even on the day of the murder?"

"That's right."

"You have never seen the decedent, Robert Greely, at all?"

"That's right."

"And you have never seen him entering or leaving Sheila Benton's apartment?"

"That's right."

"But he must have done so, since he was found murdered there, mustn't he?"

"I suppose so."

"Well then, can you tell me *why* it is that you have never seen the decedent, Robert Greely, entering or leaving Sheila Benton's apartment?"

"Because I mind my own business," Mrs. Rosenthal snapped.

There was a roar of laughter. It wasn't as big as the one Dirkson had gotten, but it was the best Steve could have hoped for under the circumstances. He grinned broadly.

"No further questions."

46

"DID YOUR mother ever talk about your father?"

"What?"

Steve Winslow and Sheila Benton were sitting face-to-face in the attorney-client conference room off the court. Court had recessed for lunch right after Steve's cross-examination of Mrs. Rosenthal. Steve was choosing to skip his lunch and was making Sheila skip hers.

The reason, of course, was that he was obsessed with his new theory—the theory that Greely was really Sheila's father. Not that, if Greely were, Steve really suspected Sheila might have killed him. On reflection, he had realized that that idea had just been a flash of paranoia. Even if Greely were Sheila's father, and even if he had been in a position to upset the trust, that would have posed no threat to Sheila, and she would have had no reason to want him out of the way.

But Uncle Max would have. That was the theory Steve was working on now. Sheila's living father could have been a real threat to Uncle Max. He could have upset the trust and contested the will and raised bloody hell with Uncle Max's little empire. And suppose Uncle Max had sent those letters, and then lured Greely up to Sheila's apartment on the pretext of meeting his long-lost daughter and then killed him? It would have been a perfect frame-up. There would be nothing to connect Uncle Max to the murder at all. And Sheila would take the rap.

Steve had no idea why Max would want to frame his niece, but it wasn't inconceivable. Max was her trustee. Her trust was worth millions. Max supposedly had millions of his own, but what if they were tied up in speculative investments of all types? What if Max sometimes had need for ready cash? He wouldn't be the first trustee who'd dipped into a trust for his own purposes. And then with Greely on the scene, contesting the trust, contesting the will and demanding an audit, Max could have found himself in quite a spot. A spot where killing Greely and framing Sheila would actually have been killing two birds with one stone.

So Steve was desperate for information.

"Did your mother ever talk about your father?" he repeated.

"Why? What are you getting at?"

"I don't know. Did she?"

"Not that I know of. I was very young when she died, you know."

"I know. I want you to remember back. I want you to tell me everything you can remember before your mother died."

"I don't understand."

"You don't have to understand. You just have to tell me."

Sheila's jaw set. "Oh no you don't, mister. That's the way my uncle treats me. That's why I wouldn't let him hire a lawyer for me. Now if you want something out of me you tell me why, and none of this you-wouldn't-understand-little-girl shit."

"Sorry," Steve said. "I'm a little pushed for time, and I'm getting edgy. The thing is, I don't understand either. And I need to understand. So I need some facts. And if they don't seem to make much sense, that's because I'm groping in the dark, and I don't know what *does* make sense. But I'm trying to sort it out, you see?

"So here's the thing—if you didn't kill Greely, then someone else did. And they killed him in your apartment with your knife. And there's gotta be a reason. And the only way that makes sense at all is if you tie it in with a twenty-million-dollar trust fund."

Sheila threw up her arms. "But how? Tie it in how?"

He shook his head. "I know. That's the problem. I've thoroughly gone over the provisions of the trust, and aside from that stupid licentious-behavior clause that's causing all the trouble, there's nothing in it that could possible affect any of the parties mentioned in it. I mean, it isn't even as if you were convicted of this crime, Phillip would come into forty million dollars instead of twenty. If you lose your trust, no one gains except a bunch of unnamed charities."

Sheila's eyes widened. "Wait a minute! How do you know they're unnamed?"

Steve looked at her. "I read the trust. They're not named."

"They're not named in the *trust*," she said excitedly. "But what if, somehow, someone knew that a particular charity stood to benefit?"

He waved it away. "You're grasping at straws. That's ridiculous."

"Is it?" she said indignantly. "Why? Because I thought of it? Because you didn't? What's ridiculous about it?"

"What difference would it make if a charity benefits?"

"You don't think there are people who have siphoned money out of charities?"

"And how the hell would they know?"

"Through Uncle Max, of course." Sheila was becoming more

and more animated as she built on the idea. "Can't you see it? You've met him. Can't you see him at some ritzy social club joking over a brandy with old cronies about how if I'm not a good girl, some of their organizations stand to make a few million?"

"No, I can't."

"Damn it, I'm serious. It's my neck here. The least you could do is consider it."

"Fine," Steve said, his voice rising. "Noted. I hereby promise to investigate the possibility that the United Way, acting on inside information that they stood to benefit from the trust, conspired to have a blackmailer killed in your apartment. All right? You satisfied?"

Sheila recoiled from the intensity of his outburst. "Jesus Christ!"

He grimaced, rubbed his head. "I'm sorry," he said. "I just don't have time to go off on a tangent right now. I don't think you're stupid, and I will look into this, okay? But right now I need you to answer some questions. All right?"

She looked at him for a moment. "You still haven't told me why."

"I was trying to, when—" he broke off. "Never mind. All right. Look. If no one named in the trust stands to benefit from the crime, we have to look for someone *not* named in the trust. As far as I can see, the only one who answers that description is your father."

"My *father*. But my father's dead."

"How do you know?"

Sheila stared at him. "Are you telling me my father *isn't* dead?"

"No, I'm not." He had no intention of burdening her with any of the details of Mark Taylor's investigation. "I'm doing what you're doing. I'm grasping at straws. I'm saying 'what if?' I'm considering any possibility, however remote, that anyone could benefit from your trust. So I asked about your father."

She frowned. "I see."

"And you told me you knew nothing."

"That's right."

"Your mother never spoke of him?"

"I was four when she died."

"Yeah. All right. What about your grandfather? Can you remember him at all?"

"Why?"

"I told you. I'm grasping at straws. Please?"

Sheila thought a moment. "I can't remember much. I just remember him as a kindly old man. Funny, isn't it? How a child's take on things is so limited."

"What do you mean?"

"Seeing Gramps as kindly. But as a child, that was the only side of him I ever saw."

"And he wasn't?"

She looked at him. "You read the trust."

"Yes, yes, having to wait till thirty-five and that clause and all that. But you said that was the only side of him you ever saw. What was the other side? I mean back then, when you were a kid."

"All I meant was the impressions you get when you're young. Seeing him as kindly, and then later realizing what a tyrant he really was."

"How? Give me an example. Tell me how you got this wrong impression."

"I don't know," she said. "It was just, he always treated my mother and me so kindly that I never really noticed how he treated Uncle Max and Uncle Teddy. Until later, I mean."

"And how did he treat them?"

"With an iron hand. He surrounded them, stifled them. At the time I thought it was kindness. Now I realize it was domination."

"Give me an example."

She thought a moment. "All right. Grandpa had a summer house in Vermont." She chuckled. "A summer house. Hell, it was a mansion—a huge building with a circular drive on this beautiful hillside in Vermont. It was gorgeous. My mother and I used to live there with him. I think I told you that, right?

"Well, anyway, when Uncle Teddy married, Gramps bought him a house on the property adjoining ours. See? At the time I thought that was nice. I say at the time. Actually it happened before I was born. Phillip's a year older than I am, you know."

"Yes, yes. Go on."

"All right. I was just trying to say, when I said 'at the time' I just meant when I was young. Right? When I thought about it. Back then. And I figured Gramps was just being nice. Now I realize he was just making sure Teddy would be right there where he could keep an eye on him."

"Yeah. I see. Teddy was wild in those days, wasn't he?"

"I suppose so. I never realized it at the time. At least not until he went to jail. But I think Uncle Teddy and his wife had to get married. I think that was one of the reasons Gramps was so down on him."

"What was Teddy's wife like?"

"I don't know. She died when Phillip was born."

"So Uncle Teddy brought up Phillip alone?"

"Yes. Gramps wouldn't even hire a nurse or governess to help out. Teddy had to cart Phillip around with him everywhere he went. It was a nuisance, but that's what Gramps wanted. I think he felt the responsibility of raising Phillip would force Uncle Teddy to settle down."

"Apparently it didn't work."

"Apparently not. Uncle Teddy went to jail. My mother died. Gramps died a year later. That left Uncle Max to bring up me and Phillip."

"What was he like?"

Sheila looked at him. "What do *you* think?"

47

WHEN COURT reconvened that afternoon, Dirkson stood up and said, "Call John Dutton."

Sheila Benton twisted convulsively in her chair. "No!" she said.

Steve Winslow put his hand on her arm. *"Easy."*

She grabbed his arm. "No, they can't do that."

"They *can* do that. He's not your husband, he's just your boy-friend. They can make him testify."

"But—"

"Shhh. There's nothing we can do. Just take it easy. It's all right. If he loves you as much as you think he does, he's not going to hurt you."

"Just what do you mean by that?"

"Shhh."

Heads turned as John Dutton walked to the stand. This was going to be delicious. The lover. The married man. The party to the late-night assignations testified to by Mrs. Rosenthal. And the thing was, he looked the part, too. Lean, tall, tanned, blond, and with that pretty-boy profile, John Dutton looked as if he might have just stepped off the screen of one of those beach-party movies. His entrance drew excited whispers from the crowd. This was going to be great.

"Your name?" Dirkson said.

"John Dutton."

"Occupation?"

"Stockbroker."

"Mr. Dutton, are you acquainted with the defendant, Sheila Benton?"

"I am."

"You are what might colloquially be called her boyfriend?"

John Dutton gave Dirkson what could only be considered a condescending smile. "I'm in love with her, if that's what you mean."

"It will do. Mr. Dutton, are you married?"

"Yes, I am. I am in the process of getting a divorce. When it is completed, I intend to marry Sheila."

Dirkson smiled and nodded. "Thank you very much. Let me ask you this—did you know the decedent, Robert Greely?"

John Dutton appeared to wilt on the witness stand. Sheila let out a small gasp and grabbed Steve's arm. A murmur ran through the courtroom.

Dirkson raised his voice. "Did you hear the question, Mr. Dutton? I'll repeat it. Did you know the decedent, Robert Greely?"

Dutton wet his lips. "I had met him, yes."

There was a reaction from everyone in the courtroom except Dirkson, who obviously had expected the answer.

"Under what circumstances, Mr. Dutton?"

"At a card game."

"Did you meet him on more than one occasion?"

"Yes, I did."

"When was the first time you met him?"

"I can't remember."

"About six months ago?"

"I suppose so, yes."

"And you have seen him several times since then?"

"I don't know what you mean by several."

"You tell me. How many times have you seen him?"

Dutton wet his lips again. "I got invited to a card game. It was a weekly card game. I began playing in it. Greely was a regular in the game. So I saw him on those occasions."

"A weekly game?"

"Yes."

"So you're saying you saw the decedent once a week?"

"On those weeks we were both in the game. I didn't go every week. He didn't go every week. When I went, he was often there."

"Did you ever see him outside of the game?"

"No."

"Never?"

"Never. Well, I might have walked out at the same time when the game broke up, but other than that, no."

"But you did see him at the games?"

"Yes."

"And the first time was approximately six months ago?"

"Yes."

"Mr. Dutton, an examination of your bank account reveals that during the last six months you have withdrawn over seven thousand dollars in cash over and above your usual expenditures. Is that true?"

The air in the courtroom suddenly became electric with anticipation. Harry Dirkson did nothing to spoil the effect. He just stood there, staring evenly at the witness, waiting for the answer.

John Dutton squirmed on the stand. "I . . . I would have to consult my records."

"I have subpoenaed the records from your bank. I have them right here, if you'd wish to examine them."

Dutton rubbed his forehead. "No. That won't be necessary. I withdrew the money."

"And what did you do with that money, Mr. Dutton?"

Sheila grabbed Steve's arm. "Stop him!" she said.

There was no time for Steve to weigh the pros and cons of objecting at this point. He rose to his feet. "Objection, Your Honor. Incompetent, irrelevant and immaterial. No proper foundation has been laid."

Judge Crandell looked from the defense table back to the witness. Crandell was only human. The look on Dutton's face decided the point.

"Objection overruled. Witness will answer the question."

John Dutton looked around the courtroom. He looked trapped. Desperate. Almost as if he were going to cry.

He looked back at Dirkson. "I refuse to answer on the grounds that it might incriminate me."

The court was in an uproar. Judge Crandell banged the gavel furiously, but nothing was going to stop the stampede of reporters who were charging for the exits.

48

JOHN DUTTON came out of the elevator in his luxury East Side apartment building, walked down the hallway and put the key in the door to his apartment.

A hand clamped down on his shoulder. He spun around. Steve Winslow was standing there. He was obviously in no mood to be trifled with.

"All right, Dutton," he said. "What's the story?"

"My lawyer said I shouldn't talk to you."

"I don't give a shit what your lawyer told you," Steve snapped. "Your girlfriend is going up the river on a murder rap unless you come clean. Now, I don't know what your lawyer told you, and I don't know what your legal rights are, but either you start talking or I'll kick the shit out of you."

Dutton looked at him, gave in. "All right, come in."

He unlocked the door and let Steve into the apartment.

"I'm glad you said that," Steve said, following Dutton in. "I was bluffing. I couldn't fight my way out of a paper bag. Now let's have it. It was coke, wasn't it?"

Dutton looked at him. "How'd you know?"

"Seven grand over six months is too cheap for blackmail. Besides, Greely didn't bleed people. He was a one-bite man. So it had to be coke."

"Well, you're right."

"Great. I suppose Sheila knew all about this?"

"Of course. I bought it for her."

"What about Greely?"

Dutton walked over to the couch, sat down and rubbed his head. "Just a damn coincidence. I hadn't seen him in about three weeks, since the last game I went to. I had no idea. You can imagine the shock when I recognized his picture in the paper. Robert Greely. Jesus. But I kept quiet about it. I didn't think anyone would ever find out."

"You thought wrong. What about Sheila? Did she know you knew Greely?"

"Not then. I told her when I saw her yesterday."

"And you told her not to tell me, right?"

"My lawyer didn't want me to tell even her. We had no idea it would ever come out."

Dutton rubbed his head some more and looked down at the floor.

Steve stood looking at him contemptuously. "Great," he said. "Can I use your phone?"

"Sure. Why?"

Steve walked over, picked up the phone and punched in a number. "Hello Mark, Steve. We missed a bet on John Dutton. Just because he flew to Reno doesn't mean he couldn't have turned around and flown back. Check all flights from Reno that would have gotten him here in time for the murder and still let him keep that appointment with his wife's attorney that seemed like such a sweet alibi. Then check all the flights back to Reno after the murder that would have gotten him there in time to catch the flight I met him on. It's time we stopped taking things for granted."

Steve hung up the phone. He had been watching John Dutton during the call. Dutton had looked at him, but had not betrayed any particular emotion. "Thanks," Steve said. He started out.

"It's a nice idea," Dutton called after him. "But you're going to draw a blank."

Steve turned back in the doorway. "That I can live with. What I can't take is any more surprises."

49

SHEILA BENTON looked at Steve Winslow through the wire screen in the visiting room at the lockup. "You're mad at me, aren't you?" she said.

Steve smiled ironically. "It would help if every now and then you would give me some little hint as to what was coming next. I might be able to plan a defense."

"Why are you so upset? I'm the one who's going to be convicted."

"Oh, you're finally starting to realize that?"

"Give me a break, will you?"

"No, I won't give you a break. This is serious. This is not fun-and-games time, like with you and Johnny baby."

"Hey!"

"The big schmuck. Where the hell does he come off telling you not to tell me he knew Greely?"

"Lay off."

"No, I won't lay off. What an asshole. The guy's supposed to love you. So what does he do? He tries to fuck up your defense in a murder trial. That's *really* love."

"Goddamn you—"

Steve threw up his hands. "Right, right. Mustn't say anything bad about dear old Johnny. He may be a schmuck, he may be an asshole, he may be a murderer, but you still love him."

"He's not a murderer."

Steve broke out laughing. "That's funny, you know it? I call him a schmuck, an asshole, and a murderer, and you contradict one of the three. It's an old vaudeville routine."

"Oh you—"

"You love him, right? That's what this is all about. You love him. No matter what. Is that true?"

"Yes . . . I love him."

"Even if he killed Greely?"

"He didn't."

"Yeah, but what if he did? Would you love him then?"

"I am not answering hypothetical questions."

"I don't blame you. That's a hard question. If he killed Greely and is letting you go to jail for it, it might make him a hard person to love."

Steve leaned back in his chair, pursed his lips and looked around the room, thinking things over.

Sheila sat and glared at him.

"Well," he said. "Any more little surprises?"

"No."

"Anything else I should know?"

For a moment she just kept glaring at him. Then she sighed, and the resistance just seemed to drain out of her. He knew why. It was the relief of being able to talk about something other than John Dutton.

"Uncle Max was just here."

"Oh?" Steve said. "What did he want? As if I didn't know."

"That's right. He wanted me to fire you. He was vehement about it. He said after what happened in court today the situation was critical and I couldn't take the risk. He wants Marston, Marston and Cramden, and he wants them now."

"What did you tell him?"

"I told him to stick it."

"How did he take it?"

"How do you think he took it? He started lecturing me on drugs, sex, my life-style, education, my choice of friends, you name it."

"What did you do?"

"I stood it for as long as I could. He was rather amusing, really. Telling me if I'd just be serious, like Phillip. Finally it got boring so I shocked him and drove him away."

"Shocked him? How?"

"Oh, I've always been able to shock him. He's such a prude, you know. That's how I deal with him. Flatter him, amuse him, kid him, shock him. Keep him off balance. It depends on whether I'm trying to get something out of him or he's trying to get something out of me."

"How did you shock him?"

"Oh. Well, you know, he always treats Phillip as if he can do no wrong. So I shook him up a little. Uncle Max had started off on a tangent about sex and promiscuity, and I broke in and said, 'Speaking of sex, did I ever tell you about the first time I ever played "doctor"? You know, children's sex games? It was with Phillip.'"

"What made you tell him that?"

"I don't know. He's just such a prude that I just love to shock him. I mean, you know, it was just a childish incident, no harm in it. I'd forgotten about it, then a couple of weeks ago I saw Phillip, and we got to talking and somehow or other it came up—I don't know what reminded me of it—but I told Phillip and he was amused. But Uncle Max almost hit the ceiling."

"What did you tell him?"

"Well, I didn't go into clinical details, if that's what you mean. I just told it was a happy reminiscence. I suppose it was my attitude that bothered him more than anything."

She chuckled softly and leaned back in her chair. Her eyes took on a dreamy, faraway look. "I remember it was a warm summer day in Vermont. I was supposed to stay around the house, but I wandered off into the meadow by myself. And then for some reason, I don't know why, I slipped through the woods to Uncle Teddy's property, and there was cousin Phillip. And we were full of mischief and played our little game. And then I remembered I wasn't supposed to leave our yard, and I wanted to get back before anybody noticed I was gone. It was funny, you know, because I wasn't worried they'd be angry at me for playing doctor, just for leaving the yard. So I hurried back through the woods.

"I remember I got back to the big circle in front of the house and there was no one there. I'd made it. And just as I got there, my mother came out the front door and picked me up and kissed me. And I realized I'd gotten away with it, and I was happy. Very happy."

Sheila broke off, and the thin smile faded. "Later that afternoon my mother was killed."

It clicked. Steve's head snapped up. "What?"

"That was the same day my mother was killed."

Steve leaned forward excitedly. "You told all this to Uncle Max?"

"Yes. I really shocked him. He got up and ran out of here—"

Steve was already tearing out of the room.

50

STEVE WINSLOW came running down the front steps of the courthouse. There was a cab with the light on coming down the street. He raced out and hailed it. He hopped in the back seat, barked out the address and the cab took off.

The light at the corner was red. The cab stopped.

"Run the light."

The cabbie, an old wizened man, half turned in the seat and gave him a look.

"It's an emergency. Run the light."

The cabbie grinned and shook his head. "Buddy, I got a license."

"Run the fucking light."

"Relax, buddy."

Steve jerked open the door of the cab and hopped out. While the driver was turned looking after him, Steve jerked open the driver's door. He grabbed the startled man by the shoulders and hurled him out of the cab.

Steve hopped in the cab, slammed the door and took off, running the red light.

The light at the next corner was red. He ran that too, almost colliding with a delivery truck. He shot on up the street.

By the next corner the lights were green. He floored it, weaving in and out of cars, streaking up the street.

Two blocks and the lights changed. And there was a jam at the intersection. No way to get through. He was going too fast to stop. He looked around desperately. Saw it. A break between the parked cars. He spun the wheel, fishtailed slightly then skidded between the cars and up onto the sidewalk. The cab sped down the sidewalk toward the intersection, half a block away. He kept his hand on the horn, scattering the pedestrians, who dove for safety.

Two cops, one fat, one thin, were having coffee and doughnuts at a diner on the block. They heard the horn and looked up to see a cab flash by the window.

"Holy shit!" the fat-cop said.

They got up and rushed out to their car.

Steve heard their siren about five blocks later. He didn't care. It was actually helpful in clearing the traffic out of his way.

He hit Houston Street and realized he'd gone too far. He hung a right, sped over to Allen, hung another right and headed back downtown.

The siren was getting closer as he hung a left off Allen and pulled up in front of the building. He left the cab standing in the middle of the street with the motor running. He hopped out and tore into the building.

The downstairs door was standing open. A break. He plunged up the stairs.

On the second-floor landing he heard a gunshot. It came from above. He didn't stop. He turned the corner, ran up the stairs.

The door to Teddy Baxter's apartment was open. Steve plunged through.

The apartment was empty. He stood there looking around.

A gust of wind moved the curtains by the opened window. Just as Steve spotted it, there came the sound of more gunshots from above.

He ran to the window and looked out. A fire escape. He climbed out onto it. Below him, in the street, the police car screeched to a stop behind the cab.

More shots from above. Steve looked up. The fire escape led to the roof.

He heard a voice call, "Hey!" He looked down and saw the cops looking up at him. He turned and climbed up the fire escape.

The fire escape's steps ended at the fourth floor, but there was a ladder to the roof. He climbed the ladder and peered over the edge of the roof.

Maxwell Baxter was about ten feet from him. He was holding a gun. He was slumped down against a chimney near the edge of the roof. He was bleeding from a bullet wound in the chest. He was shielding himself behind the chimney, and aiming the gun at the stairwell, some twenty feet away.

Steve swung himself up onto the roof.

Teddy Baxter, who had been hiding behind the stairwell, poked his head out and aimed a shot at Steve. Steve hit the roof, and the bullet went over his head.

Max fired. The bullet caught Teddy Baxter right between the eyes. He slumped to the rooftop, gushing blood.

Steve jumped up and ran to Teddy. He was clearly dying. Steve ran back to Max.

The effort of firing that last shot had done a lot to sap Max's remaining strength. He was slumped down on the roof, only the chimney keeping his head and shoulders up.

"Take it easy," Steve said. "The police are right behind me."

"Teddy?" Max gasped.

"He's dead."

"Thank god."

"He killed your sister, didn't he?" Steve said.

Max actually turned his head slightly to look at him. "How did you know?"

"The same way you did. He was supposed to have been in New York the day she was killed. But Phillip was in Vermont, and Teddy always took Phillip everywhere. He tampered with the brakes of the car, didn't he?"

"He must have. I would have suspected him then, if he hadn't had such a good alibi. He was supposed to be in New York. He was arrested there the next day. That made the two . . . tragedies seem unrelated. It was almost as if"—Max coughed—"as if he were in jail when it happened."

"He did it for the money, didn't he?"

"Yes. Father only had months to live. Alice would have gotten the bulk of the estate. She would have been his trustee. He thought with her gone he'd be next in line. He would have been too, if he hadn't gone to jail." Max coughed again. He looked at Steve. "You seem to know all this anyway."

"Most of it. Sheila reminded Phillip about playing doctor, and Phillip told Teddy. Teddy knew if Sheila mentioned the incident to you you'd figure it out. So he had to get rid of Sheila. But killing her was too risky. There was too great a chance he'd be connected up somehow. So he needed a more indirect method— one that would leave him in the clear. Framing Sheila seemed to be the perfect solution."

Max's eyes closed, then lifted open again. "That's right . . . and the son of a bitch almost got away with it."

Steve looked at him. "You really love Sheila, don't you?"

"I should," Max said weakly. He looked up at Steve. "I'm her father."

Steve just blinked at him. He couldn't think of anything to say. Even a simple "what?" sounded wrong.

Max's face contorted with pain. The pain passed. The features relaxed. He looked back at Steve.

"Sheila doesn't know," he said. "Even Teddy never knew. Father did. That's why he was such a stickler for morality. That's why he put that asinine provision in the trust."

"Why are you telling me this?"

"Because I know what you're doing." Max's voice had fallen to a whisper. "My detectives have told me. You're looking for Sheila's father. You're planning on springing the idea that he isn't dead on the jury. That would make for a lot of sensational headlines, get you a lot of publicity, and maybe even get her off." A pause for another spell of pain. "You don't have to do that now. Stop looking for Sheila's father. Go to the D.A. and explain what happened here. Except of course, what I just told you. But everything else. You handle it right, and he'll drop the case."

Steve frowned. "Yeah, maybe," he said dubiously.

Max looked at him, and almost managed a grin. "I know what you're thinking. That way you lose your . . . your brilliant courtroom finale. But that way Sheila never has to know. You save her a lot of unnecessary grief. A lot of grief."

Max coughed and almost lost consciousness. He rallied, and locked eyes with Steve, taunting him, challenging him to do the right thing. "Can you do that, counselor? Whose interests come first? Your client's or your own?"

Max's eyes glazed over and his head fell back.

Steve touched his wrist, feeling for a pulse. He wasn't sure how to do it, but he *was* sure that there would be none.

He slowly got to his feet. He stood there on the roof, not looking at either of the two bodies, just looking off into space.

So, it had come down to this. If he went back into court, he could clear the case up in spectacular fashion. He could make a name for himself. He'd be the hero, the winner, the courageous attorney who'd figured the whole thing out, who'd gotten his client off.

But at a price. It would take time. It would drag on. And meanwhile there was a chance those trails he'd started in California would be followed up, if not by the police then by zealous reporters sensing they hadn't gotten the whole story. They'd follow the leads in California and find out what he had—that Sheila's father was someone from the East Coast. A whole area of speculation would open up. And maybe—and Steve knew it was a slim chance—just maybe the real truth would come out.

If he did what Max said, if he took his story to the D.A., it would work. Steve was sure of it. The trial would be over. Sheila would be released, the case would be solved, and the cops would grab all the credit. And that would be the end of it. There would be no reason for anyone to ever find out about the California end of it at all. Sheila would be safe.

But for a price. Because the press and the public would be left with the image of Steve Winslow that he had adopted in his client's behalf. The clown. The fool. He would remain a joke. The inexperienced young attorney whose client would have been convicted if the police hadn't happened to break the case. It would be, to all intents and purposes, the end of his career.

Steve sighed. Yeah. That was the choice.

There came the clang of a metal door banging and a voice said, "All right! Hold it right there!"

Steve looked around to see the fat cop attempting to flatten himself against the stairwell as he leveled a gun on him.

Steve suddenly felt exhausted, too tired even to raise his hands. If the cop shot him, that was just tough.

He smiled, slightly. "It's all right officer. They're both dead."

51

DISTRICT ATTORNEY Harry Dirkson leaned back in his chair and exchanged glances with Lieutenant Farron. Farron's face was cautiously neutral, giving nothing away. Dirkson had known it would be—Farron was waiting to follow his lead. Dirkson gave it to him now—an ironic smile. Farron tried to match it, but to Dirkson it seemed a trifle forced, which suddenly made his smile seem forced too.

Dirkson didn't let on, veteran campaigner that he was. Having chosen his course, he plunged ahead. He cocked his head at Steve Winslow and said, "That's a fantastic story."

"It happens to be true," Steve said.

"Yeah, sure," Dirkson said. "Now that Max and Teddy are dead you can make up any stories you want about them."

Steve was sorely tempted to walk out. It was bad enough giving it to these guys, without having to force it on them.

"You don't believe me?"

"Why should I?"

"Okay. *You* tell *me* why Uncle Max and Uncle Teddy decided to go up on the roof and blow each other's brains out."

"It doesn't matter. Even if Teddy did kill Sheila's mother, it doesn't mean he killed Greely."

"Sure it does. Look at the evidence."

"What evidence?"

"The blackmail letter, for one thing."

"What about it?"

"The letter was cut from the newspaper so it couldn't be traced. But the envelope was typed on Greely's machine. Greely's a smart blackmailer. He had to be, to keep doing it and have no police record. Do you really think he'd make a dumb slip like that? Of course not. Uncle Teddy typed the envelope on that machine because he *wanted* the letter traced to Greely so it would prove Sheila's motive for the murder."

Dirkson frowned. "Yeah, but if this was all Teddy's idea, how did Greely get involved in the first place?"

Steve shrugged. "Hey, I can't do all your work for you. But if you were to dig into Greely's background far enough, I bet eventually you'd find a connection.

"And besides, Greely wasn't really involved. At least, he had no idea of what was really going on. I'm sure Teddy was the one who sent the letters. He may have had Greely make the phone call—he probably did—but what Teddy told him to get him to make it, I have no idea. But there's no reason to think it was the truth.

"Greely was a patsy. Teddy's fall guy. Teddy set him up. Teddy had killed his sister. He was scared to death that Sheila was going to blab to Uncle Max about Phillip being in Vermont on that day. He knew if that happened Max would figure it out. He had to stop her. So he framed her for murder."

"That's all very nice," Dirkson said. "But if that's true, then how does John Dutton fit into all this? He knew Greely. You want me to believe that was just an outrageous coincidence?"

Steve shook his head. "Not at all. The way I figure it, he triggered the whole thing."

Dirkson frowned. "What do you mean?"

"Well," Steve said. "Uncle Teddy and Greely are both dead, so we'll probably never know, but we can make a pretty good guess. The way I see it is this—Let's assume Uncle Teddy and Greely knew each other from way back. It would have to be from way back, because Teddy wouldn't want to take a chance on his connection with Greely ever coming out. But say they knew each other. Not that unlikely a supposition, when you think about it. Greely was a blackmailer. Teddy, in his youth, was a confidence man. So assume the connection.

"All right. Uncle Teddy's favorite line was that he'd been screwed out of his inheritance—that he would be a wealthy man if he hadn't made one mistake and his father hadn't cut him out of the will and put all the money into trusts. So Greely would have known about that, and would have known that Teddy's son, Phillip Baxter, and his niece, Sheila Benton, had a lot of money tied up in trusts. Being a blackmailer, he would have filed that information away.

"So what happened? Say six months ago Greely is playing in a poker game, and some young stud named John Dutton, who is a pretty boy and an egotistical asshole, is shooting off his mouth about how he's got a thing going with an heiress. And Greely, who's always on the lookout for something like that, tunes right in and finds out the girl's name is Sheila Benton.

"Which rings a very big bell. So Greely asks a few questions and pokes around some, and finds out this John Dutton is very much married. So now Greely has an heiress with a trust fund playing around with a married man, music to the ears of a blackmailer.

"So Greely goes to Uncle Teddy and says, 'Hey, I got all this dope on your niece. You know all about how her trust is set up. If you can figure any way we can shoot this information, I'll go halves with you.'

"And Uncle Teddy tells him it's hopeless. Sheila has no money of her own, there's no way she can touch the money in her trust, the only one who can get the money out of the trust is Uncle Max, and if he knew about it Sheila would lose the trust, so what's the point?

"Now, this is all conjecture, but I would imagine at this point Greely considers blackmailing Dutton. But Dutton doesn't have that kind of money—he's a fortune hunter himself, figuring he can retire a millionaire in ten years by hooking up with Sheila. So

Greely and Uncle Teddy figure that's not worthwhile, and Uncle
Teddy convinces Greely that they should hang onto the information and then maybe the situation would change and they could
shoot it at a later time."

Steve shrugged. "So that's it. The matter drops. They let it slide.

"And then something happens. What happens is, Sheila sees
cousin Phillip and kids him about the time they played doctor
together. And Phillip tells Teddy. And the key part of the story is
the fact that it happened the same day Sheila's mother was killed.
Because Phillip went everywhere Teddy went. And Teddy was
supposed to be in New York that day. But he wasn't. He was up in
Vermont, tampering with the brakes of his sister's car so she'd go
off the road and he'd inherit the whole bundle.

"So when Teddy hears this he's hysterical. He knows if Sheila
tells Uncle Max, Uncle Max will start thinking and figure out
what happened.

"So he's got to shut Sheila up. So he figures to involve her in a
mess, 'cause if her life is all screwed up, and she's in a position
where she has to protect herself, she won't be needling her Uncle
Max with any cutesy-poo childhood memories.

"So he remembers Greely. What if he had Greely blackmail
her? Wouldn't that do the trick? Sure. But he realizes that's not
good enough. Because there *is* no way to blackmail her, and
Greely would eventually find that out, and wonder what the hell
was going on. And Teddy's not going to tell Greely the real reason
he wants to do it.

"So he gets another idea. What if he frames her for murder? Of
Greely? Great. No problem there. Greely's dead, so he can't find
out the blackmail was bogus. Or get caught and blurt out his
connection with Teddy. It's perfect.

"So he calls Greely and tells him he's figured out how to make
the blackmail work. While Greely's in the john, or out buying
beer, or whatever, Teddy types the envelope. He tells Greely his
scheme, which is just a bunch of bullshit. But Greely doesn't
know that, and he has no reason to suspect anything. He thinks
he's going to make a killing. So Teddy gets Greely to make the

anonymous phone call. And he arranges to meet Greely at Shei-la's apartment, presumably to make the shakedown. He lures him up there, and he kills him.

"And the beauty of the thing is John Dutton. Because Greely met John Dutton at that poker game, Teddy knows that if the cops start trying to trace Greely's background, they'll trace him back to Dutton, not to him. Which they did."

Dirkson frowned. "Yeah, but . . ." He stopped. Tried to think of a "but." Got one. "But why go through all that? Teddy, I mean. If he wanted to shut Sheila up, why not just kill her?"

Steve sighed. He shrugged and smiled. "I don't know. Your guess is as good as mine. This isn't some TV show where the plot threads get tied up nice and tidy. The principals in this case are all dead, so we'll probably never know.

"You want theories? I can give you theories. I talked to Teddy Baxter. I think in spite of everything, he had genuine affection for Sheila and couldn't bring himself to kill her."

"But he didn't mind framing her for murder," Dirkson said sarcastically.

"Don't like that one? Try this—He knew if Sheila were killed, Uncle Max would move heaven and earth to find out who did it, and he was afraid the trail would lead back to him. Whereas, he figured no one would ever connect him with Sheila killing a blackmailer. Particularly when he knew the blackmailer could be traced back to John Dutton."

"Aw, you're just making up stuff off the top of your head," Dirkson said. "You've got nothing but wild guesses."

"Right," Steve said. "You got anything better?"

Dirkson rubbed his forehead. He carefully avoided looking at Lieutenant Farron. He was a poker player, playing them close to the vest. "You got anything else to support this?"

"Sure. The key in Greely's pocket. There was nothing else in his pockets. Why? Because Teddy took everything out of his pockets except the key. Why? Because he wanted to make sure the police would investigate the key and find out that Greely had the key to Sheila's apartment."

"But the locksmith says Greely was the one who copied the key."

"Sure. Uncle Teddy gave him a key to copy. Check up and you'll find that some time or other when Sheila took a vacation she gave Uncle Teddy a key to feed her goldfish, or whatever. At any rate, he had a key."

"But you can't prove Teddy Baxter killed Greely."

"Uncle Max told me he did."

"That's hearsay."

Steve grinned. "No, it's a dying declaration. Read your law."

Dirkson looked at him narrowly. "Surely you don't intend to put yourself on the stand to testify to what Max told you."

"I don't have to," Steve said. "You see, we're sitting here, and you're asking me my theories, and I'm giving 'em to you, and you're telling me they're bullshit, and that's all well and good. But the thing is, when we get into court, *I* don't have to explain everything, *you* do. You have to prove Sheila guilty beyond all reasonable doubt. Fat chance. Wanna know how it's gonna go?"

Steve leaned back in his chair, crossed his legs and cocked his head at Dirkson. "When you rest your case, I'll call Uncle Max as my first witness. Then you can explain to the jury why he isn't available."

Steve paused while Dirkson thought that over. He watched Dirkson, and he liked what he saw. He smiled, and shrugged his shoulders. "Then I'll rest my case right there and we'll proceed to the argument. The judge will instruct the jury that if I can explain the facts of the case by any reasonable hypothesis other than that of guilt, they must find the defendant not guilty. I'll give them a reasonable hypothesis."

This time Dirkson couldn't help exchanging glances with Farron. Neither man liked what he saw.

"If that's what you want, fine," Steve went on, airily. "Sheila will get off anyway, the police will look like a bunch of incompetent bunglers and it probably won't do your political career any good. I, on the other hand, will come off smelling like the proverbial rose."

Steve let that sink in, then changed his tack. He uncrossed his legs and leaned in to Dirkson. "But if you want to get smart," he said in an almost conspiratorial voice, "dismiss the case and release the girl. Then call in the press and issue a statement about how you, working in conjunction with the police department, cracked the Benton case. It'd be a hell of a story. Make you guys look real good." Steve paused, smiled. "Probably get you reelected."

52

SHEILA BENTON entered her apartment flanked by John Dutton and Steve Winslow. Each had a hand on her shoulder and a hand on her arm. The hands were for guidance, rather than support. Sheila could walk, she just seemed to have no real idea where she was going.

Sheila was a mess. Her blond hair was wet and stringy. Her eyes were red and dull and glassy looking. Her face was lined and caked with tears. She looked like an accident victim, which, in a way, she was.

They led her over to the couch and sat her down between them, Dutton on her right, and Steve on her left. Dutton immediately installed himself in the role of chief consoler, putting his arm around her shoulders. Steve withdrew his arm.

"There you are," Dutton said softly. "It's all right now. It's all right."

Sheila blinked and looked around. For a moment she was all right. Then her lip contorted, and the tears came again.

Dutton put his other arm around her and hugged her to him. "Easy," he said. "Just take it easy."

She lay on his chest for a few seconds, then twisted away and sat up.

"No," she said. "I'm all right. I'm all right." She took a deep breath and exhaled. "It's just hard to believe."

"Easy now," Dutton said.

"It's just I've known Uncle Teddy all my life. To think he killed my mo—" She broke off, crying again.

Dutton put his arm around her again, but she pushed it away.

"No," she said. "No, I'm not going to cry. I'm all right." She turned to Steve. "I have to know. Uncle Teddy really framed me for the murder?"

Steve nodded. "Yes. The story you told Phillip scared him to death. He knew if you told Uncle Max, Max would suspect what had happened. He had to get you out of the way."

"But Phillip knew too," Dutton said. "How was he going to silence him?"

"He didn't have to. Phillip was away at college most of the time, anyway. And Phillip, the diligent student, would never have repeated a conversation of that sort to his straight-laced old uncle. On the other hand, it was just the sort of thing Sheila would love to throw in Max's face."

"And I did," Sheila said miserably. "Poor Uncle Max. I guess he meant well. But he wanted me to fire you. And now you got me off."

"I didn't get you off," Steve said. "Uncle Max got you off. If the case had gone to the jury, you would have been convicted. That would have happened if Uncle Max hadn't figured it out."

Sheila looked up at him. Distracted as she was, she was still sensitive enough to pick up on what he had just said, and it puzzled her. "Why are you running yourself down? You figured it out too."

"Uncle Max figured it out from what you told him. I figured it out from *his reaction* to what you told him. What you told me he did. Jumping up and running out. That wasn't a shocked and embarrassed reaction. That was the reaction of someone who's had a revelation, who's just realized something. And as soon as I realized that, I knew what the revelation had to be. Even then, I was too late. If he hadn't had to go home to pick up his gun, I never would have caught up with him."

"He was still alive when you got there?"

"Yes."

"Did he say anything?"

Steve sighed and looked her in the eye. "Just that he was glad that Teddy was dead. He couldn't forgive him for what he did to you and your mother."

Sheila looked away. Tears came to her eyes again. "Poor Uncle Max. I guess in his own way he really loved me."

"Yeah. I guess he did."

She lowered her head and looked at the table. She was trying hard not to cry.

Dutton took the opportunity to change the subject. "What's going to happen to *me* now?"

"What do you mean?"

"About refusing to answer questions."

"You have your own lawyer."

"Yeah," Dutton said dryly. "We discussed him earlier."

Steve sighed. "You were within your legal rights not to answer questions. Now that there's no trial, they can't ask you any more questions. They could still charge you with something if they could figure out which law you broke. But who's gonna tell 'em?"

Sheila had recovered during this. She looked up at Steve. "So what will you do now?" she asked. "Go back to a normal law practice?"

Steve chuckled mirthlessly. "I *have* no law practice. And after this case, who would hire me? I do have two nice pieces of work ahead of me, however. Winding up your trust and probating Uncle Max's will." He smiled then, and tried bantering with her a little. "Unless you'd prefer to hire some other lawyer in whom you'd have more confidence."

He'd judged right. She smiled back. "The job is yours."

They held each other's eyes for a few moments.

John Dutton saw this and didn't like it. *He* was supposed to be the one who had that special understanding, who shared those special knowing looks.

To break the mood, he played his trump card. He reached in his pocket and took out a small plastic packet and a straw.

Steve saw this and sighed.

Sheila turned and realized what Johnny was doing. To her surprise, she was embarrassed. In front of Steve Winslow, for Christ's sake. She felt angry and defensive. "Put that away," she snapped. Then, "I'm sorry, Johnny, but, Jesus, now of all times." She shook her head. "I can't handle that now. I've got to get off that shit, you know?"

Dutton knew. He looked as if he'd been slapped. As if all his powers had suddenly been stripped away.

Steve watched with satisfaction. "Well," he said. "I'm sure you kids have a lot to talk over, so I'll be pushing off."

He got up and walked to the door. He turned back in the doorway. Sheila was looking after him and their eyes met. Just for a moment he thought he caught a wistful look. He smiled and nodded, and she smiled back.

Steve went out the front door of Sheila Benton's building and headed for Broadway, to catch the subway home. He felt surprisingly good. All right, so he didn't have a law practice. But he'd had a case. A real case. And he'd gotten his client off. So what if nobody knew it? He knew it. And it felt damn good.

He walked by a newsstand. The New York *Post* had gotten out an extra. "BAXTER SHOT DEAD!—BENTON FREED!" ran the headline. A smaller-print headline underneath ran: "D.A. CRACKS GREELY CASE!" Underneath were a glamour shot of Sheila Benton, and a stock head-shot of Maxwell Baxter. An inset photo showed a grinning Harry Dirkson and Lieutenant Farron issuing a joint statement to the press.

Steve didn't buy the paper. He just smiled and walked off down the street toward the subway.